# Murder
# of a
# Good Man

# Murder
# of a
# Good Man

## A Piney Woods Mystery

## TERESA TRENT

CAMEL
**PRESS**
Seattle, WA

## PRESS

Camel Press
PO Box 70515
Seattle, WA 98127

For more information go to: www.Camelpress.com
www.TeresaTrent.com

Cover design by Sabrina Sun

Murder of A Good Man
Copyright © 2018 by Teresa Trent

ISBN: 978-1-60381-635-9 (Trade Paper)
ISBN: 978-1-60381-636-6 (eBook)

Library of Congress Control Number: 2017951296

Printed in the United States of America

To my brother, Brian

# Acknowledgments

———

A BIG THANK you to my brother Brian, who has spent over twenty years working in the hotel industry. I have loved hearing your stories and getting firsthand knowledge of the hospitality business.

# Chapter 1

‹◦›

Blinking to keep her tears at bay, Nora reached into her pocket for a tissue. Just as she brought it up to her damp cheek, a red pickup, apparently tired of her snail's pace, swerved around to pass her. Without considering the passing driver, Nora hit the gas pedal to get back up to speed with traffic. When the red truck re-entered the lane, he nearly ran into her, causing Nora to veer off the country road. She slammed on the brakes, taking deep breaths as her heart thumped in her chest.

With shaking hands, she moved farther over to the side of the road as her heart rate returned to normal. The jolt had opened the cut on her hand from that morning's moving of the boxes and furniture from her mother's place to the storage unit. The bandage had dislodged itself, and she used her cotton shirt to stop the flow of blood until she could open the first-aid kit on the seat of the car. Thank goodness she was wearing a T-shirt underneath.

Just as she got everything fixed up, a man in a white pickup with a gun rack in the back slowed and rolled down his window. "You okay there, missy?"

Nora straightened up and smiled, not wanting to accept help from a strange man. "Fine, just fine."

"Okay then. I got a little something for you." Nora wasn't sure she wanted to see what that was. He extended his arm out of the cab window and slapped a bumper sticker into her hand. The bright red letters spelled out, BUBBY FOR PINEY WOODS PIONEER.

"Uh, thank you."

"Name's Bubby Tidwell and I can see you are about to enter the fair city of Piney Woods, Texas. While you're there, I'd appreciate it if you cast your vote for me, as the Piney Woods Pioneer. I have personally saved fourteen of our citizens, three cats, and a hamster in my days as a firefighter. They only choose people who have contributed to improving our little community, and even though you don't know me, I'd sure appreciate your support. You drive safe now." He waved and headed on down the road.

Nora put the bumper sticker in the passenger seat and stared in the rearview mirror. She had hopped into the car determined to fulfill her mother's last wish. Now that she was getting close to her destination, she realized she must look pretty rough. She rearranged her hair to create a side braid à la Disney princess while arranging silky strands of auburn hair to frame her face. Pulling a tube of concealer out of her bag, she did her best to repair her makeup. After a few minutes of fussing, she hoped she looked presentable.

She had to do this thing. She had to know. Her mother left her instructions on delivering the letter.

As Nora neared Piney Woods, Texas, two giant eyes bored into her from a lighted billboard with the words VOTE FOR BUBBY in glitter letters at the bottom. PINEY WOODS' FINEST CITIZEN was written under the face of the round-cheeked man with the Cheshire Cat smile. A hundred feet down the road was another billboard with BROCKWELL INDUSTRIES—PINEY WOODS' TRUE PIONEER NEEDS

YOUR VOTE. Brockwell was the name she was looking for, so she knew she was getting close. As she entered town, the election signs multiplied. VOTE FOR BUBBY was on a park bench, VOTE FOR BROCKWELL was on a lamppost, but it was going too far when a blue Porta-Potty sported signs from both sides. Nora guessed they wanted the people of Piney Woods to think about who they were voting for while using the blue plastic necessity. Nothing like a captive audience.

Nora drove down a main street that looked as if it belonged to an earlier time. The two-story brick buildings held lovely little stores, a restaurant, and a coffee shop. The oak and elm trees on either side of the street were so large, they nearly touched branches in some areas, framing the picturesque town with their deep-red and gold leaves. At the end of the main road in Piney Woods was the largest house on the block. The two-story brick structure looked more like the public library or a courthouse than someone's home. Nora double-checked to make sure there wasn't a book drop by the front door. No, someone actually lived there. The enormous house had a wraparound porch and windows taller than the height of the average man. What would it be like to sit on the porch, listening to the crickets, on a warm summer's evening? Nora examined the numbers on the mailbox. This was the address her mother had printed in careful letters on the envelope. Not only was the intended recipient of this letter mysterious, but he was also rich.

After driving all the way from south Louisiana to Texas, she was here. All she had to do was park in the cobblestone driveway, ring the doorbell, deliver the letter, gas up, and go home. So why was she nervous? Why hadn't her mother mailed the letter before her death? What was the big secret about Adam Brockwell? Since her father's death, Nora had never even seen her mother go on a single date.

If Kay Alexander had a boyfriend, it would have to be someone like a table-calculating insurance adjuster figuring the chances of them ever having a good time. Her mother had a way with figures right up until her death. Nora had been told how much they depended on her bookkeeping skills at the home improvement center where she had worked for so many years.

Nora's mother had an answer for everything, and most of the time that meant Nora needed to stay inside the little bubble she had created for the two of them. When Nora rebelled, as most young people eventually do, she hadn't just strayed from the course. She'd found herself a whole new ocean. Kay Alexander's cancer had steadily worsened.

Once a healthy, vibrant fifty-one-year-old woman, the woman in the bed next to Nora had appeared gaunt and tired. Her red hair, what was left of it, was covered in a brightly colored wrap. It was the brightest thing in the room, as if pink and yellow flowers could dispel the pall of her mother's illness. It was as if she was holding onto the last threads of color, her attire the one pleasure cancer couldn't drain out of her. The doctors had promised that the pain and discomfort from the chemo would pay off in the end. Nothing had worked. So here they were, mother and daughter, holding on for time.

Other than her father, Kay Alexander had never trusted men. She had been so strange before she died. Pulling an envelope out of her bedside table, she pressed it in Nora's hands.

"I need you to deliver this to the man at this address."

Nora examined the letter. The address was in Texas. "Why? Can't you mail it?"

"No, it's important this man sees you."

"Again, why?"

"Let's just say he's about to be honored with something and I … want to put in my two cents."

"How do you know this about a man I've never heard of who lives in another state?"

Kay put her hand to her chest and coughed. "I … I … just know. That's all."

Her mother's words still echoed in her ears as her phone GPS informed her she had reached her destination. Whoever this guy was and why he was important to her mother, Nora would never know until the letter was opened. She came close to the driveway and started to pull in, but then checked her watch. It was nearly seven. Maybe it would be better to deliver the letter the next day when she could be sure to catch Mr. Brockwell.

She needed to find a place to stay for the night. Piney Woods was so small, she doubted there was a chain hotel anywhere near. Turning around, she went back down the main street and found the Piney Woods Bed and Breakfast.

She walked up to the front counter in the lovely two-story home and tapped the bell. From a connecting room, a television blared with game show buzzers and canned applause.

"I think that was the bell, Tatty," a male voice said.

"It can't be. You locked the door, right?"

"Uh, I'll be right back." A small, wiry man came through the doorway to the front desk and immediately jumped back.

"Oh, man, you scared me, *chica*." He cleared his throat and stood a little straighter, though he was still not a tall man. She estimated his height at five feet seven or so. "I'm Ed Tovar, owner of Piney Woods' premier bed and breakfast. Can I help you?"

A trim woman with soft brown skin poked her head around the corner. She looked to be in her sixties. "We are the *only* bed and breakfast and he's part-owner, my forgetful husband meant to say. I'm Tatty. Did you need a room?"

"Yes. Do you have any vacancies? I don't have a reservation or anything."

"Well, we are pretty booked," Ed said, clucking his tongue. Tatty flapped her hand past her husband.

"Give it up, Ed. You don't get to charge her more just because she thinks we're full up. We're without guests tonight and awfully glad to see you." Tatty's warmth made Nora feel at home. A few minutes later they showed her to a room on the second floor.

"This will be your room, dear." Mrs. Tovar pulled open the green-striped drapes, revealing a view of the side yard that held a giant oak tree full of the burnt-orange found in pumpkin pies and autumn fires.

Aside from the yard, could see a section of Piney Woods' main street. Tatty Tovar flipped the light switch as Ed Tovar busied himself about the room like a squirrel running from branch to branch. His antsiness only served to emphasize his wife's calmness. With the treatment she was getting, Nora felt more like a beloved relative on a visit than someone paying to rent a room. Did they act like this with all their guests? If so, this town was a lot different from where she had been living.

"There is a bathroom down the hall." Ed pointed it out as if having to share a bathroom was a deluxe feature.

Tatty opened the window a crack. "Leave the window open a bit to air out the room. How long will you be staying with us?"

Nora set her weathered suitcase and a leather bag next to the bed. "Just a day or two, I guess."

Tatty fluffed a pillow and set it back down. "Are you here on business?"

Nora sighed. "Sort of. I'm carrying out a final wish for my mother. She just passed away."

Tatty stopped her busy work, walked over, and took Nora's hands. "Oh, my dear. You poor thing."

She was overcome by Tatty's kindness, and also a little uncomfortable. Even though Nora was thirty-three, she felt as vulnerable as a small child. She barely knew this couple. Placing her hand on Tatty's arm, Nora pulled away. "Thank you."

"If I may ask, what was her final wish?"

"She left a letter to be delivered to Mr. Adam Brockwell," Nora blurted out.

"A letter? For Mr. Brockwell?" Ed asked. "What kind of letter?"

"I don't know," she said. She was surprised that she had told this couple so much after just meeting them. Though their interest felt sincere.

"Adam Brockwell is *the* man around here," Ed said. "He's being considered for the Piney Woods Hall of Fame. That's a big deal. You have to be close to sainthood to get that one. Maybe he owed her money for something? Bills are the only things that outlive all of us."

Tatty put her hands together under her chin, staring up as if imagining it all. "Oh, this is so romantic. Just like something out of a Nicholas Sparks movie."

"Oh, God, don't get the woman started on that gobbledygook." Ed steered his wife toward the door. "Well, if there's anything you need, and I mean anything at all, you just dial zero on the phone, and I'll be at your door."

"Got it," Nora said.

The Tovars left, and Nora plopped down on the bed, which responded with a tortured squeak. Obviously, this wasn't the honeymoon suite. She'd been so focused on driving to Piney Woods and delivering her mother's letter, she'd never considered what to do next. Why was she in such a hurry to return, anyway? She'd cleaned out her mother's house, and in the process tripped on an uneven place in the sidewalk. Upon landing, she'd put a gash in her hand. Nora was relieved to have completed that part of handling her mother's estate—putting her things safely in storage. Her hand was healing, but she had to watch it. The thought of returning home exhausted her.

A strange clanging sound echoed outside her window. This town was so small, perhaps they had to use a trash can lid to alert the fire department?

She rose and peered through the glass. A block down, a man had fallen into a metal trash can. He stumbled under a streetlight next to an old two-story brick building. A passerby was trying to help him stand. In the quiet of the autumn evening, Nora heard bits of their conversation.

"I'm all right. Jus' took a misstep."

The man lending aid was trying to get the wobbly drunk to his feet, holding him by the elbow. "How much have you had to drink today, Dad?"

The drunk was old, painfully thin, and nearly bald. His cheeks were sunken and his eyes bugged from their sockets. The young man appeared to be a healthier version of the old man, with a receding hairline and a paunch.

The drunk tottered to the side. "Why? What do you mean? I'm perfectly fine. Finer'n fine. I'm *final.*"

"Yes, well, you must have started early today."

"Early to bed, early to rise makes a man healthy … uh … healthy …." He scratched his head as the old phrase escaped him. "Uh … healthy …."

"Okay. I get it. Why don't you let me help you get home?" the younger man asked.

"Shertainly."

The son guided his father toward a pickup truck parked in front of the run-down structure. Nora realized the building was a hotel. Now it looked more like a home for vagrants. Had the drunken man planned on checking in? The hotel was dark, except for a faint light from a nearby streetlamp. Other than the drunk and his longsuffering son, there was no other activity in or around the hotel. An ancient sign above the front entry read, TUNIE HOTEL, with a star sitting between the two words. Nora blinked when, just for a second, the unlit star seemed to twinkle in the moonlight.

# Chapter 2

———

Aꜰᴛᴇʀ ɢᴇᴛᴛɪɴɢ ꜱᴇᴛᴛʟᴇᴅ in, Nora felt her stomach growl. It was around eight, and she was happy to find a Cajun Restaurant called Jumbo Gumbo still open. Having traveled all the way from River Ridge, a suburb of New Orleans, Nora found it ironic that the first restaurant she was to dine in served dishes from Louisiana. Jumbo Gumbo was situated across the street from the run-down old hotel Nora had viewed from her window.

Considering the many heavy drinkers Nora had encountered as a waitress, she was surprised she couldn't get the vision of the old drunk out of her mind.

"Ma'am?"

Nora jumped in her seat, startled by the waitress standing next to her table holding a hot plate.

"Your dinner. Be careful. That sauce can run right off the plate. We have us a temporary fill-in chef tonight, and if I have it my way, it'll be very temporary." She placed a white plate heaping with shrimp étouffée in front of her. The smell of the Cajun spices was wonderful and reminded Nora of home.

"I can tell that if I stay here too long, I'll put on ten extra pounds."

The waitress, whose black polyester uniform was pulling a bit at the waist, eyed Nora's figure. "And what would be wrong with gaining a little weight, honey? You could use a few pounds. What do they say—it's all about that bass?" She wiggled her ample hips and laughed. "Sorry, we don't have the gumbo tonight, with our regular cook out sick. Kind of silly to be called Jumbo Gumbo with no gumbo."

"Well, I hope he's better soon."

"Thank you, but you're preachin' to the choir."

Nora raised her hand as the waitress plodded back to the kitchen. "Oh, just one more thing. Could I have some more ice water with a slice of lime in it this time?"

"You got it." The waitress headed toward the kitchen.

Nora started eating her dinner. In the background, she recognized Frank Sinatra's voice. This "true love" the guy was singing about, it was a mystery to her. She was beginning to question whether that particular miracle would ever happen for her.

The bell on the door rang, and a man entered, pulling off a weathered denim jacket. He had dark, curly hair trimmed closely at his neck and temples. Even so, a precision cut wasn't enough to contain all the curl. He had the trace of a beard and an air of authority. If she had to guess, she'd say he was probably a lawyer or local politician. He struck Nora as the kind of guy people would go to in a crisis. The man observed the empty restaurant and then glanced in Nora's direction. She shifted her gaze to the table, clanking her fork on her plate. She'd been caught staring.

"Hey, Tuck." The waitress greeted the man as if he were an old friend. "As luck would have it, your table's open." She laughed at her own joke and led Tuck to a table right across from Nora, blocking Nora's view of the Tunie Hotel.

Once the man was seated, the waitress hurried back to Nora's table with a pitcher of water to refill Nora's glass.

Nora touched the waitress's arm. "Excuse me. I was just curious. I'm staying at the bed and breakfast here in town, and I noticed the old hotel across the street. Is it open?"

"Oh, the Tunie?"

"Yes. I was wondering what you could tell me about it."

"It had been closed for years, but then one of our crazier Piney Woods citizens, a woman, bought it in foreclosure. I'm not sure if it's officially open or not, but it isn't what it used to be, that's for sure. I've seen the owner over there working on it. I'll bet she's sorry she bought it now."

The man across from Nora signaled to the waitress. She grabbed her pitcher of water and walked over to take his order.

Nora picked up her glass of water and realized the waitress had forgotten her lime. Instead of gesturing to her, she walked the few steps over to the other customer's table to remind her.

The waitress was engaged in conversation with her customer. "Man, I was glad you showed up." The woman held the pitcher of ice water with one hand while gesturing with the other. "I didn't think you'd ever get there. Were you driving below the speed limit or what? Don't you have some pretty lights on that car of yours? My old man can get kind of out of control when he's mad."

Nora was about to tap the waitress on the shoulder, but instead she startled her, causing the pitcher of ice water to spill into the man's lap.

The man jumped up with a yelp.

"Oh. I'm so sorry." Nora grabbed a napkin and started cleaning up the puddle seeping across the table.

The waitress scurried to the kitchen and returned with a towel, handing it to the man.

He had quickly regained his composure. "Well, I was wondering how I could meet you." He smiled at Nora as he dabbed at his lap with the towel. "But I never expected you to come over and dump cold water on me. Talk about an ice breaker."

Nora could feel the color rise to her cheeks. "I'm *so* sorry." She turned to the waitress, who was also trying to clean up the spill. "I came over to ask if you could bring my lime slice."

"Oh, shoot. I'm sorry, honey. I forgot. I'll just go get one." She picked up her towel and headed for the kitchen.

"Well, you sure know how to get someone's attention." The man dried his hands on the towel.

Nora was mortified. Did he think she'd cooked this "accident" up? He had just caught her staring. "I know you might not believe me, but it really was an accident."

Her answer seemed to amuse him. "Okay. I'll take your word for it, this time. You look trustworthy." The man glanced over at the table where Nora had been sitting. "It seems we're both eating dinner alone tonight. Would you care to join me? With all this uninvited moisture, I'm feeling a bit of a draft. Maybe you could sit there and block the breeze for me."

The whole situation was growing increasingly awkward, and she didn't answer right away.

"Come on. I don't bite. Besides, if I did, I'd have to arrest myself. I'm Tuck Watson, Piney Woods PD."

That explained the "pretty" lights on his car. He was a cop. "Well, now that you've vetted yourself. Okay." Nora went back to her table just as the waitress returned with the lime. She saw Nora pick up her plate and smiled.

"Wonderful. You want to eat together. This is so romantic," she gushed as she set the glass across from Tuck.

"And you are …?" Tuck held out his hand.

"Nora Alexander. Nice to meet you."

Once Nora was seated, an uncomfortable silence stretched out between them.

"My father was a policeman," she blurted out.

"Was he?" Tuck bit into a shrimp po'boy sandwich.

"Yes. In New Orleans."

"I see. Is he retired now?"

"No. He was killed in the line of duty."

Tuck's gaze softened. "Sorry to hear about that."

"Thank you. It happened when I was little."

"Yes, but losing your father is tough. I hope they arrested the guy who killed him."

"It was a robbery. They caught the guy right away." Nora played with the étouffée on her plate.

"Good to hear. One thing I hate is a murder case gone cold." Tuck Watson took a piece of bread from the basket and buttered it, all the while eyeing Nora. "What brings you to Piney Woods?"

"I came to fulfill my mother's final wish. She just passed away."

"Wow, you sure have had your share of tragedies. Sorry to hear about your mom, but now I'm curious as to what would be in Piney Woods she needed doing?"

"It's a long story, but basically I'm setting something right for her. She was always there for me, so this is the least I could do."

Tuck Watson raised one eyebrow. "Well, you're a good daughter. Did you leave your family to make this trip? Where are you from?"

"New Orleans, but I guess I don't have any family left."

"No husband or kids?"

"Nope."

"So, you're just heading back to your job?"

"Don't have one of those either. I don't even have a place to live in Louisiana anymore. I am considering my next steps of where to live and work."

"Wow. Tomorrow really is the first day of the rest of your life. So what do you think of Texas? "

"Other than the fact that you drive like crazy people, it seems like a nice place."

"Uh-oh. You're merging into my official day job. What happened? Do I need to arrest somebody?"

"No. I was driving too slowly. I was avoiding another car and he swooped around me. I had to run off the road and in the process, slammed on the breaks. Just about gave myself a heart attack."

"I wouldn't have taken you for an under-the-speed-limit type."

"I had a lot on my mind." Nora took a bite of her dinner. She glanced at Tuck, who seemed to be watching her eat. She set down her spoon and ran her hand through her hair to push it behind her ear.

Tuck took a sip of wine and then set the glass down. "So, how long have you been in Piney Woods?"

"Not long. I just got here. I walked over from the Piney Woods Bed and Breakfast."

"Oh, Tatty and Ed's. Two of our town's most upstanding citizens."

"I was just lucky to be able to find a place for the night. Piney Woods is an awfully small town."

"Wasn't always that way." He dabbed at his lips with his handkerchief. "This used to be a town where oil flowed. It made men rich. All the houses you see on Fifth Street were built when the oil wells were bringing in money by the barrel. But then that ended."

"Really?"

"The oil dried up, and so did the money. Then the people started leaving."

Tuck laid his hand on the table against the grain of the red plaid tablecloth.

"How long ago did this happen?"

"Probably thirty years."

Nora glanced out the window, her gaze drifting from the hotel to farther down the street. "It doesn't look like a ghost town."

"Yes, well, it found a way to keep on going. We have some thriving industry now, including a big warehousing operation that employs half the town. We don't have to rely on the luck of oil anymore. Piney Woods is a survivor."

Nora finished her dinner, set her plate to the side, and laid her napkin on the table. On her drive down here she had promised herself she would take things slowly with new people and places. Still grieving for her mother, she felt too vulnerable. She was determined not to get involved again, but this man was like a plateful of freshly baked chocolate chip cookies before dinner. She was having a hard time resisting.

Tuck's gaze never left her.

"This has been lovely." Nora reached for her bag.

"I've enjoyed it too," he said. "I can't believe I had a conversation with somebody, and my phone didn't ring. You don't know how unusual that is. Anything goes wrong in this town, they call me."

Nora smiled. "It was very nice meeting you."

After they paid their separate checks, Tuck turned back to the waitress. "Thanks for dinner. See you later."

The waitress grinned. "Don't do anything I wouldn't do."

"That leaves us with an awfully short list," Tuck joked.

Nora rose to leave.

"Let me walk you back to Tatty and Ed's," Tuck said. "As the local law enforcement, I feel like I need to protect you."

The heat rose on Nora's neck. "You don't have to do that. I'm fine. I think half your town must be asleep."

His amused smile widened. "Gee, is *Jeopardy* over already? We are pretty dull around here. Let me phrase it differently. May I walk you home?" Tuck offered his arm.

Her cheeks had to be blazing. When she fitted her hand into the crook of his arm, the warmth of his body radiated into hers.

A full moon made the street appear as if it had been specially lit for the occasion. The temperature had gone down some with the sun, and it was almost chilly. Nora crossed her arms for warmth. "It's starting to get a little colder. Do you get snow here?"

Tuck looked at her and then burst out laughing. "Of course,

we do. Probably not the same kind of snow you see in the Christmas movies, but we get a little every year."

"That must be nice. Just enough to enjoy, but not so much you have to shovel it."

"That's about how it is. So, tell me about your life in New Orleans."

"Not much to tell. I've waited tables, worked the drive-thru. I even worked front desk at a hotel, and if you've ever worked in the hospitality industry during Mardi Gras, you know how crazy that is."

"That kind of surprises me. You didn't go to college?"

"Yes and no. I was a liberal arts major with no real defined focus. Kind of hard to turn a generalization into a career. Besides, why would I do anything to make my mother happy like that?"

Tuck's chest shook as he laughed. "Oh, you're that kind of daughter."

She laughed too. "Probably so. I turned eighteen and just wanted to be out in the world. College was my way of doing that. It worked pretty well for four years. Then I had to go and graduate with a degree and no job skills."

They walked a few more steps, their feet beating a pleasant rhythm on the pavement. They passed by several old buildings where antiques were sold, then a hardware store, finally arriving at the Piney Woods Bed and Breakfast front porch in companionable silence. In the moonlight, the gingerbread bric-a-brac made dancing outlines on the lawn. As they reached the top step, Nora's heart plummeted at the realization their time together was ending. Her disappointment was short-lived, for Tuck slid his arm around her and leaned down to kiss her. The kiss was as tender and light as the evening breeze.

"Sorry. Don't know why I did that. I don't usually kiss people on their first day in town." His voice was gruff.

Nora straightened and stepped back. "You're quite the welcome wagon, Officer," she said in a shaky voice. "I should go. It's been a long day. I'll be leaving in the morning to go back to Louisiana."

What she really wanted to do was invite him inside. It was unbelievable. She'd just met the man. She had to realign her focus. She wasn't boyfriend shopping—she was only here to take care of her mother's final wish.

"Sure you don't want to stay just one more day?" Tuck's phone rang. He looked down at the caller ID and grimaced. "Sorry, have to run. It's been so nice … meeting you, Nora Alexander. You can spill ice water on me anytime." He gave Nora a heart-stopping grin, then walked away with the phone pressed to his ear.

# Chapter 3

THE NEXT DAY, Nora parked in Adam Brockwell's driveway and headed up the steps onto the imposing porch she had seen from the street. Hopefully, she would find him at home and be able to deliver her mother's letter. Her original plan had been to meet Mr. Brockwell and then head back to Louisiana. After her dinner last night with Tuck Watson, somehow that decision seemed a little hasty. Just as she was about to knock on the looming double doors, one of them yanked opened.

"Oh!" A man in tennis shorts and a white polo shirt jumped back. He had thick, tawny-gold hair and his profile spoke of privilege and money. "I'm sorry. I was just going out and didn't hear you on the porch. Can I help you?"

"Um … I think so. I'm looking for a Mr. Brockwell?" Nora clutched the satchel, thinking of the letter inside.

"Well, this is a dream come true. A beautiful woman comes to my front door and wants to talk to me." His lips parted as he smiled, revealing white teeth not to be outdone by any Hollywood actor.

Nora was a little taken aback by this attractive man. He was much younger than her mother. Who knew she had it in her?

"I know this is sort of strange." The weight of the letter in her bag weighed her down.

"Would you like to come in, then?" Mr. Brockwell opened the door wider.

They entered a foyer, apparently the landing area for many different rooms in the house. An Hispanic woman mopping the expansive area looked up and smiled. Nora's head swiveled as her eyes followed the gray and white marble staircase. The young man waited while she surveyed her surroundings.

Nora, gawking like a tourist, was suddenly embarrassed. "Oh. I'm sorry. It's just such a big house. Let me introduce myself. I'm Nora Alexander. I've driven here from New Orleans."

"Nice to meet you. I'm Corey Brockwell. What brings you to Texas?"

"*Corey* Brockwell?" Corey wasn't the right name. Her letter was for Adam Brockwell. An incredible relief washed over her. This man wasn't her mother's secret lover. He didn't fit her idea of someone her mother would pen her final words to. For one thing, he was too young. Then again, her mother had one secret, why not two? Not all insurance adjusters were old and ugly.

Nora pulled out the envelope. "As I said, I've driven all the way from New Orleans. My mother just passed away, and she asked me to deliver this letter. It's addressed to someone named Adam Brockwell. Do you know him?"

"Adam Brockwell is my father."

Now she was getting somewhere. "I heard your father is up for Piney Woods Pioneer. Congratulations."

"Thank you very much. As long as the judging committee doesn't dig too deep, I think he might actually win."

Nora smiled. This guy was rich, handsome, and humble. "If you don't mind, I would like to deliver this letter to him in person."

"My condolences for your loss, but you know, we have this marvelous new invention called the U.S. Postal Service. Why didn't you just mail it to him? You've driven a long way. It's almost four hundred miles from here to New Orleans."

He was right. It would have been simpler to put a stamp on the envelope, pop it in the mail, and never think about it again. Still, her mother had kept this letter until the final moments of her life. It had to be very important. If Adam Brockwell was a man her mother was involved with at some time, she'd had no choice but to drive here.

"It's a long story. I really would like to hand this personally to your father."

"Don't be silly. I can deliver it for you, and you can be on your way back home."

As charming as this man was, Nora had come too far to be thwarted now. "No. I'd like to meet your father."

Corey nodded. "Well, okay. I think he's with someone right now, but if you can wait a minute, I'm sure he'll talk to you. He has a thing for redheads."

Nora smiled. "Thank you."

"It's the least I can do, especially because you're carrying some mysterious letter. Any idea what's in it?"

"Nope. I'm figuring maybe my mother and your father might have been …." She stumbled over her words.

"Lovers?" Corey laughed.

The housekeeper stopped mopping for just an instant and then continued.

"That old dog. I can't wait to hear my old man explain this one." He stopped short and turned to her. "Uh, we're not brother and sister, are we?"

"No. Adam Brockwell is not my father."

"That's a relief," Corey said with just a touch of a Texas twang. "Come on along. I'll take you to his study. Excuse us, Mrs. Rodriguez. Right this way."

He led Nora down a hallway to a room with two sliding pocket doors.

*What is it with this house? Two doors for everything. I'll bet even the doghouse has a couple.*

They walked into a paneled study with partially open red-velvet drapes revealing windows that started near the floor and extended to the ceiling. An old man was dwarfed by the large, dark cherry wood desk he sat behind. It was littered with paper.

The old man held up a grizzled hand. "Just a minute, Corey. I'll be right with you."

In the corner of the room, a young African-American woman in her twenties sat in a straight-backed chair with a briefcase on her lap. The woman glanced at the new arrivals and returned to texting on her cellphone.

A man with a clerical collar swirled brown liquid in a shot glass. His dark hair was perfectly combed over his forehead with just a touch of gray on each side. He relaxed in a red-leather chair across from the man at the desk. "I know you have trust in the Lord, Adam, but I'm telling you, as a friend, you need to put in an alarm system. These are hard times economically."

"Mighty true, but I don't need any newfangled camera taking pictures of me throughout my house. Who could hack in? Don't you know the government's watching those idiots with surveillance cameras nailed up all over their houses? Nope. I have a rifle and enough nerve to shoot it. That's all any burglar needs to know."

"Father," Corey interrupted him, "you have a visitor from New Orleans."

Mr. Brockwell put the paper down, pushed his glasses up on his nose, and turned to look at Nora. His eyes widened, and then his breath hitched slightly. Because of her red hair and pale complexion, Nora was used to men pausing to take in her unusual coloring when they first met her. However, this was the first man to look frightened by her appearance. Was her makeup splotched in a way that made her look deranged? No, it couldn't be, or Corey would have had a different reaction to her arrival.

"All the way from New Orleans? Well, this is an honor." He rose and took Nora's hand, surrounding it with his warm, bony fingers. "My son didn't introduce me, but I'm Adam Brockwell, and this fine gentleman is Reverend Alton Siddons. The lovely young lady there, the one who's been hypnotized by her phone, is my financial counselor Lucy Cooper. You have business with me? What might your name be? With your auburn hair, I'm putty in your hands. I've always been a sucker for redheads."

This was going better than Nora expected. If this man was an old boyfriend, she approved. "Thank you. My name is Nora Alexander. I get the hair from my mother. I think you knew her? Her name was Kay Alexander." She waited for a glimpse of recognition in the old man's face.

"Kay Alexander? Her name was Kay?"

*Oh no.* What if her mother was in love with him and he didn't even remember her? Nora was glad she wasn't here to see this.

"Well, sir …." Nora shuffled a bit. "You see, she died a month ago."

"Oh … dear child. I'm so sorry to hear about your mother." His voice was gentle. He was kind, considering he didn't remember her.

"Before she died, she wrote a letter and addressed it to you."

The old man's furry eyebrows went up. "She did? She left a letter for me?"

"Yes."

"Well, this is a surprise." Adam Brockwell straightened the glasses on his nose.

Corey whispered in Nora's ear, "You know, my dad helps people all the time. Sometimes he doesn't remember their names."

"Helping other people is the least I can do. God blessed me with a little extra." Adam's hearing must have been better than his son thought.

"Truly, you have, and that's why you're a shoo-in as the Piney Woods Pioneer this year." The pastor nodded in agreement.

Nora detected a slight shake in Adam Brockwell's grasp. Was he excited or was his shaking due to age? She couldn't tell.

"Well, let's see this letter then, young lady." Adam released her hand and stepped back.

Nora pulled the tattered envelope out of her bag, and stepping forward, handed it to Adam Brockwell. He held it for just a second, studying the address on the front. Once it was in his hands, he turned the envelope from side to side. Then he opened it and began to read. Nora smiled at Corey. From the tenderness his father had just exhibited over the envelope, it might be a love note.

"Can you read it aloud, Dad?" Corey asked.

Adam Brockwell took a deep breath, not answering his son.

The old man returned to his chair. Then he put the letter down, his hand splayed across the top, covering the words Nora's mother had written.

"Would you mind?" Nora asked. "It's just, after coming such a long way, I'm curious as to why my mother wrote to you."

"I think you'd better leave." Adam Brockwell placed his other hand over his heart. His bottom lip quivered. "I'm feeling tired now."

As Nora followed Corey out, she glanced back over her shoulder. Adam Brockwell picked up the letter and began to read it again.

She wished she'd found a way to read the letter before she had handed it over Adam Brockwell. She has obeyed her mother's instructions to the letter but now was left with an unsettled feeling about the whole situation. She would have to think what her next steps would be. She scribbled her number down on a piece of note paper and gave it to Corey. "In case you need to reach me," she said.

# Chapter 4

N ORA STAYED THE rest of the day in Piney Woods waiting for a call back from Mr. Brockwell. Either Mr. Brockwell, Adam, or Corey. She paced the rented room for an hour and then decided they wouldn't call. Why should they? It wasn't as if she had been involved in the matter. Nora waited out the rest of the day and accepted Tatty's kind offer of dinner that evening.

Tatty leaned forward as she passed the rolls to Nora. "So? What did it say?"

"Yeah. What did your mother want Mr. Brockwell to know?" Ed echoed. "We've been waiting all day to hear and you're as shut down as liquor store in a dry county."

Nora took a bite of her roll, chewed, and swallowed. "I don't know. He wouldn't tell me. After he read it, he just asked me to leave."

"What? Are you serious? Not a word about what was in the letter?"

"Nope. Not a word. He did look upset, though."

"Oh, man!" Ed hit his knee. "Someone told off the great

Adam Brockwell. A nominee for Piney Woods Pioneer. I'm loving this."

Nora frowned. "I'm not. I really wanted to know what was in that letter. It was my mother's last piece of unfinished business so it had to be important to her."

"Why don't you call him up and ask him?" Ed said.

Nora considered that option. She could call him, but she would rather Adam Brockwell called her. Maybe tonight. She would wait a little longer.

WHEN THE NEXT morning arrived with still no information from Adam Brockwell, Nora checked out of the Piney Woods Bed and Breakfast, determined to return to New Orleans. She drove by the old hotel once more, now seeing some light in the lobby. Renovating a hotel had to be the world's biggest DIY project. Definitely not anything she would ever dream of doing. She finally settled in at Dudley's Brew, a little coffee shop situated on the end of a row of downtown businesses. She rationalized being well-caffeinated would help her to hit the road and pick up the pieces of her life. Three cups later, along with a slight eye twitch from the caffeine raging through her bloodstream, she knew what she had to do. She'd thought for sure that she would have answers once she delivered the letter to Adam Brockwell. Now she didn't know what to do next. Deciding not to act on something was just a decision not to act. Nora found herself wallowing in stasis. She couldn't go back home and she couldn't stay. She could find out about the letter or never find out about the letter.

Ten minutes later, Nora was driving out of Piney Woods, headed for New Orleans. She came to a stop sign, and instead of driving forward, did a U-Turn and pointed herself in the direction of Adam Brockwell's home. She had made a decision. There was a good chance Mr. Brockwell wouldn't tell her what the letter said, but she had to ask. When she parked her car on the circular drive in front of the Brockwell estate, she began to feel silly. On her way to the doorway, she lost her resolve and turned back toward the car.

As she opened her car door, Corey Brockwell, looking haggard and hung over, climbed out of a black Jaguar, now parked behind Nora. He ran his fingers through his unkempt, dark-blond hair.

"Back again?" His voice was hoarse.

"Yes," Nora stammered. "I was about to leave town and I wanted …."

He smiled wickedly. "Dying to know what your mother said to my father? Then why are you heading this way? Come on!" He gestured for her to follow.

When she hesitated, Corey grabbed Nora by the elbow, dragging her toward the house. His breath reeked of stale whiskey. This time, as the two entered the house, it was eerily quiet.

Nora looked around. "Where's Mrs. Rodriguez?"

"What's today?"

"Thursday."

"Her day off. It's a big house, but how messy can two guys get? She cooks way too much food, and we eat the leftovers."

Nora gave him a long look.

"Yes, even rich people eat leftovers."

Corey let go of her elbow and headed down the hall. Nora followed him to the kitchen, wishing she could just turn around and leave.

"No coffee made? The old man must've slept in. Never thought I'd live to see the day. I'll just put on a little pot. Sound good? I know I need about a gallon." Nora's stomach lurched at the prospect of another cup of coffee.

Corey pulled a can of coffee out of a well-stocked cupboard. "You know, if he's not out of bed yet, I suppose you could come back later." Corey filled the pot with water.

Nora felt a surge of relief. "I need to head back home anyway."

"But I'd love it if you'd stay. It's my dad and your mom, so we should both know what's in that letter." The coffee maker finished and Corey pulled a cup out of the cupboard. "Would you like some?"

"No. I think I'll go. It's really none of my business."

"Okay. I should have pegged you for the herbal tea type." He continued as if they were still talking about coffee. "I mean, with your fair skin and red hair, you sort of look like a flower child. Tell you what, 'Rainbow,' we could see if the letter is still on his desk." He exuded the naughty charm of a good-looking but hung-over rich boy.

Somehow Nora felt like sneaking a peek at the letter was crossing a line. It was one thing if Adam Brockwell had offered to tell her about it, but reading it without his permission was an invasion of privacy.

"I couldn't ask you to search your dad's desk. It doesn't feel right to me. Maybe he'd rather I didn't see it. Thanks anyway."

"Come on. Are you frightened to go into my father's study?" His tone mocked her.

Nora bristled. "Of course not."

Corey grabbed her by the arm again, pulling her down the hall as he walked backward. "Come on. Let's look for it. I'm as fascinated as you are by this whole thing."

The study door was closed, and for all of his bravado and eagerness to invade his father's privacy, Corey still knocked politely before entering.

"Dad?" he rested his head on the door. After waiting a second, he turned the knob.

As the door opened, a pungent smell assailed Nora's nostrils. She stepped backward as Corey opened the door and stepped into the study. Adam Brockwell's head was resting on his desk. If it hadn't been for the dark puddles of sticky brown residue everywhere, she'd have thought he was taking a quick nap.

Corey rushed over to his father and began shaking his shoulders. "Dad?"

Dread shone in Corey's eyes.

As Corey pulled his father's body back in the chair, partially hardened bloodstains stuck to the old man's light-blue shirt. His face had turned a sickening shade of purple, as if all of the blood had run to the top of his head when it hit the desk.

A trail of blood led from Brockwell's hand to the edge of the desk. Clenched in his right hand was the letter Nora had delivered the day before. It looked mottled and stained, as if Brockwell had spilled something on it, or perhaps even shed a tear. Besides the killer, the letter was the last thing he'd seen before he died. If it were a love letter, this love story didn't have the typical happy ending.

AN HOUR LATER, Nora sat outside the study in a brown brocade chair fetched from the front room. She held a cup of the coffee Corey had made, her hands still shaking. Corey Brockwell sat across from her in a second chair, speaking in a low voice into his cellphone, alerting people to his father's death.

"Good morning. Tuck Watson, Piney Woods PD."

Nora looked up from her coffee and recognized the man she'd had dinner with her first night in town.

He found another chair and positioned it directly across from her, his knees almost touching hers. "This is a surprise. I was hoping it wasn't you out here. Still, though, when I saw the letter …."

"You and me both." Nora sat up in her chair, pulling back from Tuck.

"I need to ask you about this letter you brought to Adam Brockwell."

"Sure." Nora's voice was flat. She felt herself becoming numb from shock.

"Okay. Your mother wrote it and asked you to deliver it to Brockwell?"

"Yes. She handed it to me not long before she died."

"All the way from New Orleans?"

"I know. Her cancer and the pain medication often made her

mind fuzzy. She was adamant that I deliver this letter to Adam Brockwell." She took a sip of her coffee.

"Were you aware of the contents?"

"No. She requested that I not open the letter. It's the whole reason I came back today. It turned out I did want to know what my mother said in her letter. I thought once I had delivered it to Adam Brockwell, he might tell me. He did not. It was the last bit of communication I had from her. I just ...." Nora couldn't go on."

"I see." Tuck rose and went back into the study. He returned after a few minutes, holding the letter, now encased in a clear plastic evidence bag. He held it up. Some of the writing was almost illegible because of the clear liquid spilled on it. Nora just hoped it wasn't a bodily fluid she was trying to read through.

"You had better look at this." He sat back down in front of her.

Nora put down her coffee and began to read.

Adam,

I'm writing to you because I never had the courage to tell you in person. I've wanted to say this for some time, but was never strong enough. I was fooled by you, taken in by your charms as so many other women doubtless have been. I even thought I felt something for you, but you didn't care. You never cared for anyone but yourself. I am ashamed of how stupid you made me feel and of the ones I hurt because of you. You showed me clearly through the choice you made that I was not worthy of the great Adam Brockwell. I hear you are up for the Piney Woods Pioneer award. You are not the man everyone thinks you are. I have not forgiven you for what happened.

I have lived a good life, and now, thanks to my daughter and all she has done for me, I will be at peace.

*Leslie*

Nora's brow furrowed. She sat back and re-examined the letter. She'd been so sure it would be a love letter, but this message, in her mother's handwriting, was unforgiving. She'd never seen or heard her mother so angry. And why had she signed it "Leslie"?

"Okay. Let's start again." Tuck sighed. "The letter you gave to Adam Brockwell …. What part did you have in it?"

"What do you mean? I told you. My mother gave it to me before she died.

"Why didn't you just mail it?"

"A couple of reasons. Anything my mother would hold on to until her last breath had to be important, and I wanted to do as she asked on her death bed."

Tuck wrote in his notebook and then looked up. "You really had no idea what was in the letter?"

"None whatsoever."

"Did she ever talk to you about her hatred for Mr. Brockwell?"

"No. Never."

"How long did you stay with Brockwell after you delivered the letter?"

"Just a few minutes. I wanted to stay longer so I could find out what my mother wrote, but he didn't want to share it. He was friendly to me, but whatever it was between them, it was private."

"Where did you go after you visited Brockwell?"

"To the Piney Woods Bed and Breakfast, where I unpacked and rested for a couple of hours, and then … I had dinner with Tatty and Ed. I was staying there. As you know … since you walked me back last evening."

Corey Brockwell stopped talking on the phone, surprise registering on his unshaven face.

"You two know each other?" Corey put his phone back in his pocket.

Tuck cleared his throat. "No. We met at Jumbo Gumbo the first night she was in town."

"Sure." Corey crossed his arms.

Nora tried to take into consideration the fact that Corey had just lost his father, also that he was nursing what looked to be a giant hangover.

"We were both eating at the same restaurant and decided to eat together. Nothing more," Nora assured him.

"Yeah, right. So, good to know the man who'll be investigating my father's murder has already been compromised by a woman who wanted him dead."

"No, you're wrong." Nora wanted to say more, but it seemed Corey had already made up his mind.

Corey's phone rang. "Mother, thanks for calling me back." He paused. "No, it's not about that. I took care of that matter and thank you for your help. It's about Dad." Corey took the call in another room, but not before glaring at Nora with a look of disgust.

Watching him leave, Tuck let out a frustrated sigh and turned back to Nora. "You were about to leave town? Is that right?"

"Yes."

"Well, don't. I'm going to have more questions."

"Me? I barely knew the guy. I met him once."

"You met our victim and delivered a letter wishing him dead. Then he gets murdered. The nicest man in town."

"But I didn't even know what the letter said. Why am I being asked not to leave?"

"You keep saying that," Tuck said, "but right now I'm having a hard believing your mother harbored all this intense anger and never once shared it with you. What was your father's name?"

"Ben. Ben Alexander."

After writing down Nora's father's name, Tuck looked up. The smile from the night at Jumbo Gumbo was gone. "Don't leave town."

"And how am I supposed to do that? I have a life in New Orleans, you know."

"My problem is the man brutally stabbed in the next room. You are one of the last persons to see him alive. No one had anything but respect for Adam Brockwell. Except, I guess, you and your mother."

Nora slumped in her chair. She'd be staying in Piney Woods, Texas, after all.

# Chapter 5

———

WHEN NORA RETURNED to the Piney Woods Bed and Breakfast, Tatty was at the front desk. "Mrs. Tovar, it looks like I may be staying a few more days."

"Wonderful! Now you need to call me Tatty. Ed and I are so happy you're staying with us."

Mr. Tovar peeked around the corner from the back office. "You know, we do have a weekly rate as well."

The smell of soup was drifting from the back room. Nora hadn't realized how hungry she was. "Do I smell … chicken soup?"

Tatty smiled. "Yes. And I baked some bread this morning to go along with it. I always make my own soup. The canned stuff has too much salt for Ed and me. Would you care to join us?"

Ed stuck his head out from the office and was about to say something when his wife shushed him with one hand.

"And we won't be adding it to Nora's bill. It's on me, Ed, so put your change purse away."

Ed scowled. "Money doesn't grow on trees, Tatty."

"Neither do new friends." She opened the swinging counter door and ushered Nora into the back area. This part of the old house wasn't quite as up to date as the front room. A designer might characterize it as shabby-comfortable. Yellow and gold curtains gave the windows a warm glow, and a large lumpy couch was positioned in front of a television. A couple of TV trays were folded up in the corner, and the day's paper was on the arm of a recliner.

Nora picked up the paper as Tatty guided her to a small dining room table. "Wow. This is current."

"Just hit the stoop about ten minutes ago," Ed said.

Nora stared at the headline. "Town Legend Found Dead." Adam Brockwell stared at her from his picture.

Tatty tapped the photo. "Just in … a special edition of the town paper. Look how thin it is. I can't believe a thing like this has happened in Piney Woods." She went over to the cupboard, pulled out three bowls, and filled them with steaming soup. "I guess he was murdered."

"Dang," Ed said. "I guess that's one guy Bubby Tidwell didn't get to rescue. You know he must be kicking himself. Trip on the sidewalk around here and you'll find Bubby trying to do the mouth-to-mouth on you. This is big. Everybody owed Adam Brockwell. He did everything around here." Ed sat, waiting for his bowl.

"Let's just hope they don't want to rename the town after him. I kind of like Piney Woods." Tatty placed a bowl in front of her husband.

What would Tatty and Ed think if they knew about her involvement in Brockwell's death? Would they still extend their home to her? Their hospitality? Their chicken soup? She liked them too much not to tell them she was on the suspect list.

"I probably should let you know," she said, "I've been told to stay in town. I'm one of the last people to have seen Mr. Brockwell alive."

Tatty drew in a breath and put her hand on her ample bosom. "You stayed in town because of the letter? That's where you went off to this morning? I'm dying to know … was it a love letter?"

"No. It wasn't."

Tatty clearly wanted to ask more. She and Ed exchanged a glance and then Ed slurped his soup, his gaze never leaving Nora.

Tatty laid a hand on her husband's shoulder. "We're here for as long as you need us, dear."

Ed finished her sentiment. "Exceptin' if you land in jail."

"Thanks." Nora ate a spoonful of soup. It was as delicious as it smelled. "I hate to bring this up, but after my mom died, I had to pay off her bills. If I plan to stay in this town, I'm going to have to find a job."

"Of course." Tatty nodded. "What line of work are you in, Nora?"

"Uh …. My last job was in a hotel, but I've worked in all kinds of places. I know you have a hotel right here in town, but it doesn't look like the management is ready to hire yet. I have a knack for organization. I probably got that from my mother. Unfortunately, it doesn't always translate to paying jobs. I guess I could go back to waitressing."

"Oh." Tatty scratched her head. "I can tell you Jumbo Gumbo already has its hands full with the employees they have. Let me take a look at yesterday's paper." Tatty pulled a paper out from the cushions of Ed's chair and began to refold it to the classified ads section. She placed the folded section on the table.

Ed looked over his bowl of soup and then pointed to an ad. "Hades Alley needs a waitress."

"Certainly not. Our young lady here would never work in a sleazy bar."

"Do you know if they need help?" Nora asked.

Ed stopped mid-spoonful. "Uh, don't rightly know. I drive by the joint every once in a while. I suppose I could call them."

"Nora, dear," Tatty said, "I don't think you understand what kind of place Hade's Alley is. There are … undesirables out there. People who drink. Look here. There's one more ad. The Tunie Hotel needs people."

Ed smirked. "*That* place? It'll be closed before you get your first check. Talk about a money pit."

Given a choice between a hotel and a bar, Nora would choose the hotel, but with Ed's forecast of potential bankruptcy, she needed to think about making reliable money. "I understand, Tatty, but a bar always needs help and right now, if I'm going to pay your bill, I need a job."

Tatty shook her head. "If you're sure you can handle it, I'll have Ed drive out there with you. At least I'll know you're safe."

"If I'm going to work there, I won't be able to have Ed with me all the time. I'll be fine."

Tatty got up and pulled a business card out of a drawer. She pressed it into Nora's hand. "Take this. Our phone number is on it. If you get the job and find yourself in trouble, just call."

"Anytime between eight and five," Ed added.

"No. Anytime at all. Right, Ed?"

"Yes, dear," Ed answered on cue, but Nora couldn't miss the eye roll he gave his wife.

"Did you know Corey Brockwell already has his father's visitation set up? He was finalizing the details as we waited for the police to interview us. Will you be going?"

Tatty sighed, a sadness in her eyes. "I believe it. Not to be unkind, but his son would probably want to hurry things along. The whole town knows he has a gambling problem. The sooner he has the funeral, the sooner he gets his inheritance. Yes. I suppose we will. The whole town will be there. He was a great man in Piney Woods."

"Oh, yeah. The great Adam Brockwell. Now he'll be right up there with his older brother Jesus," Ed said under his breath.

"Stop it, Ed. We owe the man, just like everybody else. Piney Woods never would have survived after the oil ran out if his family hadn't set up business. We have the largest distribution warehouse in Texas. Everything shipping into Dallas or

Houston makes a stop right outside of Piney Woods first. It was all his family's doing. It was pretty much a miracle around here."

"If you ask me, there was something about the guy …. He seemed so nice when he wanted something, but if you said hello to him on the street the next day? You were dead to him. Remember when he wanted to buy my classic '65 Mustang? He was calling here night and day. I was feeling like one of the swells in this town, hobnobbin' with a Brockwell. After I gave in and sold it to him, I never heard from again."

"He paid you well for that car and I didn't ask you for a testimonial on the man, Ed." Tatty bobbed her head from side to side. "What do *you* know? You thought you could charge Nora a quarter for a cup of soup."

"You're so wrong, and frankly, I'm insulted. I was planning to charge a dollar. You undervalue yourself, my love."

Nora interrupted the comfortable banter between her new landlords. "If it's all right with you, I'd like to go along to the visitation."

Ed nodded. "Sure. The more the merrier."

Nora was warmed by his answer, although a little suspicious of his easy acquiescence.

As if to confirm her suspicions, Ed grinned mischievously and said, "Maybe the cops will bust you right there at the visitation. You're better than cable TV, *chica*."

# Chapter 6

———

"ARE YOU SURE you want to go into this joint?" Ed asked as he and Nora made their way through the maze of souped-up Harleys parked outside of Hade's Alley. Nora had planned to go alone, but Tatty was having none of that.

The building was a one-story wood-frame structure painted barn red. On each corner facing the parking lot a flag was hanging. The stars and stripes waved on one end, and the Texas state flag on another. There was a large BROCKWELL FOR PINEY WOODS PIONEER sign in the window and BUBBY TIDWELL bumper sticker that had been plastered on a barrel out front. Neon beer signs blinked through the window, and the sound of a country crooner singing and twanging on a guitar drifted through the screen door.

Nora shrugged, "What else can I do?"

"I'm just saying, this place ain't no tea shop. There are some rough characters in there."

"Did Tatty make you promise to warn me once we arrived?"

"Maybe," Ed admitted.

"Let's do this." As Nora pushed open the door, she stepped out of the bright, sunny September light into the dark, dingy world of Hades Alley. Across the room, a couple of guys in leather vests and bandannas were shooting pool. They both looked up at Nora, and one flashed a gold-toothed smile at the exact moment he hit two balls into the corner pocket.

A motley crew of drinkers sat at the bar, many of them in shirts missing sleeves. The men and their women were all focused on old broadcasts of football games. If they'd already seen the game and knew the score, what was the fun of watching a re-run? Clearly bar bums in Texas behaved as illogically as bar bums in New Orleans. This insane habit seemed to be universal. Behind the bar was a woman in a black tube top, a cigarette dangling from her bottom lip as she refilled a beer, pulling on a tap with ease. Her eyes roamed over to Nora and then she smiled at Ed.

"Hey, Ed. Does Tatt know you're out with another woman? Where and how did you pick this one up? She's way—I mean *way*—out of your league."

Ed blushed. "Tatty knows all about it."

"Well, then, I have to hand it to her for being so open-minded." The barkeep extinguished her cigarette in a Texas-shaped ashtray on the counter.

"She certainly is." Ed leaned forward. "This young lady is looking for a job. You need any waitresses?"

The barkeep reached under the counter, pulled out an application, and slapped it in front of Nora. "Ever waitress before?"

"Yes."

"In a … *bar*?" The barkeep extended the last word as if it were in a language Nora didn't know.

"Yes," she nodded, "in a *bar*." Nora mimicked the barkeep's inflection and threw in a little attitude for good measure.

"Super-de-duper." The barkeep pulled a tray of glasses out and started lining them up under the bar. The older woman's smirk was outlined by layers of wrinkles, most likely formed by years keeping a cigarette dangling from her mouth.

A pudgy man in a *Grand Theft Auto* T-shirt, with a chain hanging from his jeans pocket, sidled up to Nora. "Hey, don't I know you?"

If only it were the first time she'd heard that line. "I don't think so."

"Yes, you're the one!" he shouted. If the entire bar hadn't noticed the stunning redhead who'd walked in with the elderly Mexican gentleman before, they were all looking at them now.

"You're the one who gave old Adam Brockwell a letter and then stabbed him to death, aren't you?"

"No. I mean yes. I—"

"It is you. I knew it! I heard all about you."

A man sitting at the end of the bar stood and pulled his glasses out of his pocket, slipped them on and leaned forward toward Nora, holding the frames tight against his head with both hands. In the darkened room, Nora couldn't quite make him out. He pushed his beer away and ran into the men's room.

The barkeep snarled and yanked the application form back. "Adam Brockwell helped us pay off our bills here after the fire. Sorry. Not hiring."

"What do you mean?" Nora replied. "I had nothing to do with Adam Brockwell's death. Besides, I thought people were innocent until proven guilty? Or do you not believe in due process in Texas?"

"Adam Brockwell was the only good thing this oil bust town had going for it." The barkeep picked up her glasses again.

"It wasn't like I killed the man!" Nora shouted.

Ed placed a hand on Nora's sleeve. "Let's go, *chica*."

The drunken man returned from the men's room, wiping his mouth with a paper towel. From his pale countenance, she assumed he'd been throwing up. He walked up to the group gathered around Nora.

"Oh my God," the man muttered, "it just can't be." He began to shake, causing the few wispy hairs left on the back of his head to sail from side to side.

"Do you know him?" Nora whispered to Ed.

"Wiley? Don't mind him." Ed guided Nora to the door.

Nora recognized the drunk she'd seen in front of the old hotel. For some reason, he appeared to be horrified at the sight of her.

"You better get on out of here, missy," the barkeep called after her. "Ed, don't bring her back in here. She's not welcome."

# Chapter 7

WHEN NORA AND the Tovars entered Morrison's Funeral Home—a one-story, tan brick building situated on the edge of town—a lonely church bell could be heard on this September day, ringing not just once, but continuously.

Nora turned toward the sound. "Wow. They sure are whaling on the church bell."

Tatty turned also and placed a hand on Nora's arm. "It's old Piney Woods' way of telling the people about Brockwell. Before everyone had a telephone, the bell was how the town's forefathers made an announcement."

"Yeah," added Ed. "Think of it as the original Tweeter."

"It's called Twitter," Tatty corrected.

"Whatever. Just another form of being nosy I don't partake in."

"These days they only use the bell if there's an emergency like a tornado coming, or somebody's funeral like this. I'm surprised they didn't ring it when the old man was murdered."

The line of mourners for Adam Brockwell's visitation snaked out of the viewing room. Why had she wanted to come to this? She'd never known the man. Hoping no one would recognize her like they had in the bar, she'd taken the precaution of borrowing one of Tatty's hats and hidden her hair underneath it. The truth was, she'd come here because her intense curiosity about the man and her mother's letter to him had overruled her sense of safety.

Corey Brockwell, dressed in a tailored, dark-gray suit, stood next to the coffin, accepting hugs and handshakes. His face was pale and drawn, and he didn't at all resemble the man who'd led her into the study on her first day in Piney Woods. Chairs were lined up against the wall to allow more room for mourners to chat once they'd viewed the casket. All around her people spoke in hushed tones.

The young woman who was Mr. Brockwell's investment counselor sat in one of the chairs. She'd been staring at the floor when Nora entered, but now her eyes darted from side to side as if she were checking out the room from behind her tissue.

The pastor who'd been with Adam Brockwell when Nora delivered her letter walked over, hands folded at his waist.

"Nice of you to come. I saw you at Mr. Brockwell's house, but we were never formally introduced. I'm Alton Chilton. I was Mr. Brockwell's pastor. As you can see from all of the friends we have here today, Adam Brockwell was a legend in this town."

"Everyone keeps telling me just those kinds of stories about him." Nora thought of some of the things Ed and Tatty had said. "How long were you his pastor?"

Pastor Chilton let out a deep sigh. "Oh, I guess about twenty years now."

Nora had never been around a person like Pastor Chilton. Church to her was a place other people went on Sunday. Adam Brockwell was apparently a regular and seemed to possess a faith in something she could never understand. Nora recalled the conversation between Pastor Chilton and Brockwell about an alarm system. Maybe Mr. Brockwell shouldn't have put so much trust in his ability to shoot and been a little more open to his pastor's advice. Pastor Chilton went on to talk about Piney Woods and his parishioners, but Nora tuned him out. Could it be she was in the room with Adam Brockwell's murderer? Could someone be looking at her, planning to frame her for their crime?

"Excuse me," Nora interrupted him, "but did Mr. Brockwell say anything to you about the letter I left from my mother?"

Pastor Chilton's head jerked back a bit. "Hello again. No. Mr. Brockwell sent us all packing after getting that note. I offered to stay, but he would have none of it."

"I was hoping to learn more of what happened next."

"We are all reeling about what happened. It's a tragedy for this town." Pastor Chilton surveyed the room and then took Nora's hand and enveloped it in his in a quick handshake. "It was so nice of you to join us today. Excuse me." He shook Nora's hand for a second time then crossed the room.

Once again, Nora noticed the investment counselor looking her way. Nora grabbed Tatty by the elbow and nodded toward the young woman. "Do you know the name of the woman sitting over there?"

"Lucy Cooper. Her mother cleaned house for Mr. Brockwell for a few years. Now she seems to be carrying on the family tradition of being in service to him. She works over at the bank. Real nice. She helped Ed and me set up a retirement portfolio."

"You mean you have stock investments? Is it wise in a retirement package? Shouldn't you be squirreling it all away instead of risking it in the market?"

Tatty shook her head. "No, dear. She makes safe investments for old people. She's doubled some of our savings."

Pastor Chilton had his arm around Lucy's shoulders. She nodded, apparently comforted by the pastor's words.

Corey also seemed to be observing the scene as he stood next to his father's coffin. The line was moving now and Tatty, Ed, and Nora neared Adam Brockwell's still form.

"I was so sorry to hear of your father's death," Tatty said to Corey when it came time for her to express condolences.

"Thank you." Corey's response, after he'd spoken to so many well-wishers, seemed automatic. The Tovars stepped away and Nora came face-to-face with Corey once more. She glanced at the lifeless visage of Adam Brockwell. The undertaker had done a wonderful job covering the gashes made by his killer's knife.

"Miss Alexander," Corey addressed her in a formal tone. "I have to say, I'm surprised to see you here today. I thought you'd already gone back to wherever it is you came from."

"That was the plan, but now I'm not allowed to leave town."

Corey nodded with a polite smile. It seemed sincere but didn't reach his eyes. "What a pity. Thank you for coming." He shook her hand then released it and reached out to the next mourner, pushing her down the line and out of his sight.

"She's the one," an older woman whispered behind Nora. "She's the one who gave him the poison-pen letter just before he died."

Nora turned around. Two older ladies were talking behind embroidered handkerchiefs. As she met their gazes, they turned away from her. Their clothing looked like something straight out of Woodstock. One wore a gauzy top and flowing skirt, accented by beads. Her fine gray hair hung straight to her waist. The other woman wore a denim jumper with daisies embroidered at the neckline, her silver hair done up in braids on top of her head.

"I see you've titillated the Fredericks sisters. Not hard to do in this town." Tuck Watson appeared at Nora's side.

She hadn't noticed him in the room until now.

"They're talking as if I'm the reason Adam Brockwell died."

"Were you?" His immediate question surprised her.

"No." Nora bit her lip. "Not to my knowledge."

Looking back at the sisters, Tuck continued in a whisper, "Their parents were avid gardeners. They loved to grow flowers. So much so, they named their twin daughters Azalea and Violet. They're a little strange, but you can't arrest someone for being weird."

"Tucker Watson, don't tell me you finally have a date and you brought her to a funeral," a woman with short, spiky salt-and-pepper hair said as she walked up to Nora.

"Aunt Marty. Should have known you'd be here."

"Why not? Adam Brockwell had more money than God."

"Yes, and sadly he's one of the few people who didn't buy real estate through you." Tuck turned to Nora. "Aunt Marty, this is Nora Alexander. She … will be in town for a little while."

"Yes, well, he calls me 'Aunt Marty,' but I'm only ten years older than he is. I was a late child for my parents."

"Nice to meet you."

"And you as well." She tapped Tuck on the shoulder. "I like this one, sweetie." Marty grabbed her key out of her purse. "Well, I've paid my respects. I need to get back to work. I'm a little overwhelmed right now."

Tuck Watson reached over and kissed his aunt. "Don't work too hard."

Marty laughed and waved over her shoulder as she exited the funeral home.

Azalea Fredericks and her sister moved closer, as quiet as kudzu in the summer. "You came all this way to deliver your letter. What did it say, exactly?"

"Um …."

Tuck jumped in before Nora could reply. "Nothing important."

The crowd became quiet. "Who was your mother?" Violet Fredericks now asked. "Adam Brockwell was up for Piney Woods Pioneer, you know." Violet's voice was identical to her sister's.

Azalea leaned forward. "Although our vote was going to be for Bubby Tidwell. I'm one of the fourteen, you know. One of the fourteen people Bubby has rescued. He gave me mouth-to-mouth resuscitation. His lips were like pillows, they were." She started blushing and bit her bottom lip while Violet sighed. Nora tried not to think of Bubby Tidwell's lips, but it was difficult to brush that whole vision to the back of her mind. Azalea glanced around, "Where is Bubby today?"

"Getting fitted for that new suit he's going to need when he is pronounced Piney Woods Pioneer. Going back to the subject at hand?"

Nora checked Azalea's lips to be sure they weren't moving.

"I don't know," Nora answered, trying to be polite. "I didn't even know about the letter until right before she died."

Azalea started fanning herself with her hanky. "And you've come here to avenge your dead mother …."

Nora feared Azalea would get the vapors, if women still came down with vapors.

"No," Nora snapped, "of course not. I didn't know about her dislike for the man. I didn't even know that she knew him. This is all news to me."

A man in a crisp brown suit joined their cozy group. "I say, you've got a lot of nerve coming to the funeral of the man you killed."

"I did not kill him," Nora said through clenched teeth.

A woman stepped up beside him. "Of course you'd say that."

Nora feared she was about to be lynched as more of the men and women around her started closing in.

"Listen …" Nora tried to reason with the crowd.

"Quit picking on her!" a man yelled as he stepped out from the group now crowding around her.

Nora recognized him as the drunk from in front of the hotel. The same man who'd run from her at the bar. He had on a worn suit and a green-felt fedora. She smelled liquor on his breath, but he seemed to be almost sober.

The man addressed the small crowd. "This is what's wrong with this town. You're all just a bunch of bullies, starting with the man in the casket. Bullies!" The drunk walked over and put his arm around Nora. As he did so, he stepped back and gazed at her. Tears formed in his bloodshot eyes. "It's amazing," the drunk said, staring at Nora.

"What is?"

"How much you look like your mother."

"Excuse me?" Nora asked.

The man removed his tattered fedora. "Shpitting image. Just amazin'."

Tatty put a gentle hand on the drunk's shoulder. "You must be mistaken, Wiley. How much have you had to drink today?"

Wiley's glassy eyes focused on Tatty. "Just a little to take the edge off. Pacing myself so as to see the old son-of-a-bitch go into the ground."

The Fredericks sisters gasped and held on to each other.

"I blame him, you know." There was a slight break in Wiley's voice.

"Why don't we go sit down?" Tatty suggested, but before she could move, the old man placed his hand on Nora's cheek.

"You're Leslie's kid, aren't you? I'd know that face anywhere. At first I thought you *were* Leslie, and maybe I'd had too many cocktails, but then I figured it out. You're not Leslie, you're her kid." Wiley began to sob, and letting loose a howl, threw both arms around Nora. He wasn't only under the influence, he was confused.

She extricated herself from his grasp. "Kay was my mother's name."

"Leslie Kay. That's right. Was …? What do you mean 'was'?"

"She died last month, but why would you think you knew her?"

"Would you have a picture? A picture of your mama?" he asked, between sobs.

Nora pulled out her phone and found a picture of her and her mother. Wiley wiped his eyes with an old bandanna and tried to focus on the small screen. Tatty looked over the other shoulder.

"Oh, my. I can't believe it. I finally found Leslie, and now I've lost her." Wiley sat in a maroon chair provided for the mourners. He took his handkerchief and blew his nose, making Nora think of geese flying south for the winter.

She took the chair next to him. Tatty and Ed sat on the other side.

"You think you knew my mother?" Nora asked.

"Yes, I knew her. She was Leslie Kay McArdle in this town."

"You mean she had family here? She never told me anything about having anyone in Texas. She told me her family was from New Orleans and they'd all but died out."

"Don't know anything about people in New Orleans. All her folks are here."

"And you knew her? I mean, when she was young?"

"I should think so. She was my little sister." He extended his hand. "Wiley McArdle."

Nora shook his hand, thinking, *Good news, I finally find a relative of my mother's; bad news, he's the town drunk. Quite a clan, these McArdles.*

"You know, I think I saw you on Main Street and at Hade's Alley."

Wiley looked at his hands. "Did you? I don't remember. I'm a cook over at Jumbo Gumbo."

"Must have been somebody else then. So, do I have other relatives in Piney Woods?"

"Oh, not too many these days. There are a few of us left. I have a boy. He's your cousin."

"Well, well. This is a surprise, Nora. Here we were thinking you were a stranger and we find out you're a McArdle." Tatty shook her head in amazement.

"Surprise, surprise," added Ed.

Wiley scanned Nora again. "You really do look like your mother. Oh, she was beautiful when she was a young woman living here. Probably the prettiest girl in town at the time. All the boys wanted to take her out, but our daddy would have none of it. He didn't think the boys around here were good enough, don't you know."

"And she left?"

"She did. Seemed strange because she seemed so happy here. Everybody loved her."

Wiley leaned over, his watery, buggy eyes looking with kindness into Nora's.

"I guess I'm your closest relative now. Welcome to the family." Wiley's breath made her eyes water.

The Fredericks sisters stood watching them. Tuck Watson observed the entire scene, his eyes trained on Nora.

# Chapter 8

A FTER PULLING HERSELF from Wiley's tearful hug, Nora left the visitation with Tatty and Ed. How could this be happening? Nora had thought she was alone in this world. Now she'd found a family in a town she'd never heard of? Her life was becoming filled with all kinds of surprises about her mother and her previous life. She wondered what else she would discover while in this town.

Back in her rented room, Nora sat on the bed, listening to Tatty and Ed rattle around downstairs. Wiley said her mother was happy here. Why did she depart so suddenly? Why would she leave behind her family and the place she called home? Why had she started calling herself by her middle name? It was as if she wanted to disappear in a crowd. Did something happen or was it just a case of wanderlust? After living her entire life with her mother, Nora couldn't picture Kay with any kind of lust.

Kay Alexander had worked as a bookkeeper in New Orleans, never missing a day of work until last year when she became ill. Nora considered her mother the embodiment of nose to the grindstone. It was part of what infuriated Nora when she was young. How could one human being be so boring? If she had to put a color on her mother, it would be beige. It was like she wanted to be plain. To blend in to the wallpaper. What had turned Kay Alexander into a plain beige kind of woman? Nora rebelled by being just the opposite. If her mother was beige and cold, Nora was like a flame—bright, burning red. She spent so much time not being like her mother, she lost contact with who she really was. It was now clear the forty-hour-a-week, money-counting drone had been so much more than Nora assumed.

Nora thought of the years her father had been alive. Things had been happier then. Then one day he had left on a normal patrol, first promising her that they would go to the park the next day. Ben Alexander always kept his promises, and Nora had gone to bed that night dreaming of sitting in the bright orange pumpkin coach at the playground, where he would play the handsome prince escorting Cinderella to the ball. After that they would visit Storyland to go on the rides. They had been there many times, and Nora couldn't wait to visit again. His partner at the time was Delmar Dupree. Dupree's name was listed in the faded *Times Picayune* article her mother kept in her Bible about the robbery. Del Dupree had more years on the force than her father, and Nora knew he had to be tough to survive on the streets of New Orleans. Was there some insight he could share with her now? Every time he came to the house, he had barely noticed her. Had her mother ever told him about her past?

Nora pulled out her laptop to search for the name Dupree on the New Orleans PD website. There had to be some sort of directory to track him down. It turned out to be harder than she expected. There were eight districts in the New Orleans Police Department. She decided to try calling, but after being put on hold by three of them, she gave up. Pulling the clipping out of the satchel, she reread the article her mother saved after her father's shooting.

"A local policeman was killed in a shootout at a convenience store today. The assailant was arrested on the scene by the officer's partner."

It was so uninformative; it was depressing. People were killed in New Orleans almost every day. Her father was just one more. A statistic.

Putting the article back in her leather satchel, Nora stretched out on the bed. This was it. Life 101 without her mother. She'd been surviving on her own for years, but this time it felt different. As much as her mother's consistency had irritated her, she'd love to hear her reassuring voice right now. There was no phone that could reach her, no email or physical address.

Nora snapped herself back to reality. If she had to stick around, she'd need more cash. She pulled out her wallet and counted her remaining money. She was down to a few twenties and some singles. There were some things in storage back in Louisiana she could sell, assuming she could make the monthly rent payment on the unit. She needed a job, and fast. Picking up the local paper handed down from Ed, Nora spread it across the bed and opened it to the Help Wanted section. There was a job posting for a telemarketer. The tiny column of Help Wanted ads was just another reason people had trouble living in small towns. It was hard to find work. Nora gazed out the window again, her eyes resting on the crumbling hotel.

With the Tunie Hotel being so close, she already knew she could walk to work or drive the two short blocks home and save money on gas. Nora grabbed her purse and drove down the street. There had been no Help Wanted ad in today's paper, and there was no sign in the window, but hadn't Ed mentioned an ad in yesterday's paper? Right now she needed a job and maybe a little more control over her life. As she approached the hotel, she noticed there was still trash on the ground from where Wiley McArdle ran into the trash can. It might be her first duty in her new job. *What a career move.*

The two-story hotel was wedged in between other stores

in the downtown area, taking up a couple of lots. How many rooms would a hotel like this have? It wasn't as big as a Holiday Inn, so it couldn't be more than thirty or forty. Would be she be required to clean all those rooms? Her back hurt already.

# Chapter 9

---

Nora pushed on the door to the lobby of the Tunie, and to her surprise, it opened. She wasn't even sure if the hotel was operating. The deep red carpet was dingy and smelled of mold. There was a stack of towels on the front desk and Nora wasn't sure if the sound she heard behind the desk came from a person or a rodent.

"Hello?" Nora called out. "Is anyone here?"

A loud thud was followed by, "Shoot!"

"Are you okay?"

A head popped up. Behind the counter stood a disheveled woman, her short hair stiff with mousse. Nora recognized her as Tuck Watson's Aunt Marty from Adam Brockwell's visitation.

"Sorry," Marty ran her hands through her hair, "I didn't hear you." She wrinkled her nose in annoyance. "Trying to plug in this computer. We use it for reservations, and I bought it secondhand. Sometimes the only way to get it to work is to jiggle the cord. Somehow I thought the counter was higher, or at least my head did." She rubbed the top of her head. "Can I help you? We have several rooms available." Marty paused, a look of recognition spreading across her face.

"Wait. I know you. You're the girl Tuck …" she paused, "and then I heard you—"

Nora stopped her. "Yep. That's me. Your local person of interest." Was this going to end like her interview at the bar? How long before Marty asked her to leave?

Marty eyed Nora. "You don't look much like someone who could kill a man. He was a pretty tough old codger. I'll bet he could have pinned you in a wrestling match."

Nora let out a breath she hadn't realized she was holding. Maybe this woman wouldn't judge her like the rest of the town.

"I don't look like a killer because I'm not a killer. I was just in the wrong place at the wrong time."

"Lucky you, then. So, what kind of room did you need?"

"I was wondering if you're hiring. The police want me to stay in town for a while, and I'm running out of money."

"Do you have experience working in hotels?" Marty walked around the counter and into a small office off the lobby.

Nora followed. "I worked at a Hilton in New Orleans during Mardi Gras, so I've worked with people before."

"Good. I'd hate to hire someone who hasn't worked with other humans."

"You know what I mean." Nora's answer was a little too immediate. She wished she hadn't said anything. Talking back in a job interview, even an informal one, was probably not a good idea.

"Why did you leave? Didn't you like the job?"

"I liked the job plenty, but I needed money to take care of my mom, and I could make more waiting tables in the French Quarter. New Orleans is a party town. The drunker people get, the more they leave on the table. At the Hilton, I worked front desk. I hated to leave, but chemo—even with insurance—doesn't come cheap. Sadly, in my mother's case, it didn't work either, and she passed. Her letter to Mr. Brockwell is the sole reason I ended up in Texas."

To her surprise, Marty smiled. "My name's Marty Reynolds, and from what I can see of you so far, I think you'd be a breath of fresh air in this one-oil-well town. Do you have a résumé?"

Nora bit her lower lip.

"A résumé?" Marty repeated. "Sure, though not with me. It's not too impressive though. I tried to be a personal organizer."

"A what?"

"You know. I sorted people's closets for them. It was big for a while, but then people figured out they could just go to the Container Store and do it all themselves. My mother was not too happy. I spent four years in college studying liberal arts and then tried to make a living reorganizing sock drawers. Then with the advent of the internet, people had even more organizational gurus giving it away for free. It seems incredible to me, but I'm a victim of Pinterest."

Marty gave her a perfunctory smile. Being a personal organizer was right up there with "professional shopper" to some people.

Nora blew out a breath, not sure if this woman was friend or foe. Her gaze met Marty's. Sometimes, honesty was the best policy and even if it sounded desperate, she need to be truthful.

"I really need this job," Nora blurted out, hoping she didn't sound as desperate as she felt.

"Uh-huh. Well, I can see that." Marty gestured around the dark lobby. "I don't know if you noticed, but we're just getting on our feet around here. I used to work here as a kid, but now that I'm the owner and manager, I really need the help of an experienced front-desk person."

"I'm experienced."

"Yes, but you don't get tips around here. You'd be back to that same lowball salary you were making in New Orleans."

"I know."

"What about after all of this stuff about Adam Brockwell blows over? What then? Will you stay?"

Nora had to make a choice. Would she tell Marty the truth—that she wasn't sure if she would stay in town after the investigation ended—or would she tell her what she wanted to hear? That would probably get her the job, but she just couldn't. "I have to be honest with you. I really don't know what I'm planning to do. I seem to be living day to day right now. I know this sounds like a lousy deal for you, but it's all I have to offer. I'll work hard at whatever hours you need me for, and if you don't mind that I have a past in a town I've never ever been to before, I'd love to work for you."

Marty pursed her lips and nodded. Nora could tell she was mulling it over.

"Can you handle the front desk on the five to eleven shift?" Marty asked.

Nora nodded. Decision made.

As NORA LEFT the hotel, she decided to look for an ATM to make sure there wasn't any more money in her bank account back home. As she walked across the street to Piney Woods Savings and Loan, she almost ran into Lucy Cooper, Brockwell's investment counselor, who was barreling out of the plate glass door just as Nora was attempting to enter. The stack of papers Lucy was carrying flew to the ground.

"Sorry." Nora picked up what looked to be a deposit slip for $20,000.

"I'm sorry. I'm the one who wasn't looking." Lucy grasped the pile of papers close to her chest and stuffed them into a briefcase. "I should have done this in the bank."

Nora's eyes widened in amazement at the amount. "Gee, you sure make big deposits."

Lucy closed the briefcase. "I'm a financial planner. Handling people's money is my business. I was just making a deposit for a client."

"Sorry." Nora held up her hand. "None of my business."

Lucy nodded and went on her way. Something about Lucy Cooper struck Nora as off. She seemed awfully young to be a successful financial planner. Nora's instincts told her to pay attention to Lucy Cooper. Tuck Watson's investigation appeared to be focused on Nora, and the rest of the town seemed convinced she was Adam Brockwell's killer. Nora feared she'd be the only one looking for the real killer. Maybe Lucy Cooper knew something that could help.

Deciding the ATM visit could wait, Nora let Lucy walk a few steps farther down the block before she turned and headed in the same direction. This would work as long as Lucy didn't get into a car and drive off. Nora's car was parked close by on the street, but she wasn't sure she could jump into it in time without losing track of her target.

Lucy's efficient heels clicked along the sidewalk, making her easy to trail. She turned the corner and Nora feared this would be where she'd lose her. As Nora came around the building onto a side street, Lucy went into the Shady Sunsets Assisted Living Center. Who was Lucy visiting in there? A client? It would be pretty despicable if she were one of those scam artists who preyed on older people living on meager savings.

Nora climbed the wooden steps next to a wheelchair ramp positioned on the side of the entrance.

As she entered the lobby area, a lady with a drugstore shade of golden-blond hair sipped from a coffee mug with the words "Not a Morning Person" printed on it.

"Can I help you?" The woman exhaled on the last word, making Nora feel as if she were intruding.

"Uh, I was supposed to meet my friend Lucy here." She glanced at her watch to help her story. "I'm afraid I'm running a bit late. Would you know where …." Nora's mind raced. Should she assume Lucy Cooper was visiting a client or could she have a friend or a relative here?

The woman behind the counter looked at Nora over glasses

that slid down her nose. "Her mother is in the lounge on break, although most people don't invite visitors to join them for a visit to the vending machine." Her tone made Nora feel like an idiot.

"Right," Nora acknowledged. "Good ol' Mom." Nora tried to laugh it off, but her laugh sounded hollow as it bounced off the walls of the lobby.

"Down the hall, last door on your left marked 'Employees Only.'"

"Great. Thanks for your help." The woman ignored her and went back to her computer screen. Obviously she wasn't much of an afternoon person either.

Nora followed the brass-plated numbers above the doors until she found the employees' lounge. The door was open. Wanting to hear the conversation, Nora stepped closer, careful to stay out of the line of sight of either woman.

"Did you see him in the coffin?"

"Yes, Mama. I saw him. He's really dead."

"You're sure now?"

"I'm sure."

"And now he's dead. Adam Brockwell is dead." The older woman took in a sharp breath.

"Yes. I told you he was." Lucy sounded irritated.

"If I had the nerve, I'd 'a been the one to kill him."

"How can you hate this man so much?"

"I just do."

"Well, he's gone, so let's get on with our lives. The evil old goat doesn't have any power over you anymore."

A chair scooted across the floor. Nora feared Lucy was on her way out and searched for a place to hide. She darted around a corner, where the hallway intersected with a second corridor.

"I just wanted to let you know it's over." As Lucy came to the door of the lounge, she turned back and raised a hand.

"Love you, Mama."

"Love you, too."

Nora flattened herself against the wall, the palms of her hands now splayed up against it.

"What are you doing?" An old man was standing in his doorway, dressed in a maroon-plaid bathrobe. He gazed at Nora's ridiculous position. Nora could hear Lucy's heels clicking down the hall in the opposite direction.

"Uh ... this wallpaper." She stroked her hands along the wall like someone making an upright snow angel. "It's just so luxurious."

The old man sneered in disgust. "Get the heck off my wall." Nora pulled her hands from the wall in a lightning-quick movement. As she started to turn the corner toward the employees' lounge, the old man called out after her, "Weirdo."

Feeling certain Lucy had concluded her visit with her mother, Nora stepped through the open door of a small room with one chipped Formica table and several blue plastic chairs.

Arnette Cooper, a woman in her forties, her skin a deep brown, sat looking out the window, a tissue clasped in her hands.

"Mrs. Cooper?" Nora asked.

The older woman turned, and as her eyes met Nora's, a tear ran down her soft brown cheek.

"Oh, I'm so sorry," Nora apologized. "I've come at a bad time." She started to back out of the room.

"No, wait." Arnette dabbed at her wet cheek. "Just a foolish woman crying in the middle of the day." Her mouth trembled a bit as it formed a shaky smile. "What can I do for you?"

Nora stepped back into the room and pulled a chair next to Arnette's place at the table. "I'm ... a friend of your daughter's. Are you sad because Mr. Brockwell died?"

Arnette looked a little surprised at Nora's question but then gazed upward. "I'm surprised by it, but yes, I guess I am." She responded with soft laughter. "I've spent so much of my life hating the man. Guess I'll have to get myself a new hobby."

"Why? Why did you hate Adam Brockwell?"

Arnette's head bobbed a bit as her hand ran across the smooth surface of the lunch table.

"I'm sorry. You're one of Lucy's friends? She's never mentioned you."

Nora drew in a breath. Deciding to tell the truth, she plunged in, "I'm Nora Alexander."

Nothing registered on Arnette Cooper's face.

"I brought the letter to Adam Brockwell right before he was murdered."

Arnette watched Nora differently now, as if she were trying to recall something absent from her memory for years. The corners of her eyes softened.

"You look like someone …. I think I knew your mama."

"I don't think you'd have known her. We've lived in Louisiana for many years since she left Texas."

"Probably right. I worked for Mr. Brockwell."

Nora did a slow nod in understanding.

"Is it true you thought it was a love letter you were delivering?"

"Yes," Nora admitted, feeling foolish.

"Someone in love with him? Couldn't be nothin' further from the truth. This town would be surprised, but there were people around here who didn't love him. Didn't think he was the best thing since sliced bread. He might have brought in a warehouse and kept the town out of the poor house in the recession, but he had a way of taking other people's lives and turnin' 'em upside down."

Arnette checked her watch. "I gotta get back to work, honey. It's real nice meeting you. Too bad you just missed Lucy." Arnette gave Nora a closer look. Nora wondered what she was thinking.

"I should go." Nora rose and started for the door.

"Glad he's dead and I don't care who knows it. You done good. Didn't want to come back to this town. To that man. If I had been just a little stronger and a whole lot braver, God help me, I'd have done the stabbing myself."

# Chapter 10

———

A N HOUR LATER, Nora took her place at the front desk of the Tunie Hotel, with Marty Reynolds by her side.

"I don't know what I was thinking when I bought this place. I grew up coming here for special events. There used to be a little restaurant, and we used the banquet rooms for school functions. My first kiss was under the disco ball in the Stephen F. Austin Ballroom. Then later, when I went to college, I came back and worked in the hotel over the summers. By that time it was starting to get rundown. I'm just lucky I convinced Max to come back and do the night shift for me. This place was opened before I was born by a guy named Melvin Tunie. He even had these singing bellmen named the Tunieville Bellboys. Pretty hilarious, huh?"

Marty walked Nora to one of the banquet rooms. "The hotel went into foreclosure after the people who bought it from Mr. Tunie stopped paying their mortgage. I picked it up for a song. Little did I know how hard it would be to find a buyer. After months of trying to sell my 'bargain,' I decided it was fate. I was supposed to run the Tunie. I guess I bought it still thinking of the way it was when I was a kid. What do I know about running a hotel? Luckily, all the empty space in the banquet rooms has been a moneymaker." She flipped a switch and the room was flooded with light. Instead of tables covered in crisp white linens and seasonal floral arrangements, there were five long tables with rusty metal chairs lined up along them. In front of the tables was a portable podium. The curtains looked threadbare and the room was surrounded by wood fixtures dulled through years of neglect. "Not quite the Tunie grandeur of yesteryear. I've been renting out this room to a company that provides tutoring for college entrance exams. They're a little shady, but they paid in cash to use the room for the next two months. They run a session several nights a week. It was a godsend. I've been trying to cover the front desk two shifts a day. Because I had to sell my house to re-outfit the rooms, I've moved onto the property. I also used up my retirement savings. I've gone from real estate to the hospitality business. Opening this place was a crazy idea and lately I've been wondering if I'm going to make it."

"You sold real estate before you bought the Tunie?"

"I sold houses and commercial property. How else would I have found out about the Tunie? There's just something about this lumbering old money pit I couldn't resist. Guess it's my midlife crisis."

"Sounds like a big undertaking."

"You've got that right. But here I am. Some mornings I wake up and wonder what I've gotten myself into. We'd better get back to the front desk. People will start coming in for the class soon."

"Do you have any guests?"

"Right now we don't, but we've had a few. No one knows we're open, but I've asked Max to see about a website. He's an old friend. We worked here together when we were in high school. He knows all about putting things up online. If people can find us on the web and then book their rooms, we will at least be in this century."

Marty's casual manner put Nora at ease, but she tensed up again when Tuck Watson entered the lobby accompanied by a cheap-looking, lanky woman. She was more than thin, she was rail thin. She wore a red dress and her mousy-brown hair was pulled back with a rhinestone barrette. Was he here to check into a hotel room with this woman? Nora figured that in this job, she'd soon know everybody's secrets. Tuck Watson's taste in women seemed to run low-rent and scrawny, but then again, nothing about men should surprise her at this point.

An awkward moment passed as Tuck's girlfriend gave her a once-over. Nora ran her fingers through her hair, trying to straighten it somehow. Her well-rounded figure and natural hair color was a complete contrast to the woman whose scrawny fingers with their press-on nails entwined around Watson's bicep.

"This is a surprise, Marty. Is Miss Alexander a guest at your hotel?" Tuck Watson nodded to Nora.

"A guest? No way. I've hired her! Isn't it great?" Marty clapped her hands together as if she'd just landed the hottest applicant in town. She nodded at the woman next to Tuck. "Jolene."

"Glad you got somebody to help you out, Marty." Tuck leaned closer to the counter and whispered to Marty, "I hope you ran a background check."

"I didn't have to. Nora and I had a long talk. You should know me by now, Tucker. I love a lost cause. I mean, heck, I bought the Tunie Hotel. Nora here was a sister in trouble, and I was glad to be there for her. As a matter of fact, we were both in trouble. With Nora here and Max taking over the graveyard shift, at least I'm going to have my nights free from this albatross. So, what can I do for you—need a room?"

Tuck looked confused for a moment, then, picking up on how the situation appeared, he pried his arm free of Jolene's grasp. "No. I don't need a room, but Jolene here needs a job. You may know her husband has just been sent to the state prison for a few years, and she has two children to support. Do you have anything open?"

"Dang!" Jolene said. "It makes me mad I just missed out on front desk. I'm real good with strangers." She smiled, showing off the gap in her front teeth.

"It's all about timing," Marty acknowledged. "Do you have any experience in housekeeping?"

"Just my own."

"Works for me. It would be part-time to start, but when we get more guests, there will be more rooms to clean. We have forty rooms in all, so I'll be hiring more staff if I ever need them."

"Part-time. I don't know …."

Marty scrunched up her nose, as if apologizing she couldn't give her full-time. "It's the best I can offer. Take it or leave it."

Tuck answered for Jolene. "And she'll take it. Right now, any money coming in will help."

"But some minimum wage part-time job won't be enough."

Tuck cleared his throat. "Jolene thought her husband was working at Brockwell Warehousing, but he was actually spending his time at the convenience store selling recreational drugs. Now that he's been incarcerated, she's trying to adjust to a new standard of living." He faced Jolene. "It looks like you're going to need two part-time jobs. Count this as number one."

Jolene crossed her bony arms. "*Two* jobs? I do have kids, you know."

"Yes, but the housekeeping is done after checkout, so you'll be working from eleven a.m. until you finish. Now you have early mornings to work somewhere else," Marty added in a cheery tone.

Jolene didn't look too happy. "Fine. I'll be here tomorrow at eleven."

"Excellent, I can show you what needs doing." Marty came around the desk with a bounce in her step. "If I keep this up, I'll be a hotel magnate in no time. First Nora and now Jolene. I officially have a staff. Come with me, Jolene, and I'll show you where the housekeeping supplies are." Marty took Jolene over to a room off the lobby.

Once they were alone, Tuck stepped closer to Nora. "You know, I'm glad I ran into you. It saves me the trip over to the Piney Woods Bed and Breakfast. I'd like you to come in tomorrow to answer a few more questions. If you don't mind."

"Do I need a lawyer?" Nora asked.

"I don't know, do you?" Tuck answered.

"Okay. I'll be there tomorrow. I don't know what else you have left to ask me. I already told you I just dropped off the letter and left."

"Yes, you did. Still, though, there is something about your story I'm missing."

Jolene came back and took hold of Tuck's arm and squeezed it.

Marty grimaced at Jolene's temporary possession of her nephew. "When you come in tomorrow, we'll get all your paperwork done. Welcome aboard."

"Yeah, well, I may as well get paid for cleaning." Jolene squeezed Tuck's arm again.

"Thanks, Marty." Tuck held open the door for Jolene and then tipped his hat to Nora.

She bristled.

"Don't let Tuck get under your skin," Mary said after her nephew was gone. "Sometimes I think he's a little too serious about his job. I mean, look at who he's out with tonight? Before you go thinking she's his girlfriend, I can tell you he's just trying to help. I don't see her as an eager hotel maid, though. She's playing Tuck."

"Really?"

"Yes, but don't you worry. He's got her figured out. He'll drop her back at the trailer park and report to her husband she's alive and flirting."

"What you're trying to tell me is that he's a good guy?"

"Sure. You can trust him."

"I wish I could, but I can't get away from the fact I'm the prime suspect in what has to be the biggest murder case Piney Woods has ever seen."

"I'll be honest with you. This town has been humming about your involvement in Adam Brockwell's death. Don't know if you killed the old guy or if you didn't. Either way, I figure you'll be quite a draw for my little hotel." Nora laughed. She was right. They did need each other.

"I'll do all I can to bring in nosy people who want rooms."

"That's the spirit."

Marty surveyed Nora and shook her head. "Before you go thinking he's perfect, you should know he had a brother who went to jail."

Nora gave her a sideways glance. "He arrested his own brother? What is he, Robocop?"

Marty laughed. "No. He wasn't even on the force back then. His brother, Ronnie, was a sweet boy, but he started running with the wrong crowd in high school. He and his friends were the life of the party. They were doing drugs and drinking and getting into trouble. People think small towns don't have crime, but the truth is, they are full of young people with nothing to do."

"Was Ronnie Tuck's older brother?"

"Yes, so Tuck saw it all. We were worried he'd follow in his footsteps, but somehow he went the other way. You never know how these things are going to turn out. "

"So, how did he end up getting arrested?"

"He was with some guys, and they were selling drugs. Unfortunately for them, one of their newest customers was an undercover narcotics cop. They all got arrested. When the questioning started, the other guys pointed to Ronnie. You see, he didn't have anything on his record. He was a good kid. Misguided, but good. His so-called friends figured he'd get a small amount of time. The rest of them had records by then. They let him take the fall."

"So, I take it Ronnie wasn't the dealer?"

"Not at all. As a matter of fact, he'd just finished filling out his college applications. He was looking to the future. He even had a math scholarship lined up. There was no way he would've ruined his life by doing something like that."

"Did any of this come out in court?"

"Of course, but the judge didn't believe it and Ronnie got the time. He's out now and lives down in Houston."

"So, that's why Tuck became a policeman?"

"He told me he never wanted to see someone like his brother sent to jail again. He realized the justice system is flawed. An innocent man can spend the rest of his life in jail, and there's nothing he can do about it. I think it eats at his craw. Maybe that will work in your favor. If he thinks you're innocent, he'll fight for you. If he thinks you're guilty, he'll do everything he can to get you sent to jail. He's got a strong sense of right or wrong, my nephew."

"Family tragedies can do that." Nora thought of her father, whose life had been cut short so dramatically. What would her life have been like if he'd survived? Would she have been more serious about college?

"The thing is, our family lost Ronnie that year."

Nora's eyes widened.

"No, he's still alive. He comes back for holidays now and again, but it was never the same. He did end up going to college and went on to become a chemical engineer, which if you ask me is pretty ironic. We always hoped he'd settle down right here in Piney Woods, but he tells us this town is too small for him."

"What happened to his friends?"

"Oh, lucky us, they stayed around. You can see them hanging out at Hade's Alley. Some of them have been in jail, and some of them have died. None of them have come to any good. Sometimes I think Ronnie escaped just in time. He never talks about his stint in jail, but I think it must've been pretty awful."

"So, Tuck is trying to right the world, one criminal at a time?"

"That's not quite it. Tuck is trying to keep the harm that

came to his family from coming to others. Doing something like bringing Jolene here is pretty typical for him. He may put her husband in jail, but that doesn't mean he wants to see the man's family suffer."

Nora leaned on her elbow and thought for a moment. Tuck Watson was a mystery. Their first night together was so wonderful, and for a short time, she felt like her life might start again after her mother's death. He was so different from the other men she'd been with. Now she was on his "most wanted" list, and not in a good way.

"I think you've got this, Nora. I'm going to try and figure out the accounting software."

"Go right ahead. I'm fine."

Marty left her alone at the front desk.

Nora faced a wall of pictures, and next to that, a floor-to-ceiling window. One good thing about her station behind the counter was she could see all of Main Street. Tonight it was dark and quiet, with just a little mist rising off the concrete. Across the street at the courthouse, there was a light in the alley. She leaned across the front desk, squinting to see if someone was walking down the side street with a flashlight. As she leaned farther, she knocked over a box of key cards Marty had set out.

"Great." Nora knelt down to pick up the cards.

"Hello there," a voice came from above her. "Do you mind if I take a look around? I used to come to the most wonderful parties here years ago."

A slight man in a bow tie stood on the other side of the desk.

She stood. "Uh, I guess so. There's not much going on at the moment, although some young people will be arriving soon their tutoring session."

"You're new here, aren't you?" the man asked.

"Yes. My name is Nora. I'm new to town and new to the Tunie."

He nodded. "Welcome, Nora. It's nice to meet you. I'm Mr. Birdsong."

*Birdsong? What an odd name*, Nora thought.

"I've been coming to the Tunie all my life. This sweet old place has had its ups and downs."

"There was a lot of history made here," Nora said, "or so I'm told."

"You know what I really miss? The dances. We used to have the best dances in those rooms. Beautiful ladies waltzing. Wonderful food. It was magical. Are they going to be continuing the social gatherings? I'd sure love to have an elegant evening of dance."

"Maybe. Right now, though, the ballroom—that's the banquet room, right? It's being used for a college prep class."

"I see." He walked over to the wall of pictures and gently removed one. "Here's one such evening. This young lady was the belle of the ball that night." He walked back to the front desk and placed the picture in front of Nora. In the aged photo, a young woman twirled around in a flowered dress while two men admired her. Something about her was so familiar.

"Do you know her name?"

"Oh, she was quite something. Too bad the evening didn't turn out well for her."

"What happened?"

"I'm really not sure. She left with this young man," he pointed to the taller of the two men, "and then when she returned, she seemed very upset. I was about to see if there was anything I could do for her, but her brother was present, so I assumed he would help her."

"So he took her home?"

"Yes, but she seemed angry at him as well. We didn't see much of her in this town after that. I think her brother blames himself to this day."

"Do you know her name?"

He leaned closer and said in a soft voice, "You being here will be a good thing for the Tunie." He looked toward the banquet rooms. "I think I'll go see what the youth of today are learning." He saluted her and tiptoed toward the college prep session, replacing the picture on the wall as he left.

"Um, no one's arrived yet," she said, but he kept going. She didn't see the harm of him checking out the room. The Tunie Hotel was a historic landmark in Piney Woods. She would have to expect people would want to wander around the place as if it were a museum.

Nora stayed at the desk as a few students trickled in, along with an older man who looked like their teacher, but she checked the OPEN sign more than once, reflecting on the utter stillness of the lobby. She tried to concentrate on the check-in procedures in case she actually got a guest. Although if she hit a snag, she could always call Marty, who was in the back office.

Most hotels had a little corner with snacks and amenities for guests. There was an alcove off the front desk that would work perfectly for a snack bar. It was currently being used as a storage area for empty cardboard boxes and some broken-down chairs. Nora folded up the boxes and was stacking them in a corner on the discarded chairs when Marty re-emerged from her office.

She rubbed at her eyes and yawned. "Working on the computer while exhausted—not a good idea." She looked at the cleared alcove. "Uh, thank you for doing that. I was using that little area for dumping."

"I was just thinking, maybe we could put in a little shop for things our guests might need? You know, toothbrushes, pain relievers, candy bars and sodas. It wouldn't make a lot of money, but it would be convenient for our guests."

"First of all, every income stream is a good income stream, and second, it's hospitality—which is what this is all about. I'll have Max put the chairs and boxes in the Dumpster out back. Great idea, Nora. Wow. You're a natural."

"Thanks."

"It will be wonderful if we ever get any guests, and if I can figure out how to bill them with the doggone software." Marty sighed.

"Where's your sweeper? I'll do a little housekeeping here in the lobby."

Marty's eyebrows rose. "You will? Great. Working eighteen hours a day, I'm just too tired to clean up."

"Well, I'm here now. If you have a carpet cleaner, we could try to brighten up this carpet."

Marty grinned and yawned. "Yes. I think this little relationship is going to work out just fine. Welcome to the Tunie."

# Chapter 11

———

THE NEXT MORNING, still feeling a need to talk to her father's former partner, Nora tried a different tack in locating Del Dupree. She pulled out her laptop to do an internet search. Maybe he was no longer a cop. There had to be plenty of Duprees in Louisiana, but not so many Dels with just one L. Of course, she was assuming he was still in Louisiana. What popped up on the screen surprised her.

Del Dupree was no longer a policeman but the owner of Dealin' Del of the Bayou. He owned several car lots in the New Orleans area and even had commercials listed on YouTube— the "I must be crazy to make these deals" kind. Nora watched a couple of the ads and began to think maybe she was the one who was crazy for trying to contact a man about a murder from so many years ago. Dealin' Del's phone number flashed across the bottom of the screen. Nora wrote it down then looked at her watch. It was still early. She'd try to call later.

"How was your first night at the hotel?" Tatty asked Nora when she came downstairs for a breakfast of French toast and bacon.

"It was fine. I like Marty. I'm just glad she trusts me after hearing about my alleged involvement in the Adam Brockwell murder."

"I am too."

Ed put down his paper. "She was desperate. She would have hired anyone."

"Eat your breakfast, Ed," Tatty said.

"There's a lot to learn because she's so short-staffed. Marty's been doing it all, and now she wants me to learn everything. I guess I'll get to check a guest in one day."

"Just like around here." Ed poured a liberal amount of syrup over his French toast. "You think you want to be in business for yourself. Be the boss. Then you find out you're also the hired help. Bosses work harder than anybody."

"Uh-huh." Tatty smiled. She did most of the daily housecleaning and all the cooking. Ed did the maintenance work and complained most of his way through simple tasks like changing light bulbs and mowing the grass.

"Lieutenant Watson showed up last night with a woman who applied for the housekeeper job." Nora took a bite of her bacon.

"Oh, really? Who was the woman?" Ed asked.

"Brown hair. Very skinny." Nora tried to remember her name.

"Probably one of the divorcées around here. There's quite a variety to choose from." Ed grinned as if he had a list of them floating around in his head.

Tatty hit Ed with her napkin. "Ed! Get your brain out of the fifties. No one says 'divorcée' anymore."

"You want to know why? Half the county is divorced. No one stays hitched anymore either. 'Course," he hooked his thumbs under his suspenders, "they don't make 'em like me anymore."

"You are quite the blessing, Eduardo." Tatty scowled, though a slight smile was starting to sneak through.

Nora had to laugh. Still lovebirds after all these years. So much trust between them. She could only hope one day to have someone who loved and trusted her the way the two of them did each other. "Yeah, well, Lieutenant Tuck Watson made sure to tell Marty to keep an eye on me."

"It's his job, sweetheart. He still isn't sure of you."

"I suppose." Nora debated telling Ed and Tatty about her latest attempt to clear her name. "I, uh, ran into Lucy Cooper yesterday."

"You were over at the bank? It couldn't have been to count your money," Ed added, reminding Nora she was flat broke. "Did you need a free pen?"

"Well, she was also around the day Adam Brockwell died. No one else seems to have noticed that."

"Good point." Tatty's eyes brightened.

"Exactly. So I kind of followed her."

"And?"

"She went to visit her mother at the nursing home."

Tatty clucked her tongue. "Assisted living. We feel it's a better way to say it."

"Right. Then after she left, I sort of … talked to her mother."

Tatty picked up the plates and put them in the sink. "So, you talked to Arnette? Lord, I haven't spoken to her in years."

"Did you know Arnette disliked Adam Brockwell?" Nora asked.

"Really now," Tatty leaned closer, "I'd think he'd be a right nice fella to work for. He was always kind to me. Of course, there was the scandal … about Lucy and all."

"What scandal?"

"Lucy's daddy. Arnette's never been married. Even so, she was a regular at church every Sunday. What a beautiful voice she had! She was sweet on a man who was teaching at the junior high. He only taught for a year, and then no one ever saw him again. He didn't even turn in his resignation over at the school. I guess he moved on. Funny thing, though … I never would have pegged him as a runaway daddy. Seemed like a real good man." Tatty poured herself another cup of coffee. "She quit working for Mr. Brockwell, and they hired Alma Rodriguez to do her job. Still, though, it was hard to believe Arnette never went after her math teacher. Ed Junior was in one of his classes and really liked him. He passed math that year, which didn't always happen in those days."

Ed leaned back in his chair, twiddling his thumbs. "Good old Junior. Not exactly a candidate for astronaut training."

Tatty hit Ed with a dishtowel. "Now you stop. You're so proud of our Eddie working in management at Mr. Brockwell's distribution center, you can't stand it."

"Takes after me. Born leader." Ed glowed with the look of a proud parent.

"But I never could figure out the thing with Arnette. I half expected to hear wedding bells for those two, but no. The school year ended and he was gone. Lucy was born the next fall."

"Fascinating. Don't you think it's kind of odd that of all the people in town, Lucy ends up working for the same man her mother did? Especially with how Arnette feels about him?"

"Well, honey, he was the fellow with all the money around here. Makes perfect sense to me Lucy would go after it. She works on commission, you know."

"I guess you're right."

"You know, most of our friends are having to spend their golden years living in a spare bedroom in the house of one of their children. Lucy Cooper's helped a lot of folks stay in their own homes. I also heard she made an offer on the old Hemphill house. Places like that don't come cheap."

"Lucy sure must have a gift for finding money," Nora said, thinking of her mother. How would she have handled long-term care for her? How can someone so young and working on commission afford to buy a house? Nora needed to learn more, both about Lucy and the secrets her mother had been keeping.

After breakfast, Nora returned to her room to call Dealin' Del of the Bayou. After working her way through two receptionists and a personal assistant, she finally got Del Dupree on the line. His thick Southern Louisiana accent came through like a commercial for the chamber of commerce.

"My assistant is tellin' me you're the daughter of my old padnar? Is that right? The little girl with the red hair?"

"Yes, sir." Nora was beginning to feel embarrassed for calling this man after so many years.

"Well, where you at, girl?" He now sounded delighted to hear from her.

"I'm in Texas. I apologize for bothering you, but I was wondering if I could ask you a few questions about my mother. Did she ever confide in you? Did my father? I came to this little town to deliver a letter my mother had written to a man named Brockwell and then he was murdered."

Dealin' Del of the Bayou didn't answer right away. Nora wasn't sure if he was recalling a painful memory or getting ready to hang up on her.

"Terrible news, darlin', but I was your dad's partner a long time ago." His Cajun accent lightened up.

"Yes, I know. This letter my mother wrote to Adam Brockwell? It was the last thing she wrote. I think she was standing up for herself by writing it even if she did not like Adam Brockwell. Did she or my father ever tell you anything about her past?"

"Your daddy and I spent a few long nights with nothin' going on in the streets, and we had some conversations. I don't think it was ever anything important. You know, our families, our kids … that kind of thing. Sorry. Can't help you there. My condolences about your mama."

"Thank you. I just never expected to find myself in the middle of a murder investigation."

"You never know about people, darlin'. The secrets they carry year after year. There's a reason why they keep that stuff buried."

Nora sat back for a moment to think. "What's ironic about all this is that Mr. Brockwell was up for some sort of award for being an outstanding citizen here in Piney Woods. I don't think my mother would have given him any awards."

"Doesn't sound like it. Not sure if a rich guy would make much of a pioneer."

"I suppose."

There was a slight hum in the background, and Del Dupree came back on the line, his Cajun accent renewed. "Sorry, darlin', I've told you all I can. It's real nice hearin' from ya. Call back anytime, ya hear? Especially if you find out anything new."

# Chapter 12

———

"THIS IS GREAT." Max arrived at the beginning of Nora's shift to help carry in the boxes of guest amenities Marty had ordered at her request. Nora was in the alcove, unloading a box of candy bars. Max moved with grace for a man who was over three hundred pounds. He carried a carton of sodas to the corner of the alcove, stacking them out of Nora's way. "You made me a snack bar."

Nora stepped back to admire her work. With the addition of some shelves, the little alcove looked great. "That's the idea."

Max reached out toward the candy bars, and Nora pushed his hand back. "For the guests."

"Right." Max smiled.

"I left a list of products and their prices to charge our guests."

"Do I get an employee discount?" Max asked. "You know, I used to be an officer of the court. I should at least get the government employee discount."

"Don't tell me," Nora propped her chin on her fingers, "dogcatcher?"

"No." Max grimaced. "I was a bailiff for Judge Nelson here in town. I learned all about truth, justice, and the American way in that courtroom." He leaned closer. "You'll probably be surprised, but I'm studying to be a lawyer."

"Really?"

"Well, not like real law school, but I'm studying online. It's not Harvard law, but I can get my juris doctor right here in Piney Woods. So, maybe I should be getting the student discount, too!"

"You settle the amount of your discount with Marty."

His head wobbled from side to side. "Then yes, I do."

"You and Marty go way back?"

"Yeah. We both worked here in high school. Matter of fact, there's a picture of us somewhere on Mr. Tunie's wall. Old Man Tunie took a new picture of his staff at the beginning of each summer. You ought to check it out."

"I saw those pictures, but I didn't know you and Marty were in them."

"Sure. We're there, standing in front of the crowd. The old man used to ask them to stand behind us to make it look like the guests were piling up to get in. They weren't, though. Half the people in the picture worked on Main Street." He pointed to a picture on the wall and Nora drew closer.

A skinny Max and a very young Marty stood in front of a crowd of people .... Were any of those people related to her? "A picture can say anything the photographer wants it to say. Just look at Facebook."

"For sure. One thing about Mr. Tunie ... he loved his pictures. He has pictures from every decade the Tunie was open and even created a wall of heroes for the town's sons lost in wartime."

"It's good to know about the past," Nora said, thinking how ill informed she was about her own history.

"Sure, it gives us all something to talk about. So, uh, I heard about you and all the—"

"Gossip?" Nora broke in.

Max nodded and set down his cup. "Yeah. And I just wanted

to let you know, no matter what anyone else says, I don't think you're a cold-blooded killer."

"Thank you."

"Seriously, Nora. I don't think you did it, and I'm talking from the viewpoint of an online law student."

"Thanks … I think."

"The question is, if you didn't do it, who did? I mean, around here, killing Adam Brockwell is like cheating Jesus at cards."

Nora laughed. "I'm beginning to believe Adam Brockwell would, too."

"Who else would want to kill him?"

"Well, I do have someone else I've been sort of investigating."

"Really?"

"Yes. His investment adviser. She comes from humble beginnings and yet she seems to have enough cash on hand to make an offer on one of the nicer houses in town."

"How old is she?"

"Early twenties? Not only that, but she works on commission at Piney Woods Savings and Loan."

"Interesting. So how much money can one girl make working at a bank?"

"Maybe she won the lottery?"

"Possible," Max said, "but not probable. Have you ever known anyone who actually won the lottery?"

"No."

"Me neither."

"I better get back behind the desk. Still no check-ins, but between the college prep class and our little store here, I'll be busy." Nora started walking to the door.

"What house is she buying?"

"Tatty and Ed told me the old Hemphill place."

"Oh, my. That's a nice house. My mother used to know the Hemphills. I'll bet she'd know what it was worth." Max pulled out his cellphone and pushed a button.

"Hey Mom. I'm just here with my new coworker, Nora ….

Yes, *that* Nora. No, I'm perfectly safe .... Yes, I still have my mace ... anyhoo, I was wondering if you knew how much the Hemphill place was selling for .... Uh-huh." Max put his hand over the speaker, "Over two hundred. That's a lot for this town." He returned to the phone, "Thanks, Mom. That's all I needed .... Love you too .... I'm glad you got my back." He ended the call.

This new information put Lucy square in Nora's sights. She had to find a way to make Tuck Watson see her for who she really was. "Thanks, Max."

The large man swaggered a little bit. "All a part of my duties, m'lady. Now, if you don't mind, I need to head home and catch a nap before I come back for my shift at eleven. See you then."

A few minutes later, Nora was sitting behind the check-in desk, counting change and placing it in the register, when a hand slapped down on the counter, making her jump.

"Leslie, is it you? So good to see you again. My little sis. Cute as a button. I saw you from the street." Wiley staggered around the lobby.

"I'm not Leslie." Nora's voice was gentle.

Wiley was really out of it this time.

"What do you mean, you're not Leslie? Of course you are. Same red hair, same beautiful eyes. You were always too beautiful for this little town. Too beautiful." He started to trudge back to wherever he came from.

"Remember?" she called after him. "I told you, my name is Nora."

He turned back and squinted at the window. "*Nora*?" He said her name as if it left a bad taste in his mouth.

"Yes." It was as if she was speaking to him from the other side of a tunnel.

He stood for a moment. "Where is she? Is she here with you? Tell her ol' Wiley wants to see her, will ya?"

"I can't. I'm sorry. Do you remember me telling you my mom just passed away?"

Wiley started stumbling around. "Dead. She's dead. Leslie's dead. There's nobody left now, you know. Nobody from the old days. Dead. All dead." He looked at Nora, one eye bulging a bit. "Doc says I'm half dead, ya know."

Wiley was breaking Nora's heart. He was so sad. She told him, her voice soft, "I'm here because she had a letter for Adam Brockwell."

Wiley's bottom lip stuck out in mock adoration. "Oh, Mr. Bigwig Brockwell. My, my." He left off his false praise, looking confused. "Why would Leslie write Brockwell? She hated the guy."

"Listen, do you want me to call you a cab or something?"

"A cab? In Piney Woods? We've got cabs now? Well, I'll be damned. We're coming up in the world."

"When was the last time you ate anything?"

Wiley thought for a moment. "What day is it?"

"All I needed to hear. Come sit down, and I'll buy you a bag of chips."

His eyes widened at her unexpected kindness. "You will?"

"Sure. Then we'll see about getting you back home. Wherever that is."

Nora left her post and took Wiley by the arm.

He studied her with his bloodshot eyes. "You're just like her, you know. You've got a good heart. Too pretty, but a good heart. I'm glad you're back. Life hasn't been the same since you left."

"Why don't you eat something now?" She gave him a bag of chips and a candy bar. In just a few minutes he tore into the wrappers and gobbled it all down, finally passing out on the lobby couch.

When Max came in for his shift, he spied the old man snoring amid the food wrappers. "Looks like our first non-paying guest. It was nice of you to feed Wiley. His drinking has been getting worse lately. Some days he shows up here babbling about some woman."

"Do you know where he lives? I can drive him home."

"Sure. I could draw you a map, but he only lives a block from here."

Nora shook Wiley's shoulder with a gentle motion. "Wiley? Wiley, I need you to wake up."

"Huh?" The old man woke with a start.

"It's okay. It's me, Nora Alexander. Do you remember?"

He seemed to have sobered some since he wandered into the lobby earlier in the evening. He pulled himself up, and his weathered hands grasped the sides of the faded couch cushion. Nora feared for a moment he was preparing to throw up but then he surprised her.

"Nora Alexander," he repeated, like a small child getting instructions from a teacher.

"Right. I'm Kay's daughter remember? Uh … Leslie's daughter."

A light came into the old man's dazed eyes. A slight smile shone through the stubble of his day old beard. "Leslie. Yes."

"Can you stand up, Uncle Wiley?"

The old man sighed and smiled at Nora's calling him "Uncle." She shouldn't have said it, but he looked so pleased at the title.

"I can try."

Nora put her hands under his elbows and helped him to stand. "Great. I'm going to take you home. Max is drawing me a map to your house."

"There she is." Wiley became wistful as he pointed to the picture Mr. Birdsong had shown her.

"Who?" Nora asked.

"Leslie. Your mother."

Nora stepped closer to the picture. This time she looked at the young woman in a different way. She could recognize the shape of her face and the graceful bounce of her hair against her shoulders, but nothing else was familiar. Nora was given the precious gift of seeing her mother as a young woman without a care in the world. She'd bewitched the two young men in the photo, each leering at her over his glass of punch.

Kay Alexander—then known as Leslie—had the sweetest smile, and behind her trailed a flowered scarf. It looked as if she'd drop it at any moment, and when she did, the two men would jump to get it.

"I can't believe I'm looking at my mother. She's so young."

"We were all young back then. It was a very special time."

The two men also seemed familiar.

"Who is that?" she asked, pointing to the thinner of the two. He had blond hair and was wearing a striped polo shirt with the collar turned up. Wiley looked closer.

"Oh." A bitterness crept into his tone. "Brock."

"Who's Brock?"

"Well, you, of all people, should know who Brock is, seeing as how you're being accused of his murder. That's Adam Brockwell." He tapped his finger on the glass of the picture.

Adam Brockwell had been young, strong, and good-looking, much like his son was today. "Who's next to Mr. Brockwell?"

"Arnie. He's dead now. Jeep accident in basic training. Even though he never fought in a war, Mr. Tunie put his picture up. He said he figured he was one of the finest young men this town ever produced. His picture is on the hero wall over here. Good guy. Never could figure out why he liked to hang out with a guy like Brock."

The door to the lobby opened from the street and a man walked in. Nora recognized him as the burly man she'd seen help Wiley out of the trash can on her first day in Piney Woods.

"There you are." He walked over to Wiley.

"Vernon. You didn't have to come. Did they call you?"

"No. I just knew where you'd be once you tied one on, Daddy."

Max stepped forward, inserting his bulk into the conversation, blocking Nora completely from the view of Vernon McArdle.

"I was about to drive him home." Nora pushed around the wall of Max. "Guess you can take over from here."

"Wait." the old man stood his ground as his son took his elbow. "Vernon, this is your cousin."

Vernon furrowed his brow and then blinked at his father. Vernon looked Nora over as he lowered his head to lock eyes with his father. "Her?"

"She's your Aunt Leslie's daughter."

"The one who left? I thought you made her up," Vernon snorted and then grinned.

"Hi. I'm Nora." Nora extended her hand to Vernon. He wiped his hand on his jeans and shook.

"Uh … nice to meet you, Nora. I'm just sorry you had to be introduced to Daddy while he's in this state."

"Not a problem. If I may ask, why is it your father comes here when he's had too much to drink?"

"Not quite sure myself. Daddy? Maybe you can answer her question?"

Wiley McArdle looked down and mumbled, "None of your business."

With so much alcohol in his system, Wiley might have a nasty headache coming on, Nora thought.

"Well, then, let me get the old man home." He took his father by the shoulders and then turned back. "You need to come out to the house. Meet all the folks."

Why did the thought of it both thrill and terrify Nora?

"Sounds great. Can't wait." Nora hoped she sounded sincere because inside she wasn't so sure it was a good idea. "Good night now."

Vernon McArdle went back out into the pitch blackness with his father, leaving Nora to wonder just what kind of "family" she'd stumbled upon. Did she have a good, loving family or was she more likely to find moonshine stills, cousins intermarrying, and revolving-door prison sentences? It was all too much to think about.

# Chapter 13

---

As Nora started for her car, a cool evening breeze swept around her legs. It was dark, but at least she had a parking place under the streetlight.

Tuck Watson emerged from the shadows, making her jump. "Well, look who it is." He might have been viewing a freak in a sideshow, but maybe that was just her paranoia. "Glad to see you're fitting in so well in our fair city."

"You were the one who told me not to leave town." She considered sharing what she'd learned about Lucy Cooper. Would that do anything to take the heat off her? To the police, she looked like the perfect suspect. She had motive, and even better, she was from out of town. No need to arrest somebody's nephew and cause a problem.

"And I'm glad you've found a way to stay. Did you forget you were supposed to come by today to answer some questions?"

Had he been out here waiting for her? After that first evening, she might have been excited to see him. Now she was wary. She had not wanted to talk to him until she had suspects to suggest other than herself.

"I don't know what else you could ask me, Officer Watson. I already told you everything I know."

Tuck leaned on the hood of her car and crossed his arms. "Uh-huh."

"Fine," she said in a clipped voice. "What do you want to know?"

"I was just wondering why you never mentioned you had relatives in Piney Woods? When were you going to get around to telling me that little piece of information?"

"You found out when I did. This may shock you, but I was unaware I had any family in Texas."

"Seriously? Your mother is in a Piney Woods High School yearbook as homecoming queen, and you didn't know it? You must be a pretty self-centered young lady to have never bothered finding out where your mother came from."

The back of Nora's neck began to heat up. She met his accusing gaze without flinching. "My mother refused to talk about her past, if it's any of your business. All she'd say was she had a lot of painful memories growing up, Officer Watson."

Watson scratched at the stubble on his chin.

"Point made, Miss Alexander. So, you never knew you had family here, and you absolutely never knew about your mother and Adam Brockwell? Wow. Life must just be one big surprise after another for you." He stared at Nora, his curiosity piqued.

"I thought the police were supposed to investigate all the angles, not just the convenient ones. Have you looked into Lucy Cooper?"

"As pretty as you are, I can assure you I have been focusing on a few other things. We have Lucy Cooper on a list of people we plan to investigate. It's just that right now, your name keeps popping up everywhere I turn."

Tuck might have a list, but it sure did not feel like it.

"When you finally do get around to her and stop chasing me, you might want to check out how she's able to make an offer on one of the nicest houses in Piney Woods."

There was a subtle change in Tuck's demeanor. "How would you know this? Did Miss Cooper share this information with you?"

Nora started to answer and then stopped. Should she tell Tuck—a man who already didn't trust her—that she'd followed Lucy, talked to her mother under false pretenses, and then cobbled information together about her recent real estate offer? It could make things even worse for her, but if Tuck continued on his current path, she might well end up going to jail for a murder she didn't commit.

"Well?" he asked.

"I sort of followed her. I know that I did not kill Mr. Brockwell, so I took a few steps on my own to find the truth."

"You've been sneaking around after Lucy Cooper? You must really be desperate to point the finger to somebody else."

"You have no idea."

"I think I do. And how did you find out about Miss Cooper's offer? I'll say one thing for you, you Louisiana girls sure work fast."

Now he really had her hackles up. She gave a loud sniff of disgust and backed away from him. "I've had enough of this attitude," she said in an icy voice. "See you around, Tex."

"I'll be in touch, little lady." Tuck put on a Texas drawl and tipped his Stetson, eyes twinkling.

# Chapter 14

―――

THE NEXT DAY, when Nora entered Shady Sunsets, she merely nodded at the receptionist, signed in, and walked down the hall, hoping to run into Arnette. The smell of breakfast, although served earlier, still lingered in the air. The man in the plaid bathrobe eyed her and shut his door with a crisp slam.

A woman with white hair was taking up most of the space in the hall with her walker. Nora stopped to let her pass. No matter how much of a hurry she was in to talk to Arnette one more time, she could take a moment.

"Thank you, dear. I'm afraid I'm a bit of a road hog …." The woman stopped mid-sentence as she raised her gaze to Nora's face. She looked startled and upset.

"Ma'am? Are you all right?" She helped the woman to a conveniently placed bench.

Once seated, the woman curled her gnarled hands in her lap. There was a faint scent of Shalimar about her. "I'm sorry. Being old plays tricks on you."

"I'm just glad I was here. Are you okay?"

The woman attempted to straighten her shoulders. "I'm glad

you're here, too. My name is Rosalyn. It's so nice to meet you."

"I'm Nora."

"Nora," Rosalyn said, trying out the name. She gazed at her and then shrugged. She patted Nora's hand. "What a fine name. One of my favorites. If you'll help me up, I'll keep working my way down the hall."

Rosalyn laid a hand on Nora's arm, and together they got her back on her feet. The woman waved and began moving back down the hall.

When Nora found Arnette, she was vacuuming a common room that held a television and a large collection of books and games. She hunched over the sweeper, her light-blue knit uniform bulging slightly around the waist.

"Miss Cooper?" Nora said over the droning of the vacuum.

"Yes?" Arnette turned and switched off the vacuum. "You came back? Did you forget something?"

"No. I just wanted to talk to you about my mother. You see, I saw this picture of her at the hotel and I just hoped you could tell me anything ... anything at all you can remember."

Arnette shifted in her seat. "I told you, I don't recall ever knowing your mother."

Maybe this was a waste of time, she thought. "Tatty Tovar was surprised you didn't like Mr. Brockwell. She said everybody in this town loved the guy."

"She did? Why were you talking to Tatty about me?" Her hands, which had been so quiet a moment earlier now became restless and trembled slightly.

"I'm staying at her bed and breakfast. She remembers you fondly. She told me you had a beautiful voice and sang in the church choir."

Arnette gazed off for a second and then turned back to Nora. "I'm a little busy, now. Can you come back another time?"

"Sure."

Feeling defeated, Nora picked up her bag to leave. She'd so hoped to find out more about her mother, something that could convince Tuck she wasn't a murderer. It seemed like the more she tried, the more confusing the situation became. The frustration tightened her throat.

"I'm sorry," she said in slightly choked voice. "It's just, I came to this town expecting to drop off a letter and warm some old man's heart. Instead, somebody murdered him, I'm a suspect, and oh yeah, my mother had a whole secret past she never bothered to tell me about. She had a family named McArdle I knew nothing about. Still don't. I just need to know more about her life here." Nora swiped at a tear.

Arnette Cooper gazed at her. "McArdle? I'm sorry too, but if you want to know about your mother, why don't you just go down the hall and ask your grandmother, baby? You're just wasting your time with me."

"My grandmother? I have a *grandmother*?" Nora could not believe what she was hearing.

"Come on, I'll introduce you."

Arnette led Nora to a room with "Rosalyn McArdle" typed on a card beside the door. It was the same woman Nora had encountered earlier in the hallway. How many times did complete strangers meet and not know they were related by blood? How odd to think you might smile and nod at a stranger and have no idea the other person who was nodding back was family. Now Nora knew why Rosalyn had been so shocked to see her. She might have thought she was reuniting with her long-lost daughter.

Rosalyn's room was filled with pictures, and Nora recognized her mother in some of them. It was a much younger version of her mother, but there was no mistaking who it was. If Nora had any doubts she had family in this town, this collection of pictures put them to rest.

"Miss Rosalyn, I think I found you a treasure." Arnette's eyes glowed with warmth.

Upon seeing Nora again, Rosalyn's bottom lip began to tremble. "Leslie? Is it you, Leslie? How can it be you?"

"No, Rosalyn," Arnette spoke, as if to a small child. "I think this is Leslie's daughter."

"Leslie's *daughter*? Oh, my lord, no wonder." Rosalyn looked at Nora with a new sense of realization. "You're the young lady who helped me in the corridor. I knew it. I knew there was something when I saw you."

"I never knew about you. My mother never told me."

Rosalyn touched Nora's cheek and then lifted a piece of silky hair the color of autumn. "She left so suddenly. And we were so afraid something bad had happened to her. This is such a wonderful surprise. Is she here with you now? Did she come home? Where is she? I haven't heard from her in some time now."

"No. I'm so sorry. No. My mother … I'm so sorry."

Nora didn't have to explain. From Rosalyn's face, it was clear she understood.

Arnette stepped in. "She's gone, Rosalyn. That's why Nora is here."

Rosalyn nodded, as if she'd been expecting this news for the last thirty years. Her gaze drifted downward, and Nora took her hands.

"This is a lot for you to take in, I know."

"She's been gone for a long time. This just makes it official." Rosalyn's voice was shaky.

"Did you have any idea where she was?"

"My baby is gone. She was so beautiful. Like you."

"Miss Rosalyn, can I get you something? Some water?" Arnette asked.

Rosalyn raised a hanky to her cheek, wiping away a tear. She let out a short sniff. "It was so long ago, now."

"She was married, you know," I said.

"I wish I could have been there."

"I'm sure she would have loved having you there. My father is gone, too. It's just me." Nora stopped herself. "Or I thought it was just me."

Rosalyn's eyes widened and she hugged Nora again as if to make up for all she'd missed. "Oh, baby, you've had a rough time of it. Tell me about your daddy?"

"He was shot in the line of duty. He was a cop in New Orleans."

"New Orleans? She was so close." Arnette was astounded. "Lord, Rosalyn, you could have driven over in a day."

"She needed her family at a time like that. I wish she could have come home."

Nora agreed, but for some reason she still didn't understand, her mother had chosen to stay in Louisiana instead of moving back to Texas. All three women sat in silence, contemplating the fallout of Nora's mother's decision.

Finally Rosalyn said, "I've missed so much of her life. I lived with her without you, and you lived with her without me. Losing a parent is awful, and losing a child … you could never believe how empty that made me feel. I have boxes and boxes of pictures I'd be glad to share with you."

"I'd like that. I don't have too many here with me, but I can bring over what I have."

"I've been without my daughter for so many years, but now, I've been blessed with you." Rosalyn reached over, laying her hand on Nora's.

Nora placed her hand over her grandmother's, and it seemed there were three, not two, rejoicing in this reunion. Nora, her grandmother, and her mother.

"The Lord works in mysterious ways," Arnette whispered.

AFTER CHATTING WITH her newly found grandmother, Nora decided she needed a drink. A tall one. She ducked into Dudley's Brew, the coffee shop next to the courthouse. Dudley's seemed to be a mainstay for those going to court in Piney Woods.

"Give me a black coffee with sugar and make it a big one."

The teenager behind the counter had straight blond hair and wore a wrinkled Surf Galveston T-shirt under his green apron. "Whoa. You must be having a bad one." He pulled a large paper cup off a stack and dripped simmering black coffee into it. "This ought to help. Just tell old Dudley your problems, ma'am. Court's in session and we won't have a rush until all the slackers finish paying their parking tickets. My time is yours right now. All a part of the service."

Judging by the acne and the surfer-dude haircut, the kid couldn't be more than sixteen. "You're Dudley?"

"Little Dudley. Big Dudley's out."

He handed Nora the steaming cup.

"Don't worry. I've had extensive training." He pointed to a large paper number on the wall. "Twenty-seven days without a spill."

He seemed to be waiting for her story, and even though she normally wouldn't dream of confiding in a teenager, she was so emotional about finding her grandmother that she launched into the story of their meeting.

"Wow, you never knew the old chick was your grandmother?"

"No idea. I didn't even know I had family in this town."

"Instant family. Awesome. It could be a great thing ... or a curse. What if they start asking for money or stuff, like your spare kidney? You could find yourself hatched from a nest of freeloaders."

Little Dudley could be right. Wiley did seem to spend more time drinking than working. She could be in for a world of trouble.

The bell on the door jingled and Corey Brockwell entered. Dark circles ringed his eyes, and the smell of unwashed clothing drifted into Nora's nose. Losing his father seemed to have taken a devastating toll.

"Give me a large black coffee."

Little Dudley nodded. "Whoa, dude, we're having a run on giant shots of caffeine all of a sudden."

Corey looked over and spotted Nora, who was already

halfway through her coffee. "What are you doing here? I thought they arrested you."

Little Dudley's head pivoted from Nora to Corey. "Huh?"

Nora sat up, her back rigid now, as if to ward off Corey's words. "They need proof to arrest a person, Mr. Brockwell. Seeing as how I didn't murder your father, they have no proof."

"Dang." Little Dudley handed Corey his cup.

"Fine. Well, I hope they lock you up for the rest of your life, and when they do, I'll personally make sure you never see the light of day."

It was hard to believe this was the same person Nora had met on her first day in town. Corey Brockwell had morphed from pleasant to downright mean. He reached into the pocket of his wrinkled khaki pants and pulled out a wadded-up twenty to pay for the coffee. As the bill came out, so did a small piece of paper with the name of a casino printed across the top. Little Dudley bent over to pick it up for him.

"Wheeler-dealer, eh? Been doing some gambling over in Louisiana? Big Dudley goes there sometimes."

Corey wasn't in deep grief; he was returning from a gambling binge in the next state. Nora picked up her coffee and headed for the door. Maybe gambling was his way of coping. He'd treated her unfairly, but she'd excuse him. She was finding relatives—he was losing them.

A chill was in the air, and Nora's steps were brisk as she walked to her car. This was the last bit of home she had left, this rusty old car. With one hundred fifty thousand miles on the odometer, she wasn't sure how much longer it would last. Someday, when she was making a decent wage, she'd replace it with a more reliable car. The way her life was going now, that would have to wait. Nora reached for the door handle.

"Miss Alexander?" Tuck walked up from the opposite direction. What was he doing? Surveillance on her?

"Yes. I'm pretty sure we've established who I am. What can I do for you, Detective Watson?"

"I just have a question for you. I have to tell you, Miss Alexander, the more I find out about you, the less I seem to know. I just finished running a standard background check." Tuck took off his hat and scratched his head.

The more nervous she became, the calmer he seemed. It was obvious this wasn't his first rodeo.

"You've been flying pretty well under the radar. No warrants, no bankruptcies .... You don't even have a parking ticket, but I have to question how much of a motive you might have seeing your mother with so much anger toward Mr. Brockwell. It wouldn't be the first time a daughter avenged her mother."

"And I repeat: I had no idea what was in her letter."

"Sure. Nothing else you want to tell me?" When Nora didn't respond, he snapped the notebook shut with one hand. "I'm going to keep trying to find out who killed Mr. Brockwell. It's my job and something I love to do."

Nora tried to keep her voice even. "I've given you everything I know about my meeting with Adam Brockwell. We've spent more time talking about those five minutes than it took for the old guy to look at the letter and ask me to leave." Nora's glanced over at a BUBBY FOR PIONEER sticker affixed to the light post. "How about Bubby Tidwell? He had a motive. This seems like a pretty fierce competition."

"Bubby really wants to be Piney Woods Pioneer, but he's not so desperate he'd kill Adam Brockwell. Besides, I checked. He has an alibi. Bubby was getting a spray tan ...." Watson broke off as his gaze wandered to the crumpled shirt in the back of her car. Nora's head began to pound as she realized the blood on the shirt she used after her near accident was now showing through the untinted window.

"What is that?"

"What?"

"That shirt." Watson cupped his hand to the glass, now peering at the crumpled-up, blood-stained item in the backseat.

Nora had meant to throw it away, but with everything else going on, hadn't gotten around to it.

"I was almost run off the road on the way here and opened up a wound on my hand when I stopped suddenly." She held up her hand, now covered by a Band-Aid. It didn't look big enough for the amount of blood that ended up on the shirt. "It was a pretty deep cut. I probably should have gone to the doctor for stitches …." Remembering their pleasant evening together, she found it impossible to continue.

"You never said anything about almost getting run off the road. At least not until now. I certainly don't see any damage on the car."

"It was a *near* accident."

He went back to the window. "I'm going to need to take the shirt with me, Miss Alexander."

"What if I say no? It's just my blood."

"We'll see. I'll take it anyway. It just became evidence in the murder of Adam Brockwell. I'm going to need you to stop by and give us a blood sample. I suggest you find yourself a lawyer, because if the blood turns out to be Brockwell's, you're going to need one."

# Chapter 15

NORA SEARCHED THROUGH her contacts on her cellphone for Max. Marty had insisted they all exchange phone numbers in case anyone was going to be late for work.

"Max, I need your help."

"Nora?"

"I need a lawyer, Max."

"You do realize I'm a law student, not a real live lawyer, right? Worse, I'm an online law student. I go to school in my pajamas."

"Tuck Watson just found a bloody shirt in my car and took it as evidence in the Adam Brockwell investigation. What do I do?"

There was silence on the other end and then Nora heard the sound keys clicking on a computer keyboard.

"Okay. Did he have a warrant?"

"No. Should he have had one?" Nora heard more clicking.

"Was it in plain sight, or was he digging through your stuff for something?"

"It was in plain sight. He saw it through my car window."

"Then what he did was legal. Not to be too much of a stickler here, but why was there a bloody shirt in your car?"

Nora scowled as her headache took flight. "I took it off right after I stabbed Adam Brockwell."

Max was silent a moment. "You're kidding, right?"

"Oh, Max, what do you think?" Nora hung up.

As she entered the bed and breakfast a few minutes later, the smell of perfume tickled her nose. This wasn't Tatty's scent, or even Ed's. Did they have a new guest? She had to admit she'd become comfortable staying here with the older couple. Their home was starting to feel like her home.

"Nora? Is that you?" Tatty called out from the living quarters.

"Yes."

"Good. Come on back here. You've got a visitor."

Did Tuck already have enough to arrest her? Maybe she could back out before anyone noticed.

"Don't just stand out there. Come on back."

As she entered the cozy living area, she saw Tatty sitting in her high-backed chair facing her guest, Lucy Cooper. Lucy set down her cup as her gaze met Nora's. Once again she was dressed for success in a fitted gray wool suit with matching gray stilettos. It was amazing to Nora how she could walk in those things. Maybe her feet hurt, because she didn't look too happy to see her.

"I hope you don't mind my intruding like this." As polite as her words sounded, there was little truth in them.

"Not at all," Tatty answered, before Nora could respond. "It's just so good to see you again, and to hear about your mother. Isn't it, Nora?"

"I'm sure it must be. I heard your mother was once an employee of Mr. Brockwell. Small world, you working for him and all." Nora's eyebrows rose as she waited for Lucy to take the bait.

"Speaking of my mother, I was pretty shocked when she told me you paid her a visit." Lucy's lips thinned with anger.

Tatty patted a section of the well-worn couch, Nora's cue to take a seat next to Lucy.

Lucy stiffened. "Just how, exactly, did you find her and what business is it of yours?"

Should she tell Lucy she'd followed her? That wouldn't sound good, no matter how she put it.

"I know it sounds like a weird thing to do."

" 'Weird' doesn't begin to describe it," Lucy agreed.

Nora sighed. Why did she always seem to be explaining herself these days? "Okay. Since you asked and seem to think I'm out to murder everybody's parent in this town, I found your mother because I was following you."

Tatty almost choked on her tea.

"I was following you because I'm a suspect in Adam Brockwell's death. I heard you were his investment counselor—"

"You were trying to find a way to put the blame on me?" Lucy interrupted her.

She'd pretty much nailed Nora's intentions. "You have to admit it's strange a man who spent his life accumulating wealth started relying on the investment advice of a twenty-something-year-old woman."

Lucy's eyes grew cold as Tatty leaned closer. "Just what are you implying?"

"I'm just curious. What was your sales pitch that made you so darn persuasive?"

Lucy stood, knocking her knee on Tatty's coffee table and unsettling her tea cup. "You had better watch out, Miss Alexander. Curiosity killed the cat, you know." Lucy grabbed her bag and reached down to touch her bruised knee. Straightening up, she tried to regain her composure. "Oh, and stay away from my mother. With your history, you can't be trusted alone with the vulnerable."

# Chapter 16

———∼∼∼———

A FTER LUCY LEFT, Tatty said, "That certainly didn't go well." She began wiping the spilled tea off her coffee table.

"Would you have some ibuprofen? My head is killing me."

"Sure, sweetie."

Tatty left the room and Nora threw herself back onto the couch. Despair over the last few days started sinking in as she reviewed her situation. She'd delivered a letter to an old man from her mother, thinking she was doing a good thing. What harm could there be? Well, it had sure stirred up a nest of hornets, and now the man was dead by someone's hand.

"Take these. They ought to help."

Nora opened her eyes. Tatty held out her warm brown palm, which held two tablets.

"Thank you."

"You're welcome. I can't believe you told Lucy you were following her."

"Call it detective work." Nora downed the painkillers.

"It might be detective work in Louisiana, but around here they call it stalking."

"I just thought if I could prove she had a motive to kill

Brockwell for his money, it would take some heat off me. It sounds plain stupid now."

Tatty crossed her arms and pondered a moment. "It's something to think about. I'll tell you that."

"And it's all I have. Detective Watson is determined to prove I killed Adam Brockwell." Nora knew she needed to tell Tatty about her latest brush with the law. Tatty was one of the few people who believed her, and not telling her might backfire. Nora leaned in closer. "It gets worse. On my way to Piney Woods, I almost had a car accident."

Tatty gasped in surprise.

"Nothing too bad. I was daydreaming and driving too slow. Some idiot tried to pass me, cut me off, and ran me off the road. I hit the brakes and the car jolted with the impact. The sudden movement knocked open a cut on my hand. I know it doesn't look like anything now, but you wouldn't believe the amount of blood that freshly opened cut produced. I had on a blouse with a tank top underneath. The blouse already had blood on it so I took it off and put it around my hand to try to stanch the flow."

"That's terrible."

"I threw the shirt into the backseat of the car when I finished with it. I think my headache comes from the impending sense of doom I'm getting from your local police. Now he has my shirt. Will this ever end?"

"If it had blood on it, why didn't you just throw it away?"

"I was planning to but kept forgetting about it. It did not strike me as important after all that has happened. Today, Lieutenant Watson saw it through my car window and claimed it as evidence in the Adam Brockwell investigation." Nora shut her eyes and laid her head on the back of the couch. "See what I mean? I need to find out who murdered Adam Brockwell before the police decide it's me."

Tatty put her arm around Nora. After losing her mother, she felt great comfort in Tatty's simple gesture.

"Nora, they're not going to arrest you for a crime you didn't commit."

Nora hiccupped as the tears started.

She was surprised when Ed came in and sat on the other side of her. "Now you listen to me. They can check the shirt and find out whose blood is on it. I've seen it on TV. Once they establish you are telling the truth and the blood is yours, they'll have to look elsewhere. Don't you worry about it."

"Do you think so?"

"I *know* so," Tatty broke in. "Tuck Watson may be all over your business right now, but he's a good man, Nora. He's a man who wants to see justice done, even if you are the most interesting case to come along in his career with your poison-pen letter and all."

Listening to Tatty's description, Nora giggled. It was so Agatha Christie. "A poison-pen letter, really?"

Tatty grinned. She pushed at Nora's shoulder. "Hush. I'm just trying to help."

"You are helping. Both of you. More than you know. Thank you. I don't know what would have happened to me if I hadn't found you and Ed."

Ed grinned and pointed both index fingers at Nora. "Well, you sure do perk up life around here. The rest of the town is jealous. We've got the freak show living right here."

"Except I keep finding long-lost relatives. I'm more a part of this town than some of the regulars down at Dudley's Brew."

Tatty patted her on the shoulder. "With all the loss you've had in your life, child, somehow, I think it's a good thing."

"I hope so." Nora thought back to Little Dudley's ideas about a family full of freeloaders. "Actually, I met my grandmother today. She wants me to bring her pictures of my mother."

"Wonderful, but not tonight. Your *abuela* is probably all snuggled up in bed. You have a night off and you need to relax. Put your feet up. Take a bath."

Nora knew she was right. She had a family now. If she could just stop fearing the prospect of Tuck coming around the corner with a pair of handcuffs, maybe she could rest.

# Chapter 17

———

THE NEXT MORNING, the world did seem a little brighter than it had the day before. Nora dug through the pictures she'd brought with her and then decided to grab the picture off of the wall at the Tunie.

"Mind if I borrow this?" Nora asked Marty as she pulled the picture from its resting place.

"Sure. Just bring it back when you're finished. Hate to rob Piney Woods of its history." Marty gave it another look. "Oh, and could you dust it?"

A little later, Nora was taking out her pictures in her grandmother's room at Shady Sunsets when Pastor Chilton appeared in the doorway.

"Knock, knock!" He was dressed in a black shirt and pants with the white rectangle of his clerical collar showing at his throat. It seemed a little silly to Nora—a grown man saying "knock, knock"—but she supposed it kept the mood light on visits to places like this.

"May I come in?" At the sight of Nora, Pastor Chilton smiled. "I see you have a visitor. This is a great morning."

"This is my granddaughter, Pastor. Isn't it wonderful?"

"Your granddaughter? Well, now that I think about it, you're right. Leslie's daughter would be your granddaughter. Your family has been separated for so long, I forget who's related." He chuckled softly. "It does sound strange. Whatever it is, what a tremendous blessing. I've always believed God rewards those who do good, Rosalyn, and Nora here has become your treasure on earth."

Nora's face heated. *Jeez*. Yesterday they were about to put her picture up in the post office. Today she was a treasure.

Nora pulled out the picture she'd taken off the wall of the Tunie Hotel.

"Oh, my, it's her." Rosalyn gazed at the faded photo of Nora's mother. "It looks like her. Did you bring this with you from Louisiana?"

"No. I found this one at the Tunie Hotel."

"Really? I never knew. I'll bet I've walked past it ten times."

"That's my brother, you know." Pastor Chilton pointed to the young man on the left in the picture. "Right there. That's Arnie."

"Did he know my mother?"

Pastor Chilton gazed upward and smiled. "Everyone knew your mother, Nora. Prettiest girl in town back then. I suppose Arnie was as smitten with her as anyone."

Nora's gaze lingered on the photo.

"Never lose an opportunity to see anything beautiful, for beauty is God's handwriting," Chilton whispered.

"Is that from the Bible?" Nora asked.

"Nope. Ralph Waldo Emerson said it, and he was so right. Adam Brockwell believed it too. He thought your mother was the most beautiful woman he'd ever seen. I sure am going to miss him, not just for his good deeds, but as a friend. This whole town will."

Not everybody in town loved him. Nora knew that. Arnette knew that. Why didn't Pastor Chilton?

"They look so young," Chilton said, blinking away a tear. "I know very little of what happened that summer. I was ten years younger than my brother Arnie, but I do know that whatever it was, by August your mother was long gone."

"Do you have any idea?" Nora asked.

Pastor Chilton gave Nora's shoulder a comforting pat, his blue eyes crinkling at the corners.

"We may never know. Sometimes we just have to accept whatever it is life hands us and move on. Leslie was a good woman, and I'm sure she's enjoying her eternal reward in Heaven."

Nora found comfort and even peace in the pastor's words. He was right. Kay Alexander was in a better place. Best of all, her mother was there with her father, and that thought made Nora happy.

"I still think about our last conversation." Rosalyn caressed the top of the picture frame. "If I loved her, the best thing I could do was leave her alone."

Why did she feel she had to hide? Why had her mother left her family? Growing up like she did, Nora never had a sense of belonging. "I didn't even know I had a grandmother."

"You just never know how your life can change in a single day," Chilton said, taking a chair. "When did you find out Rosalyn was at Shady Sunsets?"

"Arnette Cooper told me."

Pastor Chilton's lips thinned at the mention of Arnette's name. "Lucy's mother," he acknowledged in a small-world kind of way. He had more to say but seemed to be struggling with his conscience.

"Yes," Nora continued, "what can you tell me about Mr. Brockwell and Arnette Cooper?"

Chilton cocked his head. "You've got me there."

This was disappointing. Nora had thought the pastor would be aware of someone in the community having such a dislike for another. "She was his housekeeper for a couple of years back in the eighties. I guess she really disliked him."

"She did? I find that surprising. Although in light of your mother's letter, I'm not trusting my instincts like I used to concerning Adam."

"I was speaking to Arnette to see if there was anything I could find out to help me stay off the suspect list in the Adam Brockwell investigation. I suppose you know Lieutenant Watson is doing all he can to prove I'm the killer?"

"The man must be blind. Anyone can tell you're no killer," Rosalyn chirped.

"Yes, I've heard," Pastor Chilton said, "but how could someone like Arnette help you? I feel your struggle in all this, and if there is anything I can do to help, just ask. Adam was like a brother to me, and I want to see his killer brought to justice, but I don't think we need to slay the innocent to do that."

It might have been Pastor Chilton's kind and understanding eyes or just the fact he was a man of God, but Nora confessed everything, from following Lucy, to Lucy telling her to stay away from her mother. At the end of her story, the pastor didn't offer any words of support, and Nora began to wonder if she'd said too much. Could it be everything he just said had changed, and now he was also convinced she'd killed his old friend Adam Brockwell?

Rosalyn broke the silence. "I'm sorry Lucy won't let you talk to Arnette anymore. She's a fine person."

Pastor Chilton leaned closer. Nora's confession seemed to have released whatever had been holding him back.

"I probably shouldn't share this with you, but … maybe your suspicions aren't unfounded. Lucy was up at the reception desk when I came in. She was arguing with Arnette."

"What were they arguing about?"

"I can't be sure, but it sounded like Lucy wanted her to quit her job here. Arnette didn't appear to agree with her daughter."

"Why would she want her mom to leave Shady Sunsets? Do you think it was because I'd been talking to her?" Nora asked.

"From the tone of their conversation, she was planning on leaving town. In a hurry ...." His voice was almost a whisper.

As much as she hated the thought of talking to Tuck again, Nora needed to share this information. Lucy could be the killer, and she was getting ready to leave town before anyone noticed she was gone. These were not the actions of an innocent woman, and if Nora wasn't careful, Lucy Cooper would get away and Nora would find herself arrested for another woman's crime.

# Chapter 18

———◆———

WHEN NORA APPROACHED the desk at the nursing home, she heard Lucy arguing with Arnette behind a closed door marked PRIVATE. It didn't sound like they would be finishing their conversation anytime soon, so Nora grabbed her keys and drove to the police station. The police station was a two-story gray-brick building positioned right next to the Tunie. As she gathered her purse, she looked up at the hotel, admiring how the morning sun glimmered on the freshly cleaned windows. The aging relic was changing into a successful working business. When she first came to Piney Woods, she hadn't expected to stay long enough to need a job, but now that she was working, she was pleased with her situation. This hotel had also been a part of her mother's life.

What had it been like for Kay Alexander all those years ago? Perhaps she'd attended one of those elegant evenings of dance Mr. Birdsong talked about. Piney Woods seemed like a pretty good place to Nora. Her mother had been the "it" girl of her time. She began to wonder what her life would have been like if she'd grown up in this little town. Would she have followed in her mother's footsteps? The young girl in the picture was so full of life, so far removed from the woman she knew as her mother. She was the girl everyone admired. The girl people wanted to be friends with. The girl Adam Brockwell wanted to date. Life came easy for her.

In the Piney Woods Police station, Nora glanced past the reception/dispatch area on the right, through an open door, where several officers sitting in cubicles were glued to their computers. Corey Brockwell sat in a chair next to Tuck Watson's desk. Maybe this was her lucky day and he was confessing to his father's murder.

Today Corey looked more rested than when she'd bumped into him at the coffee shop. Both men glanced up as she came through the doorway. Corey's expression turned smug, but it was almost as if Tuck was glad to see her. That couldn't be right. Maybe he thought she'd come to confess.

"Come to turn yourself in?" Corey asked.

"Just what I hoped *you* were doing." The last time she ran into Corey Brockwell, she'd been willing to cut him a break, but today he didn't seem so fragile.

"I'll be the first to admit my father and I didn't always get along, especially if it had anything to do with my mother, but I'd never kill him."

"I thought your father was the greatest man Texas ever produced." She was so sick of hearing about what a wonderful man the town had lost.

"He was. I'm sure you know my father was up for Piney Woods Pioneer. They don't give that to just anybody. He was a financial success, but the award is also for a person who shows a higher level of morality and decency in how they give to others. My father did all that. He embodied the original spirit of Texans who settled this state. Now I suppose that honor will go to Bubby Tidwell, the snake. My father was a great man for this community. It was just when my parents divorced ...." He stumbled for a moment as if reaching for words. That was interesting. This was the first time she'd heard Corey say anything about his mother.

"Well then," Tuck stroked his chin, "if you're not here to make a full confession and to help me close this case, what can I do for you?"

"I can wait."

Corey stared at her. Maybe the whole idea of telling Tuck about Lucy skipping town was silly.

"Okay then, feel free to take a seat while I finish up with Mr. Brockwell." He gestured to a tan plastic chair against the opposite wall.

Without another word, Nora sat. She was ecstatic to be able to hear Corey's conversation with Tuck.

Corey turned away from Nora. "So, you're telling me you're not even close to solving my father's murder?"

"I didn't say we weren't close. You have to understand. I have to thoroughly check out every lead." He glanced Nora's way. "We can't arrest a person without evidence."

Nora shifted in her chair. Was Tuck referring to her? If he was, he also seemed to be protecting her. Maybe Tatty was right. Maybe he was a good man.

"Fine," Corey said in a clipped voice. "I know you have to do your job, but you also need to realize there are lives hanging in the balance."

Tuck looked at him quizzically. "Lives? Do you fear the killer will try to kill again? Do you think you're in danger?"

"No! I mean, I don't think so. I was referring to legal affairs. I'm now in charge of my father's estate."

A look of understanding came over Tuck's face. "Oh. I get it. You're looking for your inheritance."

Corey paled. "I won't even begin to address the inappropriateness of your statement, Detective Watson. Certainly thought you'd be a little more sensitive to the grieving."

"You're right. I flunked out of sensitivity training. Told the teacher off." Tuck grinned.

Corey jumped up, pushing his chair back.

Nora stifled a laugh, prompting Corey to stare straight at her. "Once again, I leave the two of you, wondering if I will get any justice for my father's murder."

"Mr. Brockwell, I assure you there will be justice and an answer to this homicide soon. I take this case very seriously."

Corey slid a look of disdain Tuck's way and stomped out.

"What is it you're bursting to tell me?" Tuck leaned back, steepling his fingers. Judging by his smile, you'd think Nora had shown up with a dozen donuts.

She rose from her chair and came over to Tuck's desk.

"I am so glad you stopped by." Tuck motioned to the chair in front of his desk. "I had the most interesting phone call concerning you today."

"Concerning me?"

"Yes, your father's old partner called me."

"Oh, good. I called him the other day to see if he could give me any background on my mother and father when he knew them."

"He told me." Tuck tapped on the desk with his pen. "He also told me a few things about your mother that confirmed what you said. He seemed to think she left here for a reason. Something she was hiding? He was pretty vague and almost … crude about it."

Nora crossed her arms in front of her. "He told me he remembered very little."

"Maybe he was more comfortable talking cop to cop. He spent most of the time asking me about Adam Brockwell's investigation." He paused for a moment.

"Why would he care about that?"

"I just figured he was an old cop interested in a murder case. There's a reason they have so many true crime shows these days, you know. People are fascinated by murder."

Nora shook her head in disbelief. "This doesn't make any sense."

"Listen, Nora. I just answer the phone and try to help people. So, what brings you rushing into my office today? Ready to give me that blood sample?"

Nora cleared her mind and said, "It's Lucy Cooper."

Tuck let out an exasperated sigh. "I already told you, I plan to question her."

"Well, you'd better hurry, because she's planning to leave Piney Woods."

"Why would she want to leave town? From what I hear, she has a thriving practice here."

"Could it be she's been profiting off Adam Brockwell in some way, and now that he's dead and his financial affairs will be looked through, she is getting out of Piney Woods?"

"How do you know all this?" Tuck asked.

"Let's just say it's a feeling. She's over at Shady Sunsets right now arguing with Arnette. She wants her to quit her job and everything. Pick up and move at a moment's notice."

Tuck debated for a moment but then picked up his keys and his hat. "Do you think they're still there?"

"If we hurry."

"I'll go talk to her."

"Great. I'm coming with you." Nora rose to stand beside him. Being this close to him, she felt both wary and aware of him as a man.

He spoke in a gruff tone. "I think it might be better if you let me do my job."

Nora poked at his chest with her finger. "Sure, and get myself railroaded for a murder charge?"

"Fine. Just stay out of my way. You can wait in the car." Tuck pushed her finger away and then, placing his hand on the small of her back, opened the door for her.

# Chapter 19

———

"MAMA, DON'T WORRY about your lunch in the refrigerator. We'll go to a drive-thru on our way." Lucy Cooper stood by the open passenger side of her car as her mother slid into the seat.

Arnette Cooper looked at her daughter with a confused expression. "But I don't understand. Why do we have to leave, Lucy? I like it here. Piney Woods is our home now. What about your job? What about your clients?"

"I'd kind of like to know the answer to your question myself," Tuck Watson said as he walked up behind the two women in the parking lot.

Lucy's eyes widened, and she turned her attention from her mother, now seated in the car. Stepping away from Arnette, she smoothed the wrinkles from the skirt of her business suit.

"Just taking Mama out for lunch. Is there a law against that?" Lucy fanned herself and used her best smile on Tuck.

Nobody was fooled.

"You do know you're part of an active investigation, right?" Tuck asked.

Lucy cleared her throat. "Don't be silly. We all know that

redheaded woman with the letter murdered Adam Brockwell."

At the mention of Brockwell's name, Arnette Cooper sat up and listened. "Nora? Nice young Nora killed Adam Brockwell?"

"No, Mrs. Cooper, I did not." Nora slammed the car door shut as she exited Tuck's cruiser. Lucy bit her bottom lip, looking embarrassed that her intended scapegoat had overheard her words.

Tuck swore under his breath. Nora knew he was annoyed that she'd followed him after promising not to.

"Well, if you didn't, who did?" Arnette asked, eying Tuck.

"That's what I'm working very hard to figure out, Mrs. Cooper. It's a long and tedious process that involves asking many people many questions. For instance, why your daughter is so anxious to get out of town."

Arnette raised her eyebrows, giving her daughter a well-practiced look.

Lucy's face turned ashen as she looked at her feet. "I don't know what you're talking about."

"Lucy! Answer the man," Arnette demanded.

Lucy gave Tuck a sideways glance. "It was the money. You'd have found out eventually."

"Do you mean the investments? The investments you were advising Brockwell on?"

She stared off into the distance, down the road she'd almost made it to. "Partly. I told the old man to invest in some crap stock, and no matter what it was, he dumped cash into it. These stocks were listed everywhere as dogs. All he had to do was pick up a newspaper to see it. But it was like magic. I said it and he did it. It was so easy. I told him to give me some cash for special investments. He didn't even ask what they were. He just wrote me a check." She shook her head.

"Think about it." Lucy's eyes widened as she tried to prove what was obvious. "I'd be out of my mind to want to murder someone writing me checks to use at my discretion. Why stop the flow of cash and take the risk of getting caught?"

Nora didn't buy it. "Or he could've figured out you were trying to ruin him."

"Why?" Tuck asked. "I know a lot of people didn't care for the man, but why did you take it upon yourself to destroy his fortune?"

"For my mother, of course," Lucy said, as if the answer were obvious.

Tuck cocked his head. "Excuse me?"

Arnette raised her hand from the front seat of the car. "She did it for me."

"Did you have some sort of grievance with Adam Brockwell?" Tuck asked.

"Yes."

Tuck looked at Arnette, waiting for more information, but she'd apparently said all she intended to say. It would have been logical for her to tell her story at this point, but she remained silent.

"Mama doesn't like to talk about it. She doesn't like to bring up the past. But when you see your mother cry over a man night after night …. I needed to do something for her. Something to make it right. I just didn't know it would be so easy."

"He knew, you know. It was because he loved you, Lucy," Arnette interrupted.

Now the confusion was on Lucy's face. "*Loved* me? Why would that old man love *me*?"

Nora got it. It was so simple. Arnette hated him. The scandal when she left town, pregnant. No father for Lucy. It had never been the teacher. It was someone else. "Because Adam Brockwell was your father," she whispered.

# Chapter 20

———

"**W**HAT WOULD YOU know about my father, girl?" Lucy eyed Nora.

She looked to her mother for support. Instead, Arnette was nodding in agreement.

"Were you and Brockwell having an affair?" Watson asked.

Arnette avoided his gaze. "If that's what you want to call it. He was so charming at first, and then he changed."

"Mama! Do you mean he forced you?" Lucy leaned over, taking her mother's hand. "Why didn't you tell me?"

"No. I was willing, even though he was married. There was just something about him. He wouldn't stop asking …. I'm ashamed to even talk about it now."

Nora had a hard time believing Arnette had an affair with a married man. Adam Brockwell must have had some impressive powers of seduction. Maybe he was like his son, who seemed to be a Dr. Jekyll and Mr. Hyde. Sometimes charming, sometimes selfish and ruthless.

"You don't know. You just couldn't know, baby. Mr. Brockwell was a rich man. I was the housekeeper. With dreams of working my way through college. He was married and had the cutest little boy. His wife was what I would call a society blonde. Lots of money and the kind of activities only rich women partake in. Her world and mine were so different. I went to classes and she went to lunches at the club."

"Was that Corey's mother?"

"Sure was. She was different from the rest of the women in town. She had as much money as he did. Brockwell's daddy looked at all the local pickings and thought they were just a bunch of gold diggers. Corey's mama was nothing of the sort. It was a good marriage for the Brockwells, both financially and socially."

Lucy crossed her arms, amazed at her mother's words. "I never knew you went to college."

"For a little bit, until I had you anyway. Mr. Brockwell and his wife seemed so much in love. He gave her any little thing she wanted. Jewelry, a car, anything at all. Both of their bank accounts were pretty healthy at that time. The warehouse operation took off and the whole town spoke of him like he was some sort of hero out of a comic book."

"So, why do you hate him so much?" Lucy asked.

"Because of what he did, baby. I'm going to try to explain this to you. I should have told you years ago, but it's not something I'm proud of."

Lucy shifted uncomfortably as her eyes went to the floor.

"I guess it all started when I was working in the house. I was never one to keep my mouth shut. Every once in a while, I spouted off about one thing or another, and the thing that reeled me in was he laughed at my jokes. He thought I was funny. I was just the housekeeper. I told him how goofy the milkman looked in the morning and Mr. Brockwell just laughed and laughed, like I was some kind of comedian. I was flattered. Then they were decorating the little boy's room. His wife wanted a circus theme. She was having clowns painted on the walls and elephants and circus lion tamers. The whole nine yards. She had this one clown painted on the wall that wasn't cute. It was scary. It frightened me. One day I was vacuuming in the hall and I looked up. There he was in this bright orange clown suit, his eyes seeming to follow me. Then right up behind me Mr. Brockwell touched the small of my back.

"He whispered into my ear, 'What do you think of it?'

"A shiver ran through me. He was so close.

" 'That clown on the wall,' he said. 'There's just something wrong with it. What do you think about a circus theme in a child's room?'

" 'Oh, that's not for me to say,' I told him. I knew my place and I sure wasn't getting myself in trouble over some clown.

" 'No, just for a minute,' he said. 'If this was for your child, would you paint the walls with circus animals and clowns?'

" 'I think all those bright colors and wild animals are kind of jarring for a little one,' I replied.

"He said, 'I couldn't agree with you more. I'm going to tell my wife to repaint my son's room. It could give the little guy nightmares.' "

She smiled. "So, that was the other thing about Mr. Brockwell. He respected my opinion. Also, when he walked up from behind, he put his hand on my shoulder like we were old chums looking at a painting. It made me nervous, but there was also something about it, something so seductive."

Lucky cocked her head to one side. "I thought you had a boyfriend back then."

"Sure did. His name was Mr. Ellis and he taught math at the junior high. He was a handsome man but knew his boundaries. We dated for six months and never went any further than a good-night kiss. His mama wanted to make sure he found the right woman, and I don't think she thought I was good enough for him. Still, though, we went to the church social and potluck every week for six months. He was a wonderful man, and if I could do any part of my life over, I'd have married Mr. Ellis, but then there was that trouble with the school board. There was just so much gossip. He couldn't stay teaching in that school."

"Did he ever talk to you about getting married?" Lucy asked.

"Oh, sure. We were planning on getting married. That was before …."

"Before what?"

Arnette sighed heavily. "One day when his wife was out at some function or another, Mr. Brockwell reached over and pulled me in close. This is the part I'm truly ashamed of. I was attracted to the man. Young, handsome, and rich, he thought I was funny and seemed to like me. He kissed me and I kissed him right back. That's where it started. There I was, going to church every week and cheating with a man whose wife trusted him. It was the most awful thing I ever did."

"Oh, Mama."

"It didn't take long till I was pregnant with you."

"What did you do? Did his wife find out?"

"Yes. It hurt her to the quick, and she started talking divorce. He told her it must have been one of my boyfriends. Like I had a whole passel of men coming after me. She knew though. Little Corey had a live-in nanny and she had seen us together."

"What did Mr. Ellis say?"

"He was a gentleman. Always polite. Offered to marry me anyway. I told Mr. Brockwell that Mr. Ellis and I'd get married and we would raise you as Mr. Ellis' child. Mrs. Brockwell wasn't going to let that happen. She told the school board I was pregnant by Mr. Ellis. Mr. Brockwell stood up in that meeting and backed her up. He helped her spread that lie about me. That was when Mr. Ellis left town. You didn't want to cross Brockwell."

"So, what did you do?"

"I stayed. I had you and I put up with all of the gossip and the shame of living with a fair-skinned baby who had no daddy to speak of. Of course, the whole town assumed it was Mr. Ellis' because he was also light-skinned. I tried to get other work, but the Brockwells made sure no one would hire me.

They wanted me and my baby gone from their sight. I never understood it, because they were getting divorced anyway. Finally, Mr. Brockwell told me to leave, right to my face. I just couldn't go up against him. He was Adam Brockwell, after all. The whole town loved the man."

"Is that when we left?" Lucy said in a small voice.

"Yes. We left in the middle of the night and we didn't come back for twenty years. I wouldn't have come back at all, but my sister was sick. I had to come. She had nobody else. She died when you were finishing college and then you came back to be with me. It took good old Adam Brockwell about two seconds to realize who you were."

Lucy sighed. "So, he knew all along I was his daughter."

"Oh, yes. That's why he became one of your customers. His wife was long gone and I think he wanted to spend time with you, but he couldn't let it be known he was your father. He opened an account with you. All of a sudden, you were the whiz kid of finances."

Lucy shook her head. "I'll be darned. I had no idea."

"The day I left was one of the best days of my life. He was an evil, selfish man and I'm glad he's dead."

"Mama!" Lucy scolded.

"I don't care if the police or the FBI or anyone else hears it."

"You never collected any child support?" Nora asked.

"I thought about it, especially in the early days. No, I decided to show him I could be just fine. I didn't want him interfering. Just look at my baby. She's so beautiful. I done right by her, and that's all that matters."

"What about the embezzlement? Will Lucy have to pay the money back?" Nora asked.

"You say he willingly wrote you those checks?" Tuck asked.

"He certainly did, and if you're going to arrest me for giving bad investment advice, then you'd better arrest half the people on the New York Stock Exchange."

She had a point. Wait until smug Corey Brockwell, anxious to get his hands on his father's estate, found out he'd be splitting it with a sister.

# Chapter 21

—⁓—

"HOLY COW, NORA," Max exclaimed after hearing the story that evening at the hotel. "Do you think Lucy did it?"

Nora, who would've answered with a resounding "yes" a few days ago, was no longer so sure. Lucy had the motive and the determination, but she just didn't seem like a murderer. If she loved her mother so much she'd risk prison to take care of her, how could she be responsible for such a grisly murder? Why kill the cash cow?

"Maybe. I mean, I'm glad some of the focus of the investigation is shifting off me …."

"But …?"

"But if I don't want to see myself taking the fall for a crime I didn't commit, I sure don't want to see that happen to somebody else."

"And how do you know she didn't do it? She was already stealing from him. What would stop her from killing him when he became aware of what she was doing? Sounds like first-degree murder to me. 'A killing that is deliberate and premeditated.' " Max sounded like he was quoting from one of his many legal sources.

*Lucy was right there in the room when Brockwell received the letter*, Nora thought. She'd also admitted to guiding him into bad investments to drain some of his fortune.

"Have you ever stopped to think he let her cheat him out of money? Maybe it was a guilt thing?" asked Max.

"Arnette seemed to think so. I have no idea. The more I learn about this man, the more confused I get. On the one hand he was wonderful—a town savior—and on the other, evil, manipulative, and couldn't keep his pants zipped." Nora yawned and stretched. "It's time for me to go home. The thing is, when I work this late, I find it hard to fall asleep."

"You too, huh?" Marty rounded the corner from the stairway. She was dressed in pajamas and a robe, looking comfortable in her new home. "I'm having a little trouble nodding off myself. I can't get the bookkeeping system out of my head. I'm a real estate agent, for God's sake, but with this stuff, I feel useless. I can calculate a thirty-year mortgage with my eyes closed, but this day-to-day stuff makes me crazy."

Marty ran her hands through her hair. "Nora, have you ever had any experience keeping books?"

"I can assure you," Max quipped, "that even though our Nora here is accused of the town's most dastardly crime, she returns her library books promptly."

Marty laughed and hit Max on the shoulder with a playful hand. "Shut up, Max."

What was the past history between these two? Had Max and Marty ever been a couple, or were they just lifelong friends? There was an ease between them that seemed to come from more than just friendship.

"I thought Max did accounts at night?"

"I just do some of the bookwork. Marty does most of it," Max said.

"Well, then. Just show me what to do and I'll be glad to try."

Nora wasn't sure just what might be involved keeping track of a hotel's accounts, but given the circles under Marty's eyes, she wanted to be there for her new employer.

"Excellent. You don't know how happy you just made me. I know this is more hours for you, but if I teach you the job and we're both happy with your work, would you be willing to add it to your responsibilities? Sometimes all these numbers can make me feel a bit scatterbrained and well, you've done so well organizing things around here so far."

Marty didn't realize how her simple plea for help filled Nora with happiness. Since being unjustly accused of murder, Nora basked in Marty's trust. Other people would tell Marty she was crazy for letting Nora work on her books, but her purchase of a rundown, money-draining hotel fairly was proof enough that Marty didn't always rely on the counsel of others.

"Of course, I'll pay more," Marty added, apparently mistaking Nora's moment of silent gratitude for hesitancy.

"Yes!" Nora answered before Marty could change her mind. "Just show me what you need."

And then Marty did something Nora didn't expect. She hugged her.

"Thank you." There was a tear on Marty's face as she pulled away. "I'm sorry. It's just been a long day." She glanced at Max, who was fumbling in his pocket for a handkerchief to give to her. "I guess I was feeling a bit overwhelmed. I never should have bought this place. What was I thinking?"

Max put his arm around Marty. "I think it was a wonderful idea. The Tunie is part of the history of this town. Just because the oil is gone doesn't mean this place has to go with it. Just think of all the people who once stood right here in this lobby. LBJ, Waylon Jennings, Buddy Holly … the list goes on and on. Besides, the town's bones are here." Max gestured to the walls of photos, showing residents from the 1940s to the 1980s. "It's like a pictorial library of the people who've lived in or traveled through Piney Woods. You're the reason this hotel is getting back on its feet, Marty."

"Max is right. And without you, do you think I could have found a job?" Nora added. "Who's going to hire a murder suspect?"

"Not me. No way would I be that stupid," Max added.

Marty stifled a giggle.

"All right then," she sniffed. "I guess you're right."

Nora grabbed her notebook and put her arm around Marty. "Let's go learn about keeping hotel records."

"YOU SEE, IT's not complicated," Marty assured Nora as she sat in front of the computer in the manager's office. The software Marty was using for the Tunie turned out to be similar to the program used by the hotel where Nora had worked. The only thing confusing Nora was how Marty could keep the place. She wasn't just in the red—she was in blood-gushing red.

"I know. I know. I can see it in your face. This is the *Titanic* and we're incredibly short on lifeboats."

"Well …." Nora slid her gaze to Marty, who leaned back and crossed her arms. She could tell the dire financial situation wasn't news to her.

"I thought this would be so easy. Just open the doors and *voilà*! Instant cash flow. The only problem is, I didn't figure it would be flowing right out of *my* savings account."

Nora leaned on one elbow, gazing at the computer screen. There had been no days when the hotel covered its expenses— not one. When she'd worked for the hotel in New Orleans, they had down days, but they'd always get back in the black on Mardi Gras.

"This place has so much history for the people in Piney Woods." Marty shook her head. "When the city hall burned down, the town council used the banquet room for meetings until they rebuilt. And when Mr. Tunie ran it, I don't know …

it just felt like this was a special place to spend the evening. We dressed up like we were going to the White House."

"You don't see that anymore." Nora sighed. "I think a lot of people miss those days, Marty. People want to have a reason to dress up. In New Orleans, if they don't have a party to go to, they just make something up half the time."

"There just doesn't seem to be a reason to dress up any more. We're all stuck in perpetual casual Friday."

"True," Nora said.

"All you have to do is look at those pictures in the lobby. Coats, ties, hats and dresses."

"My mother was also a part of this place. Did you know her?" Nora asked.

Marty raised an eyebrow. "Can you show me the picture again?"

Marty followed Nora out to the lobby. Nora took the picture from the wall.

"Oh, yes, the one with Adam Brockwell in the groovy turtleneck."

"I was amazed my mother's picture was here in a place that not long ago I didn't even know existed." Nora gazed at the picture and sighed. "She was so young. Do you remember her?"

"Sorry. I was just a little kid back then. I didn't really know her."

Her mother had the will and determination to survive whatever had driven her from this town and she'd made a good life for them. Marty was a survivor too. "Too bad. I think she'd have liked you."

Marty leaned against the wall and sighed. "God, kid. Sometimes I forget that while everyone else is mourning Adam Brockwell's death, you're mourning your mother's."

"It's okay. Every day it gets a little easier. What I can't get over is there were so many secrets. I wish I knew more."

"Anything I can do to help?"

"No. It's just that my mother left this town in a hurry and I sure would like to know why."

"Who's the other guy in the picture?" Marty asked.

"Arnie Chilton. He's passed too."

"Man, they're all dead," Marty whispered as she gazed at the men and women in the photograph. "We're surrounded by dead people. Doesn't that freak you out?"

"A little. You know what is so amazing about these pictures?" Nora pointed to each of them in turn.

"What?"

"It's an occasion—a big deal. That's why they're here. It's what this hotel needs. Some kind of big event to get it off the ground."

Marty studied Nora. "True, but we don't have any big events booked."

Nora pulled a picture off the wall and flipped it over.

"What are you doing?" Marty asked.

"I knew it! Mr. Tunie wrote the names of the people in the pictures." Written in a spidery scrawl was Nora's mother's name, Leslie McArdle. She wondered why she hadn't noticed it before.

"I never thought to look at the back of the pictures." Marty took another one off the wall and dusted off the back. "This is amazing. Some of these pictures are decades old."

"How many of these people do you think are still alive?" Nora asked.

"Uh," Marty's eyes darted from frame to frame, "I don't know. It could be as high as one hundred."

"Perfect! If each person in the picture brings along a couple of family members," Nora snapped her fingers, "we have our big event."

Marty chuckled. "What?"

"A grand re-opening of the Tunie. We invite all the people in the photos who are still alive and they bring people. This will get the hotel back in the minds of the citizens of Piney Woods as a meeting place for social events and as a working hotel for out-of-towners. We pass out cards and rate sheets for booking the rooms on special occasions. We make it easy for them to plan their next big event here."

"I don't know if you've noticed, but I'm running pretty low on cash. A big party costs money. Any ideas on how we should finance your grand plan?"

"Not yet, but give me some time to think about it. Do we have any petty cash?" Nora asked.

"Two dollars and button," Marty replied.

The wheels were now officially spinning in Nora's head. "Okay, a party with no money."

"Seriously, you're going to try to pull a plan together for this?"

"Why not? It'll give me something to do while I wait for your nephew to come arrest me."

# Chapter 22

---

Nora was feeling unnerved at the man's voice on the phone of the Piney Woods Bed and Breakfast the next morning. "Miss Alexander? Miss Nora Alexander?"

Whoever it was, he sounded official.

"Yes. I'm Nora Alexander."

"My name is Harvey Mortenson. I represent the interests of the late Adam Brockwell."

She hoped his next sentence wouldn't end in a phrase like "impending lawsuit."

"I know this is going to sound strange to you, Miss Alexander, but you were named in Mr. Brockwell's will."

"Me? He'd just met me. Then he was … he died so suddenly. Why—or even when—would he have had time to put me in his will?"

"Regardless of the timing, Mr. Brockwell was a wonderful benefactor in this town. You should count yourself blessed that his kindness has touched even you."

Nora didn't miss the condescension in "*even* you."

"Aren't I the lucky one, then? Isn't it a little early to be reading the will?"

Harvey Mortenson cleared his throat. "Mr. Brockwell's son requested an informal meeting to discuss the disbursement of funds tomorrow afternoon at one. We have obtained a copy of the will to be filed with the probate court, so any payouts will come at a later date."

"You mean the reading of the will?" Nora asked.

"The will reading with all the drama only happens in the movies, Miss Alexander. The closing of Mr. Brockwell's estate is a simple series of business transactions."

"Well, darn. I was hoping for the whole dark and stormy night thing."

Nora's humor seemed lost on Harvey Mortenson. "Will you be available? We are meeting at my office in the Brockwell building."

"Wouldn't miss it." Nora hung up the phone.

Tatty came around the corner, her dark brown eyes beaming.

"*Madre de dios.* You're in Adam Brockwell's will." She turned back to the living quarters, where Ed was pulling the trash bag out of the can.

"Ed, get in here. Nora's in Adam Brockwell's will."

Ed appeared in the doorway behind Tatty. "No kidding?"

"Were you listening in on the extension?" Nora asked.

"Of course not." Tatty tried to look wounded, but Nora could tell she'd been snooping. "I just happened to be … dusting near the doorway."

"She was listening." Ed put his hand behind his ear. "She had her ear against the door. I was getting worried she'd fainted standing up she stood there so long."

"Okay," Tatty admitted. "I only heard your side of the conversation. You've been invited to the reading of the will." She glowed.

"You know, the last long-term guest we had was an electrician who was working on the power lines for the state. We thought he was interesting until we met you." Ed took the pose of a scholar, placing a finger on his temple. "I may have to take up writing. I think we could get your story on one of those Lifetime movies Tatty's always watching."

"Hush, Ed. So, what are you getting from Mr. Brockwell's estate?" Tatty asked.

Nora bounced down onto the Tovar's couch. "I have no idea. I'm a little confused as to how I ended up in his will."

"Especially since you're the one who killed him," Ed said with a smile.

"Ed!" Tatty scolded. "Innocent until proven guilty, right?"

"That's not what the rest of the town is saying."

"Well, they're wrong, and the next time you hear anybody say it, you need to straighten them out."

"Yes, dear." Ed winked in Nora's direction.


"THANK YOU ALL for coming today." Harvey Mortenson looked much smaller than Nora had imagined him to be over the phone.

Why had Adam Brockwell chosen such a diminutive man to handle his legal affairs? She'd expected a polished, corporate type. Instead, Harvey Mortenson reminded her of Piglet from *Winnie the Pooh*. His choice of such a pint-sized legal counsel was another example of the kindness the town so valued in him. Nora sat in a chair between Corey Brockwell and Lucy Cooper.

"Even though I have summoned you here, you should be aware that Pastor Chilton was designated as executor of Adam's will."

The pastor pulled at his clerical collar. He looked uncomfortable being left in charge of what might be a great sum of money. Nora figured that since money being the root of all evil was a major talking point in his profession, it couldn't be easy having this demon dropped at his doorstep.

"He trusted you, Pastor. It's a great compliment. Yes, indeed," Mortenson chirped.

"Not one I'm sure I deserve. Nevertheless, I'm honored to be named executor." Pastor Chilton looked to the corner, where Nora sat with Corey Brockwell and Lucy Cooper. "And each of you has been named as a beneficiary."

A month ago Nora hadn't even been aware of Adam Brockwell's existence. He'd apparently been aware of hers.

Corey Brockwell wore the same suit he'd worn to the funeral. Kind of a surprise a rich guy like him would choose to wear the same suit. Evidently there was a lot Nora had to learn about wealthy people.

Lucy Cooper still seemed to be in shock over the news that Brockwell was her father. It had to be tough to adjust to the idea your father was someone your mother hated, and that his despised blood was running through you.

"Okay then." Pastor Chilton picked up four portfolios from the desk, handing one to each of the beneficiaries and keeping one for himself.

"Adam, always generous, left each of you something in his will. But first things first." Chilton took out a black velvet bag and walked toward Nora. "Adam wanted you to have this, along with this letter. He stated this was a gift he bought for your mother but was never able to give it to her."

Corey leaned forward as Nora opened the drawstring of the luxuriant black velvet bag. Inside was a beautiful diamond pendant, the biggest diamond she'd ever seen. "Are you sure this goes to me?"

"Quite sure," Mortenson reassured her. "We had it appraised and its worth about a quarter of a million dollars."

Nora's mouth hung open as the light made the multi-faceted diamond pendant sparkle.

"A beautiful piece of jewelry for a beautiful woman," Pastor Chilton said.

Corey scowled at Nora, observing the whole scene with a look of great distaste.

Chilton cleared his throat and Nora detected a hint of nervousness creeping into his voice.

"Mr. Brockwell," he glanced over at Lucy, "made some poor investments late in life. Very poor."

Lucy crossed her legs and switched her gaze to her manicured nails.

"What kind of investments?" Corey Brockwell asked, not waiting for the explanation.

Harvey Mortenson looked to Lucy. "Maybe Miss Cooper can clear this matter up for us, right, dear?"

Lucy looked to Mortenson and then to Corey. "I didn't know. I really didn't know." Lucy's voice was just above a whisper.

"Didn't know *what*?" It was obvious Corey also didn't know he was sitting next to his own sister.

"The good news is all the properties are still in place." Mortenson seemed to realize Lucy was struggling with the concept. "But I'm afraid the cash on hand has … dwindled."

"What are you trying to say?" Corey asked. "Are you telling us my dad was broke?"

Pastor Chilton let out a sigh. "Not quite. To tell the truth, we won't know until all the creditors have reported in and the probate is cleared. Then we'll divvy up whatever's left."

"Divvy up? I'm the only heir. Who exactly are we divvying up with?"

Harvey Mortenson stepped forward. "Mr. Brockwell left instructions that his estate was to be divided equally between his three children."

"*Three* children? I'm an only child, Mr. Mortenson," Corey protested.

"Evidently not. Let me introduce you to your half-sister Lucy …."

Corey Brockwell's brow furrowed in confusion.

Before he could say anything, Harvey Mortenson continued, "And your other half-sister, Nora Alexander."

Corey Brockwell sat with his head in his hands. Nora, in shock herself, could just imagine what he was thinking. One week he'd lost a father, in the next week gained two sisters.

A redhead who quite possibly murdered his father, and an African-American woman who'd purposely drained his family's fortune.

"There has to be some sort of a mistake here, Harvey. My parents only had one child. There must be some mistake."

"You are correct. Your parents had one child. Your father had three."

A tense silence descended among the occupants of the room and then Corey's eyes sharpened on Nora.

"I should have known. Ever since you showed up, my life has gone to pieces. As far as I'm concerned, both of you are heartless gold diggers, and any claims you make on my father's estate will be thrown out of court."

Nora didn't like Corey now. He was nothing more than a spoiled child. One of the "entitled" generation. "Oh, good," she said, "because it sounds like our sister over here has already worked through most of it. Besides, I had a father. I had a wonderful brave father who was killed by—"

"Shut up, both of you," Lucy broke in. "None of us is happy with the situation."

"Yeah, well, how much money did you steal from my father?" Corey said.

Lucy put her hands on her hips. "Seeing as he's my daddy too, who says you get all the cash? How do you think my mama was getting by on no child support while you went to private school and worked on your backhand?"

Corey grunted, got up, and started pacing the room. Nora recalled seeing him hung over and fresh from the casino that day in Dudley's Brew. Corey was obviously desperate for cash. He had gambling debts, and from the degree of his desperation, he owed somebody big.

"You don't understand. My father *was* this town. He helped people. Everyone loved the guy."

"Obviously," Nora blurted out before she could stop herself.

She was still thunderstruck over the identity of her biological father. It was going to take some time to adjust to what she had learned.

Corey turned on Nora, towering above her.

Pastor Chilton stepped in front of Corey, stopping him mid-pace. "Corey, son, if you'd just sit down, we can continue with our business."

Corey pulled his arm away from Pastor Chilton's grasp but then let himself be led back to the chair he'd been sitting in. "I want paternity tests."

"An excellent idea. As a matter of fact, I came prepared." Harvey pulled out three paternity tests from a drugstore bag.

"If my mother knew, she'd be so hurt by all this," Corey grumbled. "That bastard."

"Your mother did know," Nora said. "Why do you think they got divorced? Maybe he wasn't the guy everybody loved." She couldn't help herself. As upset as Corey was, it was time he knew who his father really was. "I guess they can cancel the planned statue of him in the town square. Then again, the thought of the birds of Texas relieving themselves—"

"You," Corey pointed at her, "shut up before I shut you up."

"Corey," Pastor Chilton hushed him. "You need to let go and let God. God will straighten this out."

"Are you saying God punished my father for his sins by sending 'Red' over here to stab him to death?"

Now Nora stood. She'd had enough of this poor little rich boy.

This time Lucy grabbed her arm, pulling her back down.

"Yeah, well, at least her mama got her due. My mama had a Brockwell and had to sneak out of town in the middle of the night."

The more Nora heard about Adam Brockwell's involvement with Lucy's mother, the sleazier it sounded. He'd used her and then tossed her aside as if she were an old tennis racquet with a broken string. Maybe this was also what had happened to her mother. She had been seduced by this young Casanova.

"My mama told me everything. Your Piney Woods Pioneer Papa was not a good man."

Corey seemed about to jump out of his seat and throttle Lucy; instead, the color left his face.

Lucy went on, "When she found she was pregnant with me, he told the world the father was one of her boyfriends. She didn't have boyfriends like that. He made her feel dirty, like she slept with many men. It wasn't true, but when he said it, everyone believed him."

"Why should I believe you?" Corey asked.

"Your poor, dear mother." Pastor Chilton shook his head in dismay. "No wonder she wished him dead."

Harvey Mortenson stopped short. "Yes, it's news to me as well."

"With Adam Brockwell doing the accusing, she didn't stand a chance." Lucy held the paternity test in the air. "Maybe this will prove it."

Mortenson cleared his throat. "One other item. Corey, we found several promissory notes in your father's safe signed by you."

Corey rubbed his eyes. "Yes."

"Yes," Mortenson repeated. "Well, those will also need to be figured into money owed to the estate."

Corey Brockwell's response was short and harsh. "Fine. But as long as we're at it, I think Nora, the prime suspect in my father's murder, should return the diamond pendant to me. It was a gift clearly meant for my mother."

"On the contrary," Mortenson continued, "Mr. Brockwell specifically stated it was a gift he intended for Leslie McArdle, who we now know was Nora's mother."

"This is ridiculous," Corey mumbled. "I'll be hiring my own lawyer to investigate all this, and mark my words, I will get back what is rightfully mine." He slumped in his padded office chair, looking every bit the spoiled rich boy who had finally been told no. His plans for his inheritance had just gone up in smoke.

# Chapter 23

———— ༄ ————

THAT EVENING AT work, Nora continued to plan for the reunion. She called the local newspaper, which agreed to cover the event. Hopefully it would be as helpful as getting on the internet. As Nora ran through the bookkeeping software, calculating accounts payables and receivables at the hotel from the day, she still couldn't believe what had transpired. She felt in her sweater pocket for the unopened letter from the man who claimed to be her father. She'd come full circle. She'd started this nightmare of an adventure with a letter to a man she didn't know was her father. Now she had a letter from him. Adam Brockwell hadn't been a father to her. Ben Alexander was her dad. Her father was the New Orleans cop who'd died in the line of duty. It had always been her story, her tagline. Now she wasn't sure. Once again she wished her mother was here. What would it have hurt if Kay Alexander had told Nora the truth? Nora vowed that if she were ever lucky enough to have a child someday, she'd never, ever lie to her.

Sitting at the desk in the hotel office, Nora said aloud, "Adam Brockwell is my father? Really, Mom? Couldn't you have mentioned it to me at least once while you were alive?"

"No kidding. Is he?" Marty stood outside the hotel manager's office door.

"Oh. Marty. Sorry. Just sort of talking to myself."

"Uh, yeah. Is Adam Brockwell your father?"

"I don't know. He says he is."

"When did he tell you?" Marty seemed to be fighting the impulse to continue her inquiry with something like "right before you brutally stabbed him to death."

"He didn't." She pulled the letter out of her pocket. "His lawyer did. Right after he told me I was an heiress." She held up the envelope with the words "To My Child" written across it.

Marty's blue eyes flickered with interest. "What does it say?"

"I haven't had the courage to read it yet."

Marty put an arm around Nora. "You've had a lot of things piled on your plate at once. You'll open it when you're good and ready. You know, I thought I knew Adam Brockwell … from a distance, anyway. Now I'm finding out he may have fathered half the town. Maybe I need to call *my* mother."

A laugh escaped Nora's lips.

"Listen, one more thing I wanted to talk to you about. Don't get me wrong—I absolutely love the plan you have for the reunion. The only problem is I don't really have the cash to pull it off. Maybe we need to cancel it."

"Cancel it? You don't have *anything*?"

"I've run through everything, even my retirement fund. Do you have any cash?"

"Uh, no. That's kind of why I'm working here …." Nora jumped. "Wait a minute …." She dug into her purse and pulled the diamond out of its bag. "What about this?"

"What is that?"

"A little gift from my father to my mother. It's worth a quarter of a million dollars. Do you think we could offer this as collateral to get a little short-term loan?"

Marty examined the pendant. "I think we could. We probably

need about five hundred dollars or so to pull the party off. This necklace would guarantee it."

"Great. Then I'm offering the Brockwell pendant as collateral."

Marty yawned. "Alrighty then. I'm tired and going to bed now that we've solved all the Tunie's problems. I'll just leave you to your letter."

"Thanks."

"And when you do open it, if you need someone to talk to about it …."

"I know. Thanks."

TWO HOURS LATER, when the hotel was quiet, Nora sat on a red velvet bench in the lobby beneath her mother's picture, Adam Brockwell's letter in hand. Biting her lower lip, she ripped open the envelope.

> My child,
>
> If you're reading this, then you know I'm your father. This may surprise you, but I knew about your existence. I had my own family, and in the end it was better that way for the both of us. Please don't think badly of me, but you can only make so much of a casual encounter. Still, though, you are a Brockwell and legally an heir. I don't know if you'll ever get this trinket or if I'll ever meet you. I'm sure the day I do will indeed change my life.
>
> *Adam Brockwell*

Nora set down the letter. That was all Brockwell thought of her: she was the result of a "casual" encounter. It sounded like a simple lesson in biology class. Meeting her *had* changed his life, for the next day he'd been murdered. Was the nicest man in town really such an uncaring person who was so driven to fill his needs at the cost of other's lives? It sure seemed so. The way he treated Lucy's mother was telling. His son seemed to have two distinct sides to him. Could it have been the same with Adam?

She needed to know more. Pastor Chilton's brother was in the picture, but she couldn't ask him. Arnette Cooper worked in Brockwell's home but didn't have much to do with her mother's life. Her grandmother had no idea why her daughter left. The only person who might know, who was still around, was Wiley. Wiley, who couldn't stay sober for more than a few hours …. Alcoholism was a disease, but the contributing factors had to be considered. What caused Wiley to drink? What memory was he trying to drown?

# Chapter 24

—⁓—

On Saturday morning, as Nora walked into Jumbo Gumbo, the delightful smells drifting from the kitchen told her a fresh pot of gumbo was on the stove. Maybe Wiley had made it into work. A young man she hadn't seen before was wiping down the shellacked wooden tables.

"Is Wiley working today?" Nora asked.

The busboy, wearing a T-shirt advertising the videogame *Call of Duty* on his scrawny chest, merely nodded toward the door that led to the kitchen.

As Nora entered, Wiley was stirring soup in a tall stainless-steel pot.

He glanced up at her, grinned, and then looked down in embarrassment, probably recalling his sorry state the last time they met. "This is a surprise. What brings you here?" He never broke the rhythm of his stirring.

"My mother."

"Okay."

"And my father."

"Uh-huh."

"My *biological* father."

The stirring stopped. He stared at the bubbling gumbo, avoiding Nora's gaze. "You know, the secret to a good gumbo is the roux. That bubbly brown stuff is the most important part. A little flour, a little oil, a little heat. You've got to get it just right and stir it up real good or it's just another can of soup."

"I didn't know you had to stir it to get it to taste right."

"Sure." He began to stir again and his smile softened as he watched the dark brown liquid spin around in the pot. "You're like this here spoon, Nora. You stirred up the town. Brought things up from the bottom, and now you're causing the flavor of everything else to change."

"I hope it's for the better."

The old man laughed. "Jury's still out, missy."

Nora leaned in, feeling the heat of the gumbo. "Uncle Wiley, what aren't you telling me?"

"I need a drink." He reached into a pot below the counter and pulled out a half-full bottle of whiskey. Unscrewing the cap, he took a swig. Once it hit, he shut his eyes for a moment and grimaced.

"Some nights the gumbo's spicier than others," he admitted.

"I'll bet." Nora waited a moment. "So?"

He returned the bottle to its hiding place and put his hands in his apron pockets. "You know, I've been cookin' all my life. I've even been to culinary school. They said I was good. Very good. You'd never know it now. 'Cept that my gumbo recipe is delicious enough that people come from miles around to taste it. George Morrow, the owner here, would have had to close his doors years ago if it hadn't been for me. He even changed the name of the joint. It used to be called 'The Eating Place.' What a lousy name. I was the one who told him to change it. Now old George is planning his retirement, and I'm here, stirrin' the roux. That's what life gives ya. You never know if you're the roux stirrer or the gumbo eater." He went back to stirring, still not answering Nora's question.

"Please. Whatever you know, it's more than I do. I'm fighting for my life, Uncle Wiley, and it all seems to be circling back to my mother and Adam Brockwell."

Wiley put the knobby, callused fingers of his free hand over his mouth and raised his watery eyes to Nora. "It's my fault. I was such a mess back in those days. Brock was seeing your mother and Corey's mother. She wasn't anything like Leslie. She was rich and part of the country club crowd. Meanwhile, we were a little rough around the edges. Me especially. One night, me and my friends were drunk. We had a big fight in front of half the town, but you know, we were kids. We were fine in an hour and wanted to climb the water tower. You know, the one on the edge of town. We climbed to the top and my friend—Jimmy was his name—he lost his footing and fell. I tried to catch him, but from the ground it looked like I pushed him. The sheriff was about to press charges."

"So, what does that have to do with my mother and Adam Brockwell?"

"She told him she was pregnant, but the problem was he was engaged to someone else. He had made his decision and it wasn't her. He told her he'd vouch for me that night so I wouldn't be arrested for pushing Jimmy off the tower. If Adam Brockwell backed you up, the police dropped your case. The deal was, though, if she came back he would change his mind. I just wish she would have come back anyway, just to test him. She did it all for me. Left her home and her family, all for me. I never knew where she was or where you were."

His shoulders slumped as he lowered his chin to his chest. "It's why I always end up back there. Somehow, I feel closer to her here. I'm as guilty as Brockwell."

"Did you ever talk to Brockwell? Ask him about it?"

"I tried to, but in this town, going off and accusing a Brockwell can ruin your life. He never committed any crime, other than dumping my sister in her time of need. No one would believe Adam Brockwell could do anything wrong. I could have spoken up when they put Brockwell up for Piney

Woods Pioneer, but who are they going to believe? The guy who donated a children's wing to the hospital or an old drunk like me? I've got a record, you know. One more DUI, and I get put away. He knew he could put me away easy. You see how I've bungled this? I'm no good."

"Oh, Uncle Wiley. You can't blame yourself."

"She was so beautiful. Such pretty red hair and a smile that could slay you. He had to have her. Nothing but the best for him, and your mama was the best. I know now she had to get away from him. He was so possessive. I think he'd been stalking her for months before that night at the Tunie. If she'd been interested in anyone, it was Arnie Chilton. He was the one she was flirting with, not that monster Brockwell."

Nora reached over and touched Wiley on the shoulder as if she could shake some sense into him. "You have to let go of this, do you hear me? You didn't know. You couldn't be sure."

"No. No. I let my Leslie down. Sometimes, you have to act on something, even if you're not sure. I could have helped her. She didn't have to run away."

Nora pulled away from him. "We are talking about my mother, right? She was the most stubborn woman I've ever met. Once she decided on something, there was no going back."

Wiley thought for a moment and then looked at Nora. "Well, you are right about that. When you knew her, was she happy? I mean, in spite of everything?"

"Most days she seemed pretty good. I didn't help things. I was a mess growing up, but she always stood by me. I should have spent more time appreciating her while she was alive. I suppose I have some of her stubbornness, myself. Now that I know what happened, maybe I do this for her. I can start to make things right."

"How can you make things right, little girl? I'll bet they're out there commissioning a statue of that rat right now. This town isn't going to take kindly to the news that their own personal hero was nothin' but a two-bit womanizer." Returning to his gumbo, Wiley started adding onions and garlic to the roux.

"After the distribution of funds at the reading of Adam Brockwell's will today, with two extra children sitting around the table, it might be easier than you think. He did the same thing to Arnette Cooper."

"Dang." Wiley's eyes bugged out. "You mean Lucy is—"

"We're related."

He began the stirring rhythm again. "I'll be. Small world."

"You're telling me." Nora dug into her purse and pulled out the pendant. "And the lawyer gave me this. A gift for my mother, after my father died. He always wanted her to have it, but she disappeared, and he couldn't give it to her."

"Holy smokes. That thing ought to be in a museum."

"Yeah, well, for today, I'm carrying it around in my purse."

"They didn't give you no box?"

"No. I think the old man must have carried it around with him."

"Well, you'd better do something with it. A necklace like that could get you killed. Get a safe deposit box over at the bank. The Hope Diamond, there, needs its own guard."

"I will. Just as soon as the bank opens on Monday. We're going to use it for collateral to fund the reunion." Nora rose to leave.

"Nora ..." Wiley called out.

She turned back to her uncle.

"Thanks."

Her uncle's life had turned out so badly, and it all started that night at the Tunie. An idea came to Nora and she turned back.

"Uncle Wiley, have you ever considered using your talents elsewhere?"

"Excuse me? What talents?"

"Would you be willing to do a catering job for me at the hotel?"

Wiley tilted his head to one side as he dried his hands on a towel. "At the Tunie?"

"We're doing a big reunion for all the people who are in the pictures Mr. Tunie took. A re-opening of the hotel. The restaurant facilities need updating, but the stoves work. You could make it your own little audition."

"For who?" he asked.

"For Marty. Wouldn't it be wonderful if the Tunie had a working restaurant again?"

He rubbed his hand against his whiskers. "The Tunie was really something in its day. They had cuisine there. Not just burgers and fries." Wiley's eyes crinkled. "You'd trust me? I mean, I don't have a real good work history, what with—"

"I know, and I wouldn't be willing to try this unless you made me a promise."

"What is it? I'll do anything."

"Find out about the AA meetings around here."

"I can do that."

"Yeah, well, then you'll need to attend them. Every day in the beginning."

Wiley sighed. "I guess I could do that. I'll do it for you. I'll do it for Leslie. Maybe I can help her through you."

"And you won't be drinking."

"Not even a shot before the meeting? Just to take the edge off? Some of those people can get pretty annoying."

Nora wagged her finger at Wiley. "Especially not then."

"You'd take a chance on me? I've been known to be ... unreliable."

"Oh, well, if you're going to work for me, Uncle Wiley, 'Reliable' had better be your middle name."

He laughed.

"We need your artistry, Uncle Wiley. It's time to make a forty-dollar steak out of a two-dollar cut of meat and convince them it's worth it."

"You've got it, boss lady."

* * *

Nora sat in the yellow floral chair in the corner of her room at the bed and breakfast. She turned the diamond pendant so the sun's rays made each little facet sparkle. It was the most beautiful and most expensive piece of jewelry she'd ever owned. Until she could get to the bank on Monday, she'd have to find a safe place for it.

She surveyed the room. A robbery would be unusual in a town this small, but she still needed to hide the pendant. Marty was waiting on a safe Nora ordered for the hotel, because Mr. Tunie had never used one. Why would he? He trusted people. Under the mattress was too obvious. The dresser and the drawer in the bedside table might be the first place her hypothetical robber would look.

As her eyes scanned the room, she focused on the fabric poofs at the corner of her yellow drapes. It was just a bunch of material made to look like some sort of flower, but if the pendant wasn't too heavy, she could slip it into a fold.

She twirled the diamond one more time, enjoying the show the reflecting gem was giving. It was breathtaking, but it was payment for a terrible crime. As beautiful as it was, Nora didn't want to keep it. She'd cash in on it as soon as she could. She dropped the necklace into her other hand, dragged her chair to the window and slipped the pendant into the silky fold of the rounded drapery decoration. Besides helping pay for the reunion, this necklace could also pay for a good criminal lawyer if she ended up being arrested for Brockwell's murder. So she needed to keep it safe. It had just become her lifeboat.

# Chapter 25

———⁓———

ONCE THE DIAMOND was safely hidden, Nora was glad to escape to work that evening. So much was going on in her head, spending a few hours working could help get her mind off things for a while. When she came in, Marty was checking in a couple with a young child.

"Wow, we didn't even know this place was here." The man turned around, taking in the lobby. "This is wonderful. Historic Texas. So much better than some chain hotel. I feel like I'm growing spurs as we speak."

"Well, yee haw!" Marty bellowed, swinging an imaginary lariat in the air. "Enjoy your stay."

The little family gathered their bags and headed for their room on the second floor.

Once the elevator doors closed, Marty grinned from ear to ear. "Tourists. I love 'em, and when they pay for their room in advance, it's a godsend."

Nora high-fived Marty. "Yay! We have actual guests. How did that happen?"

"Max got the website up. We've been getting bookings all day." Marty pulled up the Tunie Hotel website on her computer.

"See? They can book a room right there online. It's a miracle."

"Wow. Does the computer say we have four rooms booked for tomorrow?"

"It sure does. Jolene is going to have to break a nail cleaning more than one room tomorrow," Marty gloated.

Nora laughed. "I hope she doesn't file for disability over a wrecked manicure."

"How are we doing on the Tunie reunion?"

"Pretty good. You might not be comfortable with this, but I've arranged for you to do a newspaper interview about it next week. They're going to use some of our pictures in the paper to stir up interest. I'm hoping it will be the equivalent of paid advertising. I'm also working on something for the food. Now I just need to take a close-up look at the ballroom. See where it needs to be restored."

Marty came around the front desk and the two women walked toward the darkened ballroom now used mostly as a multifunction venue. Marty turned on the lights.

Nora ran her hand along the antique wallpaper. "You know, I think with a little soap and water we should be able to get most of this dirt and grime off the walls." She walked over to the woodwork on the bar and the fireplace. "We can tackle the buildup on the finish here with some white vinegar and warm water."

"Where did you learn all this, Nora?"

"My mother was a bookkeeper for a home improvement store. She was always trying out what she picked up at work. It's not as hard as you might think, and it doesn't have to clean out your bank account either." Nora continued going from place to place in the room, ticking off inexpensive ways to improve the room.

Marty stood in place, hands on her hips. "Sounds like you're working way harder than I'm paying you for."

"Yeah, well, maybe I enjoy a lost cause as well. We can at least make the room look good for the reunion. After this is all over, you can pay a professional to redecorate, because then you'll be able to afford it."

"I like the way you think, Nora Alexander."

Nora patted her on the back. "Hopefully we'll have it all done before they send me up the river for murder."

"It would be convenient," Marty agreed.

That evening there was a special Saturday session of the college-prep course attended by a group of high school kids. A little later, Nora's weekly regular, Mr. Birdsong, appeared.

Nora pulled an announcement out from under the counter. "Mr. Birdsong, I'm so glad you're here. I wanted to let you know we're going to have a reunion of all of the people who used to come here."

He raised his bushy eyebrows and grinned. "You are? A festive occasion? Right here at the Tunie? How simply wonderful, dear."

"Yes. There's still a lot to do, but it just wouldn't be right if you weren't there."

"Thank you, Nora. You are very kind to think of me." He glanced at the banquet room where the lecturer's voice sounded tinny over the cheap sound system. Mr. Tunie sighed. "It'll be just like old times."

The phone rang and Nora ran to pick it up. "Tunie Hotel." She started pulling up the screen to make a reservation on the computer. When she looked up, Mr. Birdsong was gone. The reunion announcement was still on the counter. He never stayed long, but somehow seeing him always lifted Nora's mood.

After the high schoolers left the test-prep class, Nora pulled out the vacuum to freshen up the lobby for the next day. They had real guests now and would need to keep up appearances like a real hotel. She went into the banquet room to clean up after the class and spotted crumpled-up fast-food bags thrown under one of the folding tables.

"What pigs," she mumbled, picking up the leftover hamburger wrappers and soft drink cups. As she reached under a chair to retrieve a tattered napkin, a thump resonated behind her by the podium. Nora jumped up, knocking her kneecap on the wooden chair bottom.

"Ouch! Max, is that you?" It was close to the time Max usually came in, but only silence filled the empty room.

"Max?" Nora swore again. "Dammit, Max, if this is you, cut it out."

As she rubbed her knee, glaring at the long, red velvet curtains, waiting for Max to jump out at her, every light in the room went out. The blackness felt thick around Nora. She couldn't see anything, not even her hand in front of her face.

"Max!" she yelled out. "If it's you, this is not funny. Turn the lights back on."

A gush of cold air went past Nora, causing her to shiver. Had someone just crossed the room, going between the tables?

"Max?" Nora's voice quavered. In the back of her mind, she knew it would be difficult for Max to sneak up on her. His footsteps were heavy and she'd have heard his size thirteen feet plodding down the aisle. The only thing she was sure of was she felt a surge of cold air. A shiver ran through her. If someone else was in there with her, she didn't plan on staying to find out who it was. Feeling along the rounded backs of the seats, Nora made her way to the center of the room. As Nora bumped into tables and chairs, the room seemed to grow colder and the distance stretched before her.

She burst through the double doors into the darkened lobby. Thankfully, it was partially lit from the streetlights shining through the plate-glass windows.

"Max?" she shouted out again. She started for the door, but before she could open it, Max came in, knocking her back onto the carpet.

"Nora?" Max asked. "Jeez, I'm sorry. I was just outside

looking for the fuse box. I can't figure it out. I called the power company on my cell."

As he finished his sentence, the lights blinked back on. The office door, which Nora was sure she'd shut earlier, now stood open. On the desk lay the contents of her purse. Someone had dumped them out.

"Wow." Max surveyed the small pile. "You really shouldn't leave your purse out. Something could get stolen. Marty isn't going to be too happy about this. You should count yourself lucky she didn't wake up."

"My purse was hidden in a drawer, and the office door was closed."

"Man, this place is a mess. Are you sure you locked the door?" Max asked.

Nora tried to recall. There were so few people in the hotel at any one time, she hadn't ever worried about theft.

Most of the desk drawers were open and even the trash can was turned over. She picked up her purse and started putting the embarrassing items back in first.

"Maybe we ought to go next door and call the police?" Max suggested.

Nora checked her wallet. Her cash and single credit card—over-the-limit—were still there.

"Whoever this was wrecked the office, but it doesn't look like they took anything." Nora unlocked the desk drawer and pulled out the petty cash box. The money was still there, just waiting for someone to take it.

"I don't get it. Why break in and not steal anything?"

"Maybe they were looking for something in particular?" Pastor Chilton stood in the doorway, making both Nora and Max jump back behind the desk.

"How long have you been there, Pastor?"

"Oh, I'm sorry. I didn't mean to scare you. I got a call from a parent trying to track down his daughter. I heard a group of kids were at the test-prep class tonight, and I wondered if their daughter was with them. Tall girl? Black hair? Wears glasses with black frames."

Nora tried to recall the adolescent crowd from earlier. She remembered someone of that description at the snack shop buying a candy bar with a handful of dimes.

"Maybe. Is her name Silvia?"

"Yes! You saw her?"

"She was here, but I think she left a while ago, with everybody else. She didn't go home?"

"No, and her mother is worried sick."

Even though he'd never been a parent, Max clucked his tongue in judgment. "Not good."

"No, it's not. A lot of bad things can befall a young girl if she isn't trusting the right people. Right, Nora?"

"You bet." The events of the evening were rushing in on Nora. Who broke into the office? What had she encountered in the ballroom? She returned her gaze to Pastor Chilton. "Hope you find her."

"We will. Chances are she's gone off with one of the boys. Kids today! The internet has ruined them."

Nora remembered wanting to ask the pastor about her mother and his brother Arnie. "I was talking to my new Uncle Wiley, and he seemed to think my mother might have had a crush on your brother Arnie. Did you know anything about that?"

He shook his head. "Not a lot. I was pretty young at the time. My brother was the one who followed your mother around like a puppy dog. One of many, I'm guessing."

Nora frowned.

Pastor Chilton seemed to pick up on Nora's disappointment. "Tell you what. If you come to church for our service tomorrow, I have an old box of items that belonged to my brother. Maybe we can come up with something. What do you say?"

"Great, although, I should warn you, I'm not much of a churchgoer."

"When was the last time you attended a service?"

"This will be my first."

"I see. Well, getting you in the door ought to hike up my church-attendance statistics."

Nora laughed. "Thanks so much. Now I'm sure you need to call the other ministers to brag."

"Sure. Maybe Father Michael over at St. Joseph's is still up."

After Pastor Chilton left and Nora straightened up the office, she emptied the petty cash box to give Wiley the funds to buy supplies for the reunion party.

Max walked Nora out to her car. "You want me to call Marty and ask her to follow you home?"

"No. I'll be fine," Nora assured him.

"You sure?"

"Go," she commanded, and like a three-hundred-pound puppy, Max shuffled off to his station at the front desk.

After checking her backseat to make sure there weren't any office-rummaging killers there, Nora got into her car, locking the doors as soon as she shut them. Her brave words now rang hollow as she drove down the nearly deserted street to the Piney Woods Bed and Breakfast. Nora had a sinking feeling: what if the person who spilled out her purse was looking for the diamond pendant? What if they were breaking into her room right now? She had to check on Tatty and Ed to make sure they were all right.

Nora skidded into the gravel driveway and ran up the steps. Banging the screen door behind her, she rushed into Tatty and Ed's living room.

Tatty jolted up from the couch, her hair in curlers and her feet in pink fuzzy slippers. Soft snores could be heard from Ed in his easy chair, unaware of his wife's state of alarm.

"Nora, my goodness. What's the matter?"

"Are you okay?" Nora asked.

Tatty's hand flew to her throat. "I think I am. Shouldn't I be?"

Nora turned from the startled Tatty and ran upstairs to her

room. The door was still locked like she'd left it before going to work.

"My lord, girl. What's wrong?" Tatty had followed her, attempting to keep up with Nora's pace.

Nora opened the door an inch and peeked inside, not entirely sure what she expected to see.

The room was exactly as she'd left it. She dragged her chair to the corner of the room, feeling the folds of the flower. The diamond was still there.

"Sorry. False alarm."

Tatty cleared her throat. "Do you find yourself drawn to wanting to squeeze the drapes often?"

Nora laughed. "I'm fine, Tatty. I had a break-in at the hotel. I was worried it might have happened here, too."

"What? Did the thief get anything?"

"Nope. I should tell you I have something valuable here." Nora pulled the diamond pendant out of its hiding place in the drapery.

"My lands, is it real?" Tatty gasped.

"As far as I know, it is. I promise I'll lock it away at the bank on Monday, but until then I was going to hide it here in my room."

Tatty took the diamond. "It's heavy."

"A gift from Mr. Brockwell."

"This was from Adam Brockwell? The guy they say you stabbed to death?"

"Yes."

"Well, at least he didn't hold a grudge."

# Chapter 26

———

THE NEXT MORNING, dressed in a pair of slacks and a deep-blue sweater she borrowed from Tatty, Nora entered the First Congregational Fellowship. Tatty, gussied up in a white hat and a black and white ensemble, led the way.

To the side of the outer lobby of the church was a door with a sign stating NO UNAUTHORIZED PERSONNEL.

"Is that God's office?" Nora whispered in awe.

"Sure. It is upstairs, after all," Ed said with a knowing nod.

Tatty rolled her eyes. "No, silly. I can't take the two of you anywhere." She smiled at her houseguest. "It's the door to the steeple. Pastor Chilton doesn't want anybody ringing the bell. Sometimes the kids get up there."

Nora couldn't help but notice more than one pair of eyes following their progress toward an empty pew.

"Aren't you the Sunday special," Ed whispered. "They sure didn't expect to find themselves sitting shoulder to shoulder with Piney Woods' Most Wanted."

"Shush, Ed," Tatty scolded.

Tatty, Ed, and Nora shuffled into their seats.

The organist pumped out "Nearer my God to Thee" as

another family made their way down the aisle, looking for a seat. They stepped into Nora's pew, but then, as if afraid of seating their precious children next to a suspected murderer, the woman backed out.

"We can get a better view from the other side," she said, yanking her confused children into the aisle.

Nora shifted on the walnut bench and its unyielding hard back. So few people came to the hotel, she hadn't realized what a spectacle she'd become. As the fearful family moved a safe distance away, the whispers rose to fever pitch, causing anyone who should have been reading the bulletin to glance around the room. The back of Nora's neck grew warm as Tatty reached across Ed and patted Nora's hand.

"Never you mind them, honey." She narrowed her eyes and shot a wicked glance at a few of the gossips.

"Mind if I sit here?" Corey Brockman stood next to the vacant spot on the pew. Like crickets on a summer's night, the din of whispers rose again.

"Are you sure you want to?" Nora asked. "Seeing as how you've accused me of murder on more than one occasion?"

"It's Sunday. We're in church. Surely I can find some forgiveness in my heart." He sat next to her and pulled a blue hymnal from the shelf under the next pew.

This was crazy. She'd heard of people forgiving others of terrible crimes but never would have figured Corey Brockwell as one of those magnanimous souls.

The organ music swelled as the congregation rose to sing the first hymn, many singers hitting the notes about a second behind the rest of the crowd. Nora also rose, figuring her unfamiliarity with church in general had just been revealed. The microphone on the altar picked up Pastor Chilton's boisterous voice as he entered through a side door. He glanced up and smiled as his eyes rested on Nora. She tentatively raised her hand and then wondered if it was acceptable to wave at a minister. Chilton nodded in her direction, looking pleased to see her.

"Welcome!" Pastor Chilton stretched out his arms to his parishioners. "I'm so happy to see new faces. Please, I ask you to extend a hand of friendship to our newcomers today." The congregation turned at his command and started shaking the hands of those around them, uttering the phrase, "Peace be with you." Bubby Tidwell was also shaking hands, but Nora could hear his booming voice saying, "Thank you for your support …. Thank you for your support …." She wasn't sure if he was so grateful for Adam Brockwell's death he was thanking anyone who might have done him the favor of killing him or if he was just that centered on being the Piney Woods Pioneer. When he reached Azalea Fredericks, she almost had the vapors.

Nora turned around, expecting the greeting, but even though she was one of the new faces the pastor spoke of, no one ventured her way except for Tatty and Ed. As she turned to accept a hug from Tatty, someone tapped her on the shoulder. She turned. Corey Brockwell held out his arms for a hug.

"Really?" she asked.

"Peace be with you, Nora." He pulled her into his arms, while the rest of the group stared at them.

This forgiveness thing was getting a little uncomfortable.

"Thank you, everyone, please have a seat." Pastor Chilton motioned to the pews, palms down.

"Today our study will be centered on the parable of the prodigal son. The boy who chose to leave his family. The boy who was sure he'd made the right choice, but alas, he was terribly wrong …."

As Pastor Chilton continued on about forgiveness and God always having a place for his people to return, Nora stole a glance at Corey Brockwell. Today he looked unwrinkled, clean-shaven, and rested. She was seeing his Sunday best. It was such a contrast from the desperate man in the coffee shop or the angry heir when the will was read. It was getting to the point where she wasn't sure what Corey she'd meet the next time they crossed paths.

"Yes, we all have loved ones we wish were sitting right here next to us today," Pastor Chilton continued. "I know I do, and I'm sure you have a name or a face in your mind right now. Put out your hand of love and friendship before it's too late. Be the bigger person and reap the benefits of shared love and faith in our God for the rest of your days."

Nora thought of her mother. Had she sat right here in this church? Had Nora missed out on the person who was really her mother? The young girl who was so beautiful and vibrant that the whole town loved her?

After the service ended and the attendees stood and chatted, Nora made her way to Pastor Chilton, who now clasped hands with Violet Fredericks, donning a dress covered in large pink flowers. Her sister, Azalea, in a dress that was nearly identical except with blue flowers, stood directly behind Violet, less than an inch between them. The sisters were so slender they looked like a flowered number eleven.

"Thank you for coming today, Miss Violet."

"Your sermon was an inspiration, Pastor."

*It didn't inspire her enough to greet me*, Nora thought. It was her turn to shake Pastor Chilton's hand.

"Nora! You made it," Pastor Chilton said, as if seeing her for the first time.

Nora didn't understand his surprise. It seemed like he had been preaching right at her the entire service.

"Yes. Tatty and Ed brought me."

"Good people, those two."

"I can only agree with you there. Your sermon was nice, but I have to admit I'm more excited about digging through your brother's box. I still have so many questions."

His eyes expressed confusion and then guilt. "Oh, I'm so sorry. I'm not going to be able to make time to meet with you." He leaned closer. "With all that's been going on with the young lady who went missing last night, I confess I completely forgot."

*Great.* This man had convinced her to attend a church service where she was snubbed by half the town, and for nothing. Nora forced a smile and tried to look pleasant, although pleasant wasn't what she was feeling. "I hope she's okay."

"Yes, yes. She's fine and back home, thank you for asking. Give me just a couple more days, will you?"

"Of course she will." Nora felt Corey Brockwell's firm grip on her shoulders. "She's not going anywhere. At least not until the police clear her name."

Nervous laughter came from behind her as the churchgoers tried to act as if it was perfectly normal to have a murder suspect in their midst.

"Sure." She needed to end this conversation before Corey said anything else to embarrass her.

"So, I was wondering," he whispered into her ear, "could I buy you lunch?"

Nora pulled away from his grasp. "I don't think so."

"Come on, Nora," he said. "Weren't you listening? Think of yourself as the prodigal sister. You've come home. Let's go track down some fatted calf." He gave her a grin. He could be charming, she admitted to herself. And she might learn something about her biological father. "We are siblings after all."

"Why would that make a difference?"

"You're a Brockwell now. I know you're trying to get more information about what happened to your mother. Maybe I can be of help."

"How?"

"I can give you access to my father's files, for one."

Tatty joined them, finished with her after-church socializing. Nora debated for a moment. She didn't trust this guy, but what he was offering was just too enticing to pass up.

She turned to Tatty. "You go on. I'm going to lunch with Corey."

Tatty's lips thinned. She apparently didn't trust him either. "If you think that's wise. We're going over to Ed's sister's house for the afternoon, but if you need us, just call and we can be there in five minutes ... or less." As she finished her statement, she directed an unmistakable glare toward Corey Brockwell.

He nodded and grinned as he slid his arm around Nora's waist.

# Chapter 27

⸻

"Hope Jumbo Gumbo is okay. Being born in New Orleans, I thought you might enjoy some Cajun food." Corey pulled out Nora's chair for her.

"How thoughtful of you," Nora took her napkin off the table and set it on her lap.

Wiley came out of the kitchen, wearing a white apron. He took the order book and the menus from the waiter and walked over to Nora and Corey's table.

"Good afternoon, Nora." Wiley's lips scrunched to one side in disapproval. At least today he looked sober. "Mr. Brockwell."

Corey nodded as he opened the menu handed to him.

"What can I start you off with today?"

Nora looked up from her menu. "Iced tea is fine."

"I'll take a beer."

"Certainly." Wiley wrote down their orders.

"And a bowl of gumbo for each of us," Corey said, not bothering to ask Nora.

Fully aware of the slight, Wiley turned his back to Corey, addressing Nora. "And you, Nora?"

"Gumbo is fine, I guess."

"Terrific." Wiley snapped up the menus and passed through the swinging door to the kitchen.

Corey clucked his tongue. "What's his problem?"

"It might have something to do with you being a Brockwell."

"What? It can't be. The Brockwell family is well loved in this town. If my father hadn't brought in the warehouse distribution plan, this town would have shriveled up and blown away when the oil went bust."

"So I've heard." *Ad infinitum*, Nora wanted to add. The Brockwells seemed to be their own personal PR firm.

"Besides, you're one of us now. So, is he going to take a dislike to you, too?"

Would she lose one family for the other? She'd come to Piney Woods alone, but found a family. Then she'd found a second family. The McArdles were middle class and the Brockwells were upper class. She never thought she'd admit it, but she'd been happier belonging to the poorer of the two.

She felt a sudden need to talk to Wiley. She grabbed her bag. "Excuse me for a moment. I need to use the restroom."

Corey stood as she left, displaying his best country-club manners. The restrooms were right by the kitchen. Corey was checking messages on his phone. She made a beeline for the kitchen.

Wiley was chopping onions and whacking the knife down on the cutting board as she entered.

"What are you doing out with Corey Brockwell? Are you on a date? For goodness' sake, girl, do you know what kind of trouble you may be getting yourself into?"

"You mean the same kind of trouble my mother got into? You were there for that one, too, right?" It was out before she could take it back.

He flinched. Her words had hurt him. Still, though, she didn't have a lot of time to smooth it over.

"Lower your voice," Nora whispered as if Corey were standing right there. "He thinks I'm in the bathroom."

Wiley wiped his hands on his apron and reached out to Nora. "Please tell me you're not on a date?"

"It would be pretty awful, seeing as how I just found out we may be brother and sister."

He squeezed Nora's arm. "I'm only going to say this once. The Brockwells ain't never done us any favors. You're playing with fire. These people should be struck down. They look good on the outside, but inside they're evil people."

Nora pulled back. "Thank you for your warnings, but I'm a grown woman and capable of making my own decisions."

His eyes softened a little and some of the crazy seem to vanish. "I know you are, but you're Leslie's little girl to me. Whether you like it or not, I'm lookin' after you now."

Would that be when he was sober, or all the time? "Fine."

"Nora, I've been thinking about what you want me to do. I almost went into an AA meeting, but I'm not sure I really want to stop drinking. It's my only hobby."

"I think you can do this."

He took in a breath. "It's been a while since anyone thought I was good for anything." Wiley stood up a little straighter and saluted Nora. "Okay. I'll make you proud. I'll do it for you and I'll do it for Leslie … uh … your mama."

The door behind them squeaked open and Wiley brought his hand down from his right temple.

Corey leaned in. "Nora?"

Wiley picked up the knife and began slaughtering the onions.

"You were gone so long I was starting to worry."

"Oh, I was just … telling Wiley here how much I love onions." Corey raised an eyebrow. "Okay."

Nora pushed in front of him and returned to their table.

"Tell me about your father." She gestured for Corey to sit.

"My father," he sighed, "was loved by everyone. If someone needed anything in this town, they came to my dad. If he thought he could help, he would. The new playground they just put up at the elementary school? My father felt the old equipment was unsafe, so he replaced it with top-of-the-line stuff. He did that kind of thing all the time. Like I said, everybody loved him."

Nora couldn't help herself. "Well, almost everyone."

"True," Corey conceded.

"What about your mother? We've talked about mine, but how about yours?"

A cloud came across Corey's well-schooled countenance. "My mother spends most of her time in the Palm Beach house since the divorce."

"What were the grounds for divorce?" Nora asked.

"I'm not comfortable answering such a personal question. Let's just say irreconcilable differences. Now that I've learned about you and Lucy, I'm sure it was one of you that ruined my parents' marriage."

Nora didn't know what to say. She couldn't be sure what kind of impact she had on Adam Brockwell's marriage.

Corey looked uncomfortable. "I'd rather not discuss my parents' marriage. "So, Nora, what do you think of our fair city?"

"Piney Woods is nice. Ed and Tatty have been wonderful. I feel at home there, and I was lucky enough to get a job at the Tunie."

"You did end up staying at the bed and breakfast. I wondered. I heard Ed put a lot of work into the old place. It used to be the house of an old friend of mine. His parents lost all their money with the oil bust. They were going to tear it down, so the Tovars picked it up for a song."

"You never stop to think about all the memories involved in one old house. Did they do all the decorating themselves?"

"As far as I know, they painted and papered for six months at least."

"It is beautiful. Do they get enough lodgers to pay the mortgage? I've been the only guest since I arrived."

"Sure. You're here in the slow season." His eyes widened.

"Say, I'd love to see what they've done with the place. How about you give me a tour right after lunch?"

"I'm not sure if I'm qualified to give tours. I mean, I haven't even been living there long."

His shoulders slumped. "I suppose you're right. I just wanted to go back to see it. It kind of reminds me of better days. Well, never mind. I guess after losing a loved one, a person wants to go back in time."

Now Nora felt guilty. What harm could a fifty-cent tour do? "Okay. Sure, I'd be glad to show you around."

The door jingled behind them. Tuck Watson stepped in, taking off his Stetson. The waiter brought out a to-go bag as Tuck fished money out of his wallet.

"Detective Watson," Corey said, waving from across the room. "This is a nice surprise. I was hoping for an update, and now I don't have to track you down."

Tuck handed his money over to the waiter and then joined Corey and Nora at their table.

"Miss Alexander." Tuck nodded in her direction.

Nora smiled. "Hello."

"Didn't expect to see you two out together. You must've patched things up."

"Well, we attended church together and forgiveness filled our hearts. Isn't that right, Nora?" Corey placed his hand on Nora's and squeezed.

Nora feared she'd throw up if he laid it on any thicker. "Corey promised to tell me more about his father." Nora pulled her hand out from under Corey's.

"And has he?" Tuck Watson asked.

"A little." *Like the fact his father was cheating on his mother*, Nora wanted to say.

Tuck grinned. "A little information can lead to all sorts of things. I see it every day. Unfortunately, I don't have anything new to tell you today. It is Sunday, after all. But we hope to have the DNA back sometime next week."

"Well, then, I guess we wait. Right, Sis?" Corey reached out to squeeze her hand and Nora's creepy meter went off the charts.

# Chapter 28

---

"AMAZING TRANSFORMATION." COREY'S eyes widened as Nora led him through the lobby of the Piney Woods Bed and Breakfast. "Bill's parents never had it looking this good." He hopped over and fingered the drape in the breakfast area off the lobby.

"Tatty really has an eye for color," Nora agreed. "I just wish she and Ed were back from lunch already so she could hear your compliments. It would mean so much to them."

"Well, she *is* talented." Corey surveyed the room, looking from place to place, spinning around like a decorator on a do-it-yourself channel. At the end of his last twirl, he grabbed Nora by the arm. "I'd love to see what they did with the bedrooms. Would you be willing to show me yours?"

Normally, Nora wouldn't consider taking a man to her bedroom after such a corny line, but Corey was her brother, after all. He drew her closer to him, the rich smell of cologne drifting her way. Why did rich guys always smell so good?

"Please?" he whispered, close to her ear.

"I guess," she answered, a touch of hesitancy in her voice.

"Great!" He gestured toward the stairway. "You lead the way."

Nora pulled her key out of her jacket pocket and ascended the stairs. Corey was hot on her heels.

Once she opened the door, she was thankful she'd taken a moment before church to make the bed. Corey stepped inside behind her.

"Nice." His voice was lower now. This time his smile didn't quite reach his eyes.

As he scanned the room, Nora realized he wasn't looking at the décor any more. He was searching.

He backed up to the door, shutting it behind him. "Where is it?"

"What?"

Corey stepped forward, grabbing her arm. He wrenched it with his powerful grasp, sending a shooting pain through her bicep.

"My mother's necklace. Why else do you think I'd want to be here? Not to see how much Kmart crap Tatty can cram into one house."

Nora tried to pull her arm free from his grip, but he only tightened his hold, causing more pain. All of those tennis lessons at the club had paid off.

"It's not yours anymore. Your father left it to me."

"Because he thought you were one of his bastards. The tests aren't back yet. I'm the only true heir," he growled.

Nora decided the smell of his cologne wasn't rich, but cloying. "Did you break into the office at the hotel to steal it?"

"What if I did? No one's going to arrest the son of the man who saved this town." He pulled her arm back again, sending a new rush of searing pain through Nora.

She waited for the inevitable snap.

He dragged her over to the window and pulled back the drape, searching along the window box.

"Where is it?" he shouted again. As he groped to gauge the depth of each fold in the drape, Nora felt his grip on her arm loosen just a bit. If only she could pull away before he broke her arm ....

"Where is it!" he screamed and yanked the entire window covering off of the wall.

Tatty wasn't going to be happy about this. As the curtain came down, the pendant tumbled from its hiding place. Upon seeing it, Corey threw Nora to the floor.

He held it up by the chain and examined it. Shifting his cold, gray eyes to Nora, he said, "You have no right to this."

Rubbing her arm, Nora blurted out, "Yeah, well, I never asked for it, or you, or this town, or your father, the self-appointed ladies' man. Tell me, Corey, is that your technique too? Do you think the diamond pendant will cover all the money you owe your daddy for those promissory notes? Oh, yeah, we come from real good stock."

Corey stepped forward, depositing the pendant in his pocket.

"You disgust me," he muttered under his breath. "Go back to whatever rock you crawled out from under."

"You jerk!" Nora said. "You got what you wanted. Get out."

Corey leaned down and yelled, "I don't want to hear you ran to the police to report this. It could turn out badly for you. Very badly. They might just decide to keep you. Oh, and then there are your good friends, Tatty and Ed. You know, this old place could go up with just one match. I've seen it happen before. What a shame that would be. Just remember, you talk to your little boyfriend Tuck Watson, and Tatty and Ed lose their home." He stared down at her as he exited the room, leaving her alone.

# Chapter 29

---

"Nora?" Tatty knocked on the door an hour later. Nora had spent the time after Corey Brockwell left trying to put the room back in order. She'd failed in her attempt to reattach the hardware holding up the curtains.

"Nora, can I come in?" Tatty asked.

"Um, I'm not dressed." Nora was hoping Tatty would just go away.

"Oh. Well, okay. Ed and I brought you some cheesecake. I'll just leave it in the fridge for you."

"Thanks." She waited in vain for the sound of Tatty's footsteps going back down the hall.

"Are you okay? You don't sound right."

"I'm fine." Nora needed time for the swelling to go down. This was all her fault for ever trusting a snake like Corey Brockwell. She'd dragged this poor woman into enough already.

"Okay, then." After a slight pause, Tatty moved away from the door.

Nora sat down and surveyed the damage to her body. She would have aches and bruises for sure. At least Marty had given her the night off. There were no test-prep classes on weekends.

That would give her twenty-four hours to heal. She took some pain relievers and waited for them to take effect. It would give her time to figure out what to tell Tatty and Ed.

After a couple of hours of being in her room, Nora opened the door and tiptoed down the hallway to the restroom. When she came out, there was no one there. Tatty hadn't heard her. Maybe she and Ed had gone out again? Nora decided to grab the cheesecake in the refrigerator and sneak back upstairs. As she placed her foot down on each step, her heart sank. A game show was blaring on the television, which meant they were home. Maybe the TV was loud enough that they couldn't hear her. After what seemed like an eternity of working her way down the stairs, she made it to the kitchen. She opened the refrigerator door just a little so the light wouldn't illuminate the rest of the room. With the delicacy of a bomb technician, she reached in and grabbed a white carton with her name on it.

Light flooded the room. "Here you are, Nora. I was getting worried ..." Tatty stopped mid-sentence. "Good lord, girl. What is going on?"

From Tatty's expression, she obviously knew something was wrong. If Nora told Tatty what had happened, she'd insist on going to the police. If the police went after Corey, what would stop him carrying out his threat? The phrase "just one match" flashed through her mind. She was starting to understand some of what had motivated her mother. She would have to tell Tatty and Ed.

"Um …." Tears trickled down her face.

"Where do you hurt? What happened? Let's get in the car right now and go to the emergency room."

"No. I fell trying to put the necklace back. I'm sorry, I kind of messed up your curtains."

As Tatty examined Nora's injury, she narrowed her eyes, panic fading and common sense kicking in. "You fell and hurt yourself? How?"

"Sure, clumsy me," Nora laughed, neither one of them believing it.

"I'm going to get you some ice and then I want you to show me the curtain." Tatty reached into a drawer, pulled out a plastic bag and filled it with ice from the freezer. Wrapping the bag in a dishtowel, she handed it to Nora. "Take this and march. You can eat your cheesecake later."

Obeying Tatty, Nora climbed the stairs, holding the ice to her lips. Once they entered her room, she walked over to the window.

"I tried to fix it. I'm afraid part of it ripped. I'll pay for any damages."

Tatty closed the door and leaned on it, reminding Nora of Corey just a few hours earlier. "Fine, but before you go writing me a check to buy a new curtain, why don't you tell me what really happened."

"I just told you. I fell."

"Sure you did. I've been around long enough to know when people are hurt from a fall."

Nora stared at the floor as if she could find the answer there. Finally, she eked out in a whisper, "Please. This is so hard and I am so scared."

Tatty drew Nora close and put an arm around her, hitting the bruise caused by the dresser. Nora jerked back.

Tatty helped Nora sit on the bed and ran her light brown hands through Nora's red curls. "Listen to me. If somebody hurt you, we need to tell the police."

Nora didn't answer.

"The last time we were together, you were going to lunch with Mr. Brockwell. Now you look like this." She stopped for a moment and Nora knew she was piecing it together. "Did Corey Brockwell do this? Surely not." Even Tatty bought into the Brockwell family PR machine.

"Oh my God." Tatty looked at the poorly repaired curtain. "Where's the diamond necklace?"

She reached up into Nora's hiding place. When she didn't find the pendant, she turned back, incredulous. "What an awful boy. He took your mother's necklace, didn't he?"

Nora nodded but then held up her hand. "You can't tell anyone."

"Why not? The necklace was given to you, and it's legally yours."

"Please, just please promise." Nora couldn't bear to tell her about the threats to their inn.

"Did he do anything else? I mean, you know .... I never would have thought to ask before, but now I know about his daddy ...."

"No. Nothing else. He just took the necklace, and when I tried to stop him, he pushed me to the floor."

"That's all? I have your word?"

"You do."

Tatty sighed. "I don't know why you feel this way, but if it's what you want, I'll hold off."

"It is."

"Then so be it." Tatty pulled Nora back in for a hug and she was embarrassed to feel tears start again.

Nora realized it was more than just being hurt by her half-brother and having the diamond stolen. These were the first real tears she'd cried since her mother passed. Now that the floodgates were unlocked, she just hoped she could shut them off again.

LYING IN BED that night, Nora thought about the amount of security the money from the diamond pendant would have brought her. She could've afforded to move her things out of storage and maybe even begin her life again right here in Piney Woods. She would keep her promise about the party at the Tunie Hotel.

Even though it was only money, it would have afforded her the luxury of thinking beyond getting through from one day to the next. Would she need a criminal attorney? After the altercation with Corey, she had no doubt he could have killed Adam Brockwell. Still, if it came down to his word against hers, his well-funded lawyer against her public defender, her chances of winning or even proving her innocence were small. But what would she tell Marty? Their plans to finance the reunion and turn around the old hotel's bottom line was ruined.

THE NEXT MORNING, Nora climbed out of bed and sat in the window seat to watch the sun rise over Piney Woods, Texas. It really was a beautiful little town. It must've been hard for her mother to go away and then stay away, even after Nora's father died. It would have been the time she felt the most vulnerable, but instead of running home to her family, she'd done just the opposite. She'd stayed. Coming back to Piney Woods and the comfort of family just wasn't worth it if she had to face Adam Brockwell again.

In the months after her father died, all Nora could remember was the silence. An overwhelming silence. Nora had been about eleven then, and she and her mother had holed up in a web of silence. They didn't talk at meals, they simply nodded as they passed each other, mechanically going about their business. Kay Alexander had been numb, and even though friends called to check in on her, she'd never accepted their kind invitations. It had been the saddest time Nora had ever known. Her father had always brought the laughter into their house. Nora remembered when she and her dad hid in the closet to play a joke on her mother. They giggled as they heard her key in the lock, and as she put down her bag, they jumped out, shouting, "Surprise!"

Kay had stepped back in terror, but then a smile had played at the corners of her lips. Nora could tell she wanted to be angry at her father, but she just couldn't be. Nobody could stay mad at Ben Alexander for long.

Nora jumped when her cellphone rang.

She picked it up off the night table. "Hello."

"Good morning, Miss Alexander, or should I stay McArdle? What name are you using these days? So hard to keep up with those pesky labels on files." Tuck Watson sounded full of life and caffeine.

"Alexander is fine. How can I help you?"

"I was wondering if you could come in. The two of us could sort out some questions I still have. Oh, and I'm still waiting for a blood sample. Best to get these little things cleared up."

Nora hadn't looked in the mirror yet, but she didn't think she looked her best. "To tell the truth, today isn't a good day."

"Oh, I see. Do you already have an appointment? Oh, right! I heard about the giant rock Brockwell left you. I'll bet you have to get it appraised and cashed out this morning."

"No. I'm just a little under the weather. I could drop by tomorrow."

"Oh, come on, Nora, now that you're in league with your newfound brother, I think I know you by now. Your ship just came in, isn't that right?"

"No, it has not come in the way you think. I am just finding out that I have a family here, a biological father, and two half-siblings. I have gone out of my way to point out other suspects, and while we're on the subject, how much have you looked into Corey Brockwell? I might have the bloodline, but what has he been up to all these years? Time for me to say goodbye. See you tomorrow."

Nora punched the end key. Detective Watson wouldn't be getting an interview today.

# Chapter 30

———⁓———

NORA STOPPED AT the drugstore to pick up some more pain medicine. Her body ached, but she was moving better than last evening. There were a few noticeable bruises on her arm, and some Arnica gel for those bruises might help them go away sooner.

She turned up her collar, although she didn't expect to see anyone she knew in the store. She was wandering down the aisles when a familiar voice spoke up behind her.

Lucy Cooper was standing in the makeup aisle, green plastic shopping basket hung over her arm. "Oh my, big sister. What happened to you? Did you get into a fight?"

Nora began wishing she was an only child again. "Something like that." Nora tried to smile.

"Whatever you say. Whatever happened, I'd have to surmise you lost." Lucy's eyes softened and then she linked her arm carefully through Nora's. "What do you say I buy you a cup of coffee and you can tell me all about it? Someday I'll tell you about my old boyfriend Jasper, and why I now have a concealed carry permit."

Nora hesitated.

Lucy reached up to touch Nora's cheek. "Come on, girlfriend. It's the least you can do after following me around to prove I was murdering someone."

The clerk at the register nearly dropped a bottle of cologne she'd been putting into a glass case.

Even though Lucy had singlehandedly set out to swindle their father, she kind of liked the girl. Something in Nora's attitude toward her changed.

"Coffee sounds good."

A few minutes later they sat with piping hot cups of coffee, looking out the window of Dudley's Brew.

"Are you going to tell me about it, or do I have to drag it out of you?"

Nora blew on her coffee. "You remember the necklace left to me?"

"Remember it? How can I forget it? It had more lights on it than the Eiffel Tower."

"Well, it's gone now."

"You were robbed? Oh my God. Did you call the police?"

"No."

"Why not?"

"Corey took it. He said it should have been his mother's."

"What a jerk."

"Funny. I said the same thing, after he pushed to the floor."

"Dang, girl. You're lucky he didn't do more. I'm still missing the part about why you didn't report him to the cops?"

"He said that if I did, something might happen to me, which I could take, but then he started threatening Tatty and Ed. I can count my friends in this town on one hand. I can't put them in harm's way."

Lucy folded her arms across her chest, clearly looking at Nora in a new light. "What an ass. You know I always wanted a brother, and I'll admit I never wished it was a white brother. Now I know my new brother is Corey, I can very well do without."

"I'm with you. Still, you have to look at it from his perspective. A month ago he was a happy-go-lucky heir to a fortune."

"From the best family and the best man in town," Lucy added.

"And then there's the fact he's lousy at cards. And now, he has to share what little he has. Something Corey Brockwell has never had to do."

"Not true. I think he's been sharing his papa for a long time." Lucy chuckled.

"Adam Brockwell seemed to be a very shrewd man. I'm just a little more than interested in how you bilked him out of so much money." She took a sip of her coffee as Lucy stared out the window.

"I was more surprised than anybody when I got away with it. The first day I came home and told Mama that Mr. Adam Brockwell came into my bank asking for financial advice, something in her changed. She told me to stay away from him. It would be a big mistake to enter into any kind of a relationship with that man. I thought she was crazy. 'He's just a bank customer,' I told her."

"So then what happened?"

"He just kept coming into the bank. He signed up as a new client and we went into financial counseling. I know he didn't reveal all his holdings, but he gave me an amount he'd like to invest. I counseled him, like anybody else. Pointed him toward the funds where I got significant commissions. He seemed to be on board with everything. It was wonderful. I made every sale. When I told my mother, she blurted out how much she hated the man. He'd done something bad to her years ago and she wished we'd never come back to Piney Woods. She just would not tell me why. I wondered, of course."

"Don't tell me, let me guess. This is where you came up with your evil plan."

"Yes. I wanted to ruin him. He was making my mother crazy, and it hurt me to see her like that. So, I started with one bad stock. It was kind of an accident. I mean, I just assumed he knew it was bad and would correct me. After he lost money on it, I couldn't believe how easy it was. I'm ashamed to admit how good it made me feel. I thought he'd slow down on investing, but instead, he started inviting me to come 'consult' with him at his house."

"Did you tell your mother what you did?"

"Oh, no. That would've really flipped her out. My mother has a pretty strong moral code. Something like that would have sent her over the edge. Besides, I figured he might be losing some of his mental acuity, so if anybody asked, I could tell them I advised against it. Maybe he wasn't as on top of his game as he used to be. The old guy had to be close to sixty."

Nora nodded. "So, what happened then?"

"He was always offering me gifts. He even offered to buy me a new cellphone once. He said he needed to keep me happy so I could give him great financial advice."

"Did you meet Corey when you were visiting Adam Brockwell in his home?"

"Did I ever. First he came on to me, but when he saw I wasn't interested, he was just cold. He was pretty unhappy about the investments I was making for his dad. He didn't even try to hide it. He kept coming into his daddy's office, asking for money. Talk about a guy who plays to an inside straight. He was openly rude to me in front of his father."

"So, what did Adam do?"

"It was really interesting. He told his son to be nice to me, after all … and then he didn't say anything else."

"Corey's not too happy now. Not only does his daddy not have as much money as he thought, but now he has to share what's left with us. This couldn't get any better."

"True. You know, by the time the estate is cleared, Corey will come up with a way to keep us out of it."

"Like what?"

"Oh, like a second will or life insurance policy or something. The guy is desperate for cash."

Nora reached up and felt her swollen lip. "You should've seen the look on his face. At first he was charming and talked about what a wonderful job Tatty and Ed had done redecorating the bed and breakfast. Then he convinced me to take him to my room, closed the door, and flipped out."

"Not unlike our ... father." Lucy leaned closer. "Now that Mama has told us about how he used Mr. Ellis, it just breaks my heart. I could have had a daddy. A real daddy."

"I had one. I still miss him."

She stared off into the distance. "I wonder where Mr. Ellis is today? Did he marry someone else and have his own children?"

"Probably. It's been a long time."

Lucy tapped at the table with her nails. "Maybe I can find him."

"Do you know his first name?"

"No, but he has to be in some yearbook around here."

"Even if you find him, what will you say to the man?"

"I don't know. Something like 'I'm sorry Mr. Brockwell ruined your life. He had control over my mother and you were just a casualty.' "

"One thing I'm learning about Adam Brockwell was he might have been generous to every charity around, but deep down he was a greedy man. He wanted my mother, your mother, and you."

"And you." Lucy nodded.

"Was there ever anyone else in your mother's life?"

"Not really. The thing is, she never dated anyone all these years. Not one man. We left town and she went to work cleaning houses for somebody else, but all her passion seemed to be centered on me. She worked to pay for my college, and she came to every concert, ballgame, and dance recital. It was all about me. Now I wonder what she might have wanted for herself."

"Once you get Mr. Ellis' first name, you can google the guy."

"And if we do and find out he wasn't the star teacher everyone said he was? He might have some anger issues of his own, you know."

Nora frowned. "Then we don't tell your mother. If he's an okay guy, we go from there."

"Interesting." Lucy gave Nora a sidelong look.

"What?"

"All the 'we's' you're using. So, what are we, family now?"

Nora smiled and put her hands up. "Why not? I'm related to the rest of the town. At least you don't have a drinking problem."

"Hello, ladies." Little Dudley came by with a coffeepot. "I see you're enjoying our audacious brew."

"Yes, thank you." Nora held up her cup for a refill.

"News has it you are two of the richest ladies in town these days." Dudley smiled and bobbed his head with its straight bleached hair as if he'd just served celebrities.

Lucy tapped her manicured nails against the table. "Well, the paternity tests are still out. We may still be poor folk."

"Sounds like Mr. Good Brock wasn't so good."

"Seems like it."

"Well, if you do come into a wad of cash, just remember to tip your bodacious waiter." Little Dudley bowed and looked at the counter where Big Dudley rolled his eyes and motioned to him to return to the kitchen.

"Will do, dude." Lucy gave him a thumbs-up.

Once Little Dudley had left, Nora leaned closer to Lucy. "You know, I was planning on taking the necklace to the bank today. Guess I have no reason to visit your workplace now."

"Corey won't either. Adam had a safe. Our baby brother will put it in there. He certainly can't show it anywhere in town after it was officially given to you."

"You know," Nora looked both ways to make sure no one was listening, "there is one thing I've been dying to do."

"What?"

"Visit our new mansion. We could measure it for drapes. If the necklace is in the study, we could take it back."

Lucy's eyes shone. "I can't believe I'm hearing this. Or saying what I'm about to say: good idea. If Corey is up to something, we might just catch him at it."

"Drink up, Lucy. It's time we made a visit to Daddy's house."

# Chapter 31

—✦—

"How do you propose we enter without a key?" Lucy asked after Nora rang the doorbell for the fourth time.

She had expected Brockwell's housekeeper to open the door and then she could talk her way into the study.

Nora looked around. "My guess is once Corey knew there was a lot less money to spend, he let the housekeeper go."

"I think you're right. One good thing—Corey's car isn't here, so we know he's not home."

"Yeah, but we're still locked out. So what does it matter?"

The grounds were empty and no one could see them from the street, unless they drove up the tree-lined drive. Nora walked across the porch and started trying the windows.

"What are you doing?"

"You've heard of the servants' entrance? Well, this is the illegitimate daughters' entrance."

The fourth window she tried opened. They were in.

"Unbelievable. Half the windows in Texas don't even open anymore and you find a porch full."

"Got to love these old houses." Nora hiked a blue-jeaned leg over the windowsill. "You coming?"

"Why not." Lucy slipped off her heels, hiked up her skirt and climbed in. "I think you're a bad influence on me, Nora Alexander."

"What are big sisters for?" Nora was whispering, even though the house seemed empty. They saw further evidence of the absence of a housekeeper. Jackets were tossed over chairs and dust had gathered on the antique furniture. Still, just in case the house wasn't empty, Nora and Lucy tiptoed to the study.

"Where's the safe?" Nora asked. "Is it behind some portrait of Brockwell's granddaddy?"

"You're close, but this being Texas …." Lucy walked over to the gun rack, which held an impressive collection of rifles. She ran her finger along the edge of the shelving unit until there was a distinct click. The rack folded out, revealing a wall safe behind it.

"You have to be kidding me." Nora stood back, arms crossed. "Would you happen to know the combination?"

Lucy bit her bottom lip and collapsed in the overstuffed soft leather chair. "No. Maybe he kept it taped under his drawer. I saw it in a movie once." She felt along the underside of the drawer. "Nothing here."

"Would he have left the combination for someone else?"

"Like who?"

"His lawyer, maybe?" Nora leaned over the desk from the other side, resting her elbows on Brockwell's monthly calendar pad. "Try this."

Lucy rose and put her hands on the dial of the safe.

"Try eight, six, sixty-six."

Lucy spun through the numbers one by one. The safe clicked open.

"God, girl. What did you do? Pick those numbers out of the air?"

"I figured it would be a date important to Adam Brockwell. August sixth was my mother's birthday."

"Impressive."

"I'd like to take complete credit, but it's also written here on a sticky note."

Lucy laughed. "Corey had to write it down to remember it." She reached into the safe.

"Ha." She pulled out the diamond pendant. "I do believe you're back in business, girl."

Nora tapped her index finger against her lip. "If we take it, he'll know we were here."

"Yeah, but what is he going to do about it? Report a stolen necklace he already took from you?"

"Good point." She paused. "He might carry out his other threats, though. But somehow we'll make sure that doesn't happen."

Nora sat at the gigantic polished desk and reached into the bottom drawer to pull out a green leather checkbook. No online checking for Adam Brockwell. This thing was the classic three checks per page with check stubs for recording by hand. Nora started looking through the checks Brockwell had written over the last six months.

She was amazed at how many checks were written to charities like the hospital fund and Pastor Chilton's church, but there were also many checks written to Corey. Nora did a little math and found he was averaging about ten grand a week. Lucy pulled up a chair next to her.

"Majestic Investments." Lucy pointed at a stub. "That was me."

"And he believed you were actually making profitable investments for him?"

Lucy let out a sigh. "Oh, I thought I was the one who was doing the tricking. Now I'm beginning to think the joke was on me."

"It was guilt money, Lucy. Like my mother's necklace. I think, in his old age, the guy finally developed a conscience. Something must have changed him or there would be even more of us running around. Then again, maybe it just didn't fit in with this big reputation he was building."

"Yeah, you'd expect the finest citizen of Piney Woods wouldn't want his legions of adorers to find out."

"This is interesting." Nora ran her finger along the register. "Corey was getting a check every week until about a month ago. Then, nothing."

"Do you think Daddy cut him off?"

"Had to be the case. Seriously, who tells their father they need such an incredible amount of money every week for expenses?"

Lucy shrugged. "Rich kids?"

Nora shook her head. "There's not a whole lot to buy around here."

Lucy raised her eyebrows and cocked her head to the side. "Unless you're stupid enough to bet on an inside straight."

Nora continued to page through the check stubs and then stopped.

"What?" Lucy asked.

"Can't be. It just doesn't make any sense." Nora's finger rested on a name scrawled on a check stub.

Lucy squinted at the name. "Who is Delmar Dupree?"

Nora shuddered. "My father's former partner in the police force, now a car salesman."

# Chapter 32

———

"**N**ORA? WHAT HAPPENED?" Tuck Watson asked when she and Lucy entered the police station. He moved a stack of papers out of one of the two spare chairs in front of his desk, stacking them on a nearby filing cabinet.

Nora and Lucy sat in front of Tuck, Lucy straightening the hem of her skirt.

Nora tilted her head down, trying to hide her fat lip. "Uh, it's a long story and one I don't have time to go into right now."

"I have all the time in the world. Who did that to you?" He was starting to sound angry and Nora couldn't tell if it was at her or the person who had given her a fat lip.

"Look, you wanted me to come in so you could grill me even more. Here I am."

Tuck shook his head in frustration and leaned on one elbow as he observed her. Nora felt like she was under a microscope. "You are the most confusing woman ... *suspect* I've ever met. Half the time I don't know whether to put you in a safe house or arrest you."

Nora was warmed by Tuck's urge to protect her. She imagined

how nice it would be to rest safely in his arms, warm and snug, the world outside not a concern.

"Nora, tell him," Lucy urged, pulling her out of her dream state. How had she slipped away so easily?

"We just found out something to help you in your investigation."

Watson rolled his eyes. "Oh my. Nancy Drew and her able assistant—"

"Foxy Brown," Lucy crossed her legs, laying her hand on one knee.

"Of course." Tuck smiled. "And what is it you found that my staff of trained investigators missed?"

Nora ignored his sarcasm. "Del Dupree. Adam Brockwell wrote him a great big check."

"Ginormous," Lucy added.

Tuck sat up, focusing on the new fact. "You bankers have quite the vocabulary. And you know this … how?"

Nora fidgeted. Telling him they just broke into Adam Brockwell's house wouldn't go over well. "I just do. Okay? You need to talk to this guy. If you're so all fired up about finding the truth, then start with him. Why would Adam Brockwell write such a large check to a complete stranger?

"I have no idea. What kind of proof do you have that this payment is anything out of the ordinary?"

Nora found her hands were shaking. "We don't have any kind of proof, but where there's smoke—"

"I think I might be able to answer your question," a voice from behind them said. A man in his sixties stood at the door, fingers hooked in his belt loops. He wore a beige suit over his bulky figure and his shiny cowboy boots clicked as he crossed the room. With his set of double chins, he reminded Nora of Jabba the Hutt.

"I expected my name might come up in this investigation, but I sure didn't expect you to be talking about me when I walked in the door. Let me introduce myself." He bent his large frame down and extended a hand, a broad smile filling his round face. "Del Dupree, Dealin' Del of the Bayou."

Tuck stood and shook the man's hand. "Mr. Dupree, this is a surprise. I didn't expect you to drive over here."

"I felt it was my duty. I knew Mr. Brockwell's generous gift would come up under your thorough investigation."

Tuck shot a glance at Nora, who was now giving him a look of annoyance.

"Okay. Once again, a simple phone call would have sufficed." Tuck snapped his fingers. "But then again, I forget you people would rather just drive somewhere than clear up a problem using modern conveniences. I thought Louisiana was supposed to be a fun place."

Del sighed as his eyes traveled over Nora. There was a sadness in his appraisal. Almost as if he felt sorry for her. "You are so like your mama." As his eyes continued to roam over her, Nora grew increasingly uncomfortable. With a little smile, Del pulled up a third chair beside Tuck Watson's cluttered desk.

"Seriously?" Lucy's eyes widened. "Why don't you tell us why you took a big fat check from Adam Brockwell?"

"I'd be glad to, young lady. And you are …?"

"His financial planner."

"Is that right?" He licked his lips and leered at her. "I'm sure there must be something I need to invest."

"I only take local clients."

"Well, then, I'm surprised you didn't know about my payment. It sounds like Mr. Brockwell didn't fill you in on everything. Did he?"

"You got that right," Lucy answered.

"The Fallen Officers Association solicits funds from both Louisiana and Texas. Our call center reached out to him, his generosity being legendary. The check was made out to me, because I was in charge of the center that day. We got on the phone and talked about our men in blue. Great man, that Brockwell. Too bad someone went and murdered him."

Dupree put his hand across his heart. "It has been my honor to distribute those funds yearly to the beloved families of our officers."

Nora crossed her arms, a chill now in the room. The coincidental phone call seemed a little much, but when she glanced at Tuck, he seemed to be buying it. Had she been wrong about Dupree? Had Adam Brockwell given him the money as yet another one of his good causes to support?

"So," Tuck Watson asked, "Adam Brockwell donated to your fallen officer's fund?"

Dupree's face flushed red. "I bleed blue, brother. I bleed blue."

Tuck's bottom lip thinned as he listened to the big man. Nora figured Del Dupree had hit on something important. Cops did take care of other cops. Dupree was there the night her father was shot, and now the horror of the shooting seemed to be following him for the rest of his life. Nora felt awful. If there was a hole to climb into, she'd have jumped at the chance. She'd assumed Del Dupree was a bad man, but instead, he was helping people. She'd been so wrong about him.

"Well, I'm glad we have this little matter cleared up." Del pulled a small cigar out of his pocket. "I know this is going to sound strange, but I drove here wanting to see the place Adam Brockwell hailed from."

"Where have I heard that before?" Lucy grabbed Nora by the arm.

Tuck jumped up and grabbed a report from the desk. "Um, Nora, don't go yet. There's one more little thing I need to discuss with you."

Del Dupree rose. "It's been a long drive. Is there a hotel you can recommend in the area?"

"The Hotel Tunie," Nora said. "Right next door. It doesn't look open, but it is." Her voice sounded mechanical, all her hospitality training out the window. How could she have been so wrong about this man? Del shook Tuck's hand one more time and headed for the door.

As Dupree passed her on his way out, he laid his large hand on the counter. "It's so nice to finally meet you, Nora. Your father was a fine man."

As soon as the older man left, Watson turned his attention back to Nora and Lucy. "I can see the sister thing is developing. You may want to think twice about it, though, Miss Cooper. Your new half-sister is still number one on my suspect list, even though she tried to point the finger at you. I just watch and wait for the next suspect she throws my way."

Nora wished she had someone else to offer, but she didn't. She had to keep working on the Del angle, but even his motive was shaky. "Listen, I'm sorry for saying you didn't know your job about Dupree. I had no idea he was being given money to support the families of policemen. I just assumed it was a payoff. I still think it's weird that the check wasn't written to the association itself."

"Don't worry about it," Tuck said. "If I had found out what you did, I might have jumped to the same conclusion. Although, I'm still a little curious as to how you and Lucy found out."

Lucy stepped up. "Not important right now. We've taken up enough of your time."

He started to go back to his desk but then turned back to Nora. "I know a lot of people around here think you killed Adam Brockwell, but whoever hit you in the lip … they were just wrong to do it. I sure wish you'd tell me his name."

"Thanks. It's really no big deal." Nora placed her hand over her lip.

"If that's the way you want to play it. Just remember though, I'm here if you need me."

*To arrest me*, Nora thought.

# Chapter 33

---

"**I**'VE HIRED A caterer for our party."

Marty held her cellphone out to her side. "Hold on a minute, Max. The website will have to wait." Marty set her cellphone on the front-desk counter and turned back to Nora, "Who?"

"Wiley."

"You mean the same Wiley who gets drunk and collapses in front of the hotel every week? That Wiley?"

"Okay, I'll admit it doesn't sound good when you put it that way. Yes, it's that Wiley. I know you think he's a bum and an alcoholic, but you need to give him a try."

She pursed her lips.

"Marty, I know it sounds crazy, but he's spent a lifetime cooking for other people. He's really good. You've had his gumbo. He could even manage the restaurant one day."

"True, but there's a big difference in working for someone else and actually managing a restaurant. For one thing, you have to show up to work sober for more than two days in a row."

Marty was right. A month ago she hadn't even known Wiley

existed. Whatever possessed her to trust him with the reunion?

"I know it's a risk, but you trusted me when no one else would. I'm so thankful for you taking a chance on me. Let's just say I'm paying it forward."

"Technically, Marty is." Max's voice came through the speaker on the counter. "Oh, and Marty, I got the intercom working at the front desk. I can hear everything in there, clear as a bell."

"Thank you for the clarification, Max, and turn that thing off." Marty tilted her head toward the phone.

Max continued, "You're very welcome, and one more thing I'd like to add: I like Wiley's gumbo."

"Hush, Max."

"Sorry," said the disembodied voice.

Nora met Marty's gaze, her request unspoken.

Marty covered her eyes with her hands. "I must be crazy."

"No, you're just a kind person. It's why we like you," Max's tinny voice came through.

Marty laughed. "Thanks. Still crazy, but at least you like me."

AT THE END of her shift, Nora ran the sweeper across the lobby. Now that the hotel was getting cleaned regularly and aired out, it wasn't looking too shabby. She'd spent much of the evening cleaning the banquet room, which wasn't presently holding a class. With the help of a rich oil, Nora was bringing out the shine in the wood. Tomorrow night she'd work on the brass fixtures. It would take a lot of elbow grease, but she wanted the place to look as close to its original form as possible by the reunion. Everything was taking shape. Even Marty and Max noticed the difference.

Tonight she made sure the office was kept locked. Nora couldn't afford to have her name in any more police reports. She hummed as she spotted a quarter under one of the benches lining the wall. Nora debated whether the vacuum would have picked it up or not if she hadn't noticed it. Just as she neared the coin and stooped to pick it up, the sweeper shut off.

The cord in the back wall outlet was still securely in place. She hoped it wasn't broken. Marty wasn't going to be happy about another possible expense. This was an almost-new vacuum. It was then Nora realized she was standing in front of the picture again. There was her mother, frozen in time, forever skipping in the banquet room of the Tunie Hotel, with Adam Brockwell and Arnie Chilton watching.

Nora still wanted to see Pastor Chilton so she could talk to him about Brockwell and look through his box of mementos. It seemed to her Chilton was Brockwell's closest friend. If Adam Brockwell paid Del Dupree to help fallen police officers, Pastor Chilton should know. With a tired sigh, she decided to pay the good pastor another visit tomorrow.

And, even though she'd done nothing to fix the vacuum, its pleasant hum resumed.

# Chapter 34

WHEN NORA ENTERED the First Congregational Fellowship the next morning, Maisie Goodwin, a plump woman in her fifties, sat at her desk folding bulletins. Her brown hair was shoulder length, with just a few streaks of gray running through it. She wore jeans and a Texas Longhorns sweatshirt over her ample bosom.

"Oh, Pastor is still on his hospital visits. Evelyn Parker had a nasty bunion removed." Maisie placed her hand over her mouth and chuckled. "Oh, but I'm not supposed to give the details. Keep it to yourself, okay?"

"Evelyn's secret is safe with me," Nora whispered and winked at Maisie. There was a bit of a nip in the air, so Nora wore her black pullover sweater with jeans, along with a pair of black boots that had been a little too warm for New Orleans.

Maisie went on folding, never losing a beat. "Yes. She was in quite a lot of pain, poor dear." Maisie stopped for a moment and smiled at Nora. "I hear you found yourself in a peck of trouble, my dear." Her statement was so caring it surprised Nora. Even though she barely knew this woman, she felt like an old friend. Nora was at a loss for words.

Maisie continued, "Oh don't you worry. I used to know your mother in school. It was ages ago now." Nora tried to imagine Maisie as a young and silly girl, joking around with her mother.

"You knew my mother when she was in school?" Nora asked.

"Oh yes." Maisie looked up, remembering. "She was quite the cat's meow around here."

"Can I ask you, did she go out with Adam Brockwell?"

"Mr. Brockwell? I don't think so, but that doesn't mean he didn't try. He tried. They all tried. In a town this small, when you get a girl who looks like a movie star, well, it's just trouble waiting to happen."

"Did she ever talk to you about leaving?"

"No, dear. No one did. She was here one day and gone the next. It was the darndest thing." She started back on her folding and then stopped again, this time fixing Nora in her blue-eyed gaze. "I just wanted to let you know, no matter how wonderful everyone thought Adam Brockwell was and all their cries for some sort of swift justice, you are in my prayers. Your mom isn't here to pray for you anymore and the Class of '83 looks out for their own." She peered out the window as if the rest of the town were standing out there looking in, and then pulled Nora closer and whispered, "Go Tigers!"

"Go Tigers," Nora whispered back.

"Absolutely." Maisie gave a thumbs-up. "Now, Pastor usually makes a quick visit to the sanctuary after his trips to the hospital. Guess he wants to put those prayer deposits in the bank, you know." She laughed at her own joke again. This woman truly was her own best friend. "You can go in there and have a seat if you like. It's very peaceful."

Nora left Maisie's office and took a seat in the empty sanctuary. The only thing creepier than an empty banquet room had to be an empty church. She gazed around at the straight angles created by the altar cloths, unlit candles and golden frames, and each blue hymnal set exactly three inches from the next. It was hard to imagine people getting their messy lives into such a clear and clean space. The early afternoon sun was playing with the colored glass in the windows. Nora was so entranced, she didn't hear Pastor Chilton coming down the red-carpeted aisle. He reached two fingers into a waiting bowl of water and started making the sign of the cross. After he finished, he kneeled at the altar to pray.

So much pageantry for a bunion. This guy was dedicated. After just a moment, he turned toward Nora. He wore a black jacket and button-down shirt, accenting his clerical collar. His face had a slight sheen on it, making him look almost like one of the polished statues at St. Mary's back in New Orleans.

"Glad to see you, Nora. I'll bet you're here about my broken promises. Let me get his old box from the parsonage. Not much there, but maybe you'll find something interesting."

"Great. If I'm not … interrupting."

"Oh no. While something's on my mind, I try to speak to God about it. A little holy water to set it right, and I'm on my way, you know."

"Holy water. Not just for Sunday anymore," Nora agreed, trying to make a joke.

"Not at all," he said, taking her seriously.

"Before you get the box, I was wondering if you could help me with something."

Chilton stopped and patted his middle. "Anything I can do to help."

"Do you ever remember Mr. Brockwell sending money to a man named Del Dupree?"

Chilton scratched the side of his head. "Goodness. Adam gave money to a lot of people. Although he has now been accused of some pretty dastardly things, he had a generous soul. Frankly, I don't know how this town's charitable organizations will survive without him."

"Delmar Dupree was my father's partner in New Orleans. We found a stub that indicated Adam Brockwell had written him a check. It's a strange connection, don't you think? When we asked Mr. Dupree, he said it was money donated for a slain police officers' fund in New Orleans."

"You don't say. Pretty interesting, isn't it? You know, the more I find out about my old friend, the more I realize I didn't really know him. I assumed good things about Adam, but after hearing about your mother and Arnette, maybe I was wrong. I can see why you're questioning this."

Finally someone else wasn't accepting Adam Brockwell at face value. He had not been what he seemed. Nora felt a surge of relief. She'd been trying hard to believe the payment was to help others, but a seed of doubt lingered in the back of her mind. Absent the company of Dupree and Tuck Watson, her resolve seemed to be coming back.

Maybe this church was a good place to straighten out messes in one's head.

CHILTON'S BOX OF pictures turned out to be pretty disappointing for Nora. Most of the memorabilia centered on the pastor's brother, Arnie.

Nora's finger grazed a crisp photo of Arnie Chilton. "I saw his name and picture on the war remembrance wall of the hotel."

"The wall Mr. Tunie put up is a wonderful tribute to our war heroes."

"I'm beginning to think Mr. Tunie did a lot of things right. I just hope the reunion we're planning works out for us."

Chilton pulled a book from the box and dusted it off. "Have faith, Nora. You'll get the hotel back on its feet. I believe God sent you here on a mission, whether you know it or not."

"Do you think so? To be honest, I've never done anything like this before."

"Well, maybe some fresh ideas are just what the old place needs." He paged through the ancient yearbook until he came to what he was looking for.

"There she is. Our homecoming queen. Leslie McArdle. Wasn't she beautiful?"

Nora's mother was dressed in a deep-green gown with spaghetti straps. A corsage was pinned at her shoulder, and a rhinestone crown sparkled from her feathered hair. "She looks so happy. She had no idea what kind of pain she'd endure for the rest of her life."

The pastor sighed. "No high school senior ever does."

Her mother's date was a gangly young man dressed in a tuxedo with a ruffled shirt. "Is that your brother?"

"I was hoping you'd notice. He'd already graduated, but came back to take your mother to homecoming."

"So they were an item?"

"*He* thought so. I never got the feeling it was mutual though. She was a nice girl and sometimes her good heart was confused, wanting something more."

"Did she ever tell him she didn't have the same feelings he did?"

"I don't know. Won't ever know for sure."

Now that Nora knew a little more of her mother's history, she understood. Her mother thought life would be perfect, but then everything changed. Adam Brockwell changed it for her. She'd never be a naive girl again.

Chilton fixed his gaze on his brother's photo. "He was a handsome man. I'm afraid that of the two of us, he was the better man."

Nora's heart softened toward this man. "I'll bet he'd say the same of you. What you do in this community is important. He fought for our country but you fight every day for the people in Piney Woods."

Chilton's eyes glistened. "You're too kind. I have never thought of it that way, but yes, maybe you're right. I may not be a war hero, but I still have much I can do. Blessed with the work." He hugged the yearbook to his chest and then turned to

Nora. "Thank you for your words of encouragement today. My soul needed to hear them."

# Chapter 35

───※───

THE NEXT MORNING, Nora stood at the front desk of the Tunie Hotel. She'd volunteered to fill in for Marty for a couple of hours while she did the interview with the newspaper and ran some errands. Max was still in the office, completing his nightly law school homework.

Nora reflected on her meeting with Pastor Chilton the day before. He appeared to support her suspicion that Del Dupree was doing more with the money he'd received from Adam Brockwell than giving it to the families of officers killed in the line of duty. Was there a way to check on such a thing? Nora found the number she'd used to originally contact Dealin' Del of the Bayou and dialed it.

"Uh, yes, I was wondering if there's a website for Del's charity to benefit the families of policemen. I wanted to donate, but silly me, I can't seem to find where to send the check."

There was a pause on the other end. This had to be a first. Someone offering a car dealership money and the front desk didn't know what to do with it.

"I'm sorry. You said Dealin' Del runs a charity? For policemen?" The receptionist sounded puzzled.

"Yes. Can you give me some information on it?"

There was another pause, and all Nora could hear was the car lot loudspeaker in the background. "Mrs. Thibodaux, your car is ready in the service department."

"You know, I've been here at Dealin' Del's for twenty years but never heard tell of a charity for cops. Are you sure you got the right car lot? Del isn't one to let a cent stray outside his own piggy bank, if you know what I mean." The last part was whispered into the phone.

"Really?"

"I know, right? I hadn't even noticed hell freezin' over. Tell you what, give me your number. I'll check into it and call you back. Maybe Del grew a heart overnight. It happened to the Grinch, after all, didn't it?"

Nora gave the receptionist her cell number. She was just hanging up when Del Dupree stepped out of the elevator. Today he wore a white Western shirt with a bolo tie, a bronze crawfish adorning its center.

"Good morning, Mr. Dupree." Nora gave him a cheery greeting, hoping to unnerve him. He wasn't a man she wanted to cross. She wasn't sure why she was wary of him now, but she was.

As intended, her greeting seemed to catch him off guard, and he glanced around the lobby, his gaze landing on Nora at the desk.

"Good morning." He looked around as if he were searching for something or someone. "You work here?"

"Sure do. I hope you had a restful evening."

He rubbed his massive hand across his brow as if wiping off a puddle of sweat. "It was great. So you live in this town now?"

Nora threw her hands in the air in a helpless gesture. "Temporarily. After Adam Brockwell was found stabbed to death, the police insisted I stay."

"Makes sense. Quite the irony getting stabbed by your own kid, don't you think?" He walked over to the coffee bar and poured himself a cup of Tunie's Signature Brew—another one of Nora's special touches. After adding a liberal amount of artificial sweetener, Dupree sauntered over to the front desk.

"Tell me, Nora. Did you do it?" He posed the question as if fishing for the latest gossip.

"What do you think?" Nora hoped she sounded relaxed but feared he'd heard the quaver in her voice.

"I think," he ran a finger along her cheekbone, "you've gotten yourself in a heck of a mess. Just like your mama did." He gave Nora a look that was piercing and challenging.

"You want to know what I think?" Nora asked the older man, who was now lounging against her counter.

"What's that, darlin'?" The way the words rolled off his tongue made Nora think, *What a slime ball.*

"I think there's no such thing as a slain officers' fund and you were being paid off by Adam Brockwell. How did you even know I was his daughter?"

Del Dupree stiffened, and his demeanor changed from playful to angry in a split second. "You've got a lot of nerve, little girl."

"Ever since I've been in Piney Woods, my life has been filled with strange coincidences. I found a father I never knew about and a whole family who never knew about me. Now *you* show up. You've been out of my life for years and yet here you are. I'm a pretty smart girl, and I have to ask myself why Adam Brockwell wrote that check to you. Funny, your receptionist was downright shocked you were collecting donations for slain officers. Almost as if you made the whole thing up. Maybe I should tell Tuck Watson to give you another look."

Del reached over and grabbed Nora by the wrist. She flinched. "You'd best shut your mouth before someone shuts it for you." He eyed her. "Don't play with me. It will be the last mistake you ever make."

Del Dupree slammed her wrist on the counter. It hurt. She stayed calm and collected. She was not going to give in to fear.

"Stay out of it. You don't know anything." He tossed his cardboard coffee cup in the trash and stormed out into the bright morning light, passing Max, who was on his way into the lobby area.

"What's with that dude?" Max said as he walked over to the shelves Nora had loaded with snacks for the guests.

Nora plopped into the chair behind the checkout desk and rubbed her wrist. "You wouldn't believe this story. It is something else.

"Try me."

"Well, believe it or not, that's my father's old partner from the police force—a guy I haven't seen for years."

"What's he doing here?" Max surveyed the candy selection in the snack shop then reached out and took a candy bar.

"He came here to clear his name, and of all the people in the world, he collected a check from Adam Brockwell."

"Now, *that's* interesting."

"It certainly is. He told us it was for some sort of fallen officers' fund. I think he made that up. From what I hear, he's pretty much a skinflint. I found this out when I called his headquarters and they had never heard of the fund. He owns a string of car lots in New Orleans."

Max opened the wrapper of the chocolate bar. "A car salesman who's generous? Never seen that, at least not around here. The big question is why would Adam Brockwell be involved in all this?"

"I'm still working on that. The thing is, I feel like he's as dangerous as he is crooked. Del Dupree had the drop on Adam Brockwell. He knew I was illegitimate. Do you think that check might have been blackmail money?"

Max sat on a red-velvet bench, popped the rest of the candy bar into his mouth, and crumpled up the wrapper. "Adam Brockwell was up for Piney Woods Pioneer, and that committee is real picky about things like children outside of marriage. Especially when you figure in the fact that Adam

Brockwell was dropping checks off everywhere but never to the mothers of his own children. You may have just stumbled onto something, Nora." He spoke through a mouthful of nougat and nuts. "You know, this guy could be dangerous."

"You're just getting that?"

"Low blood sugar."

"Do you think the police department has any clue?"

"I don't think they do."

Max went into the office and came back out with a law textbook. He ran his finger through the table of contents. "I think all we need to do is get Del Dupree to admit he was blackmailing Adam Brockwell."

Nora laughed. "And how do you propose we do that? He isn't exactly forthcoming with this information, you know. I'm pretty sure he's planning to take it to the grave."

"I know it sounds crazy." He flipped to the page he was looking for and took a moment to read it. "If we can record him admitting he was blackmailing Adam Brockwell, then there's nothing he can do about it."

"That's the craziest thing I've heard yet."

"No, it's not. This is what we're going to do. You're going to tell him you have proof he was blackmailing Brockwell. Get him to come into the banquet room, and I'll record him on my phone. That way there will be no interruptions."

"Don't you think he'll notice you standing there with a phone pointed at him?"

Max looked around the room. "You're right. I'll have to hide behind something."

They both had a look. There was nothing big enough in either banquet room to cover Max's bulk.

"Okay, how about this. I lure him into the parking lot."

Max smiled in approval. "Excellent. I can hide behind a car."

"Or better yet, the Dumpster." Nora paused. The whole plan sounded silly to her.

"You want this guy off your back? You want him to admit why he's here and how it concerns Adam Brockwell?"

Nora looked down, starting to feel guilty for making fun of Max's plan. "Okay, fine. I'll lure Dupree into the parking lot and get him to talk."

"Great, and if this doesn't work out, at least he'll have a Dumpster handy for dumping our bodies."

"Oh, I hope it does. Work out I mean."

"Sure. The police use cellphone videos all the time as evidence now. It's the people's journalism, you know. This is going to work."

"If you say so."

"Oh, and one more thing." Max turned back on his way to the office to redeposit the law book. "I faint at the side of blood."

With their plan in place, Max left, promising to return in a few hours. Maybe it would work, but she wasn't sure about anything anymore. Nora felt surrounded. Del Dupree, Corey Brockwell, and even Tuck Watson. All three of these men had disturbed her life in some way and two of them wanted to do her bodily harm. Today, she wished she had her mother to run to, the mother she'd spent a lifetime running away from. She needed to break this down and handle one crisis at a time. Nora still hadn't found a safe place to stash the pendant in case Corey came back for it. She dabbed at the tender part of her lip, not wanting a repeat of the last time.

Ever since the break-in, Nora had hidden the pendant in an empty tampon case in her purse. She was pretty sure even Corey Brockwell wouldn't search there. What she hadn't had time to do was get to the bank. The diamond necklace was turning out to be more of a burden than a windfall. Nora's mother would never have accepted the gift from Adam Brockwell, even if he'd had the opportunity to give it to her. Nora's life would've been a whole lot easier, and a little less painful, if she'd also rejected the gift. But, it was one of the differences between Nora and Kay Alexander. Nora wasn't going to hang back. Maybe this independent streak came from her father—her real father, Adam Brockwell. No wonder her mother had seemed distant at times. Had Nora inherited the looks and mannerisms of a man Kay despised?

# Chapter 36

---

Del Dupree returned a few hours later, picking at his teeth with a toothpick. Nora texted Max, who after a brief nap had returned to sit by the door to the parking lot and was doing some studying.

"Your car lots in this town are piles of crap. I wouldn't buy a car here if you were givin' 'em away."

The back door squeaked. Max was taking his place behind the Dumpster.

"Mr. Dupree …."

"Del. Mr. Dupree was my no-account father."

"Del, I was wondering if you could take a look at my car and give me an idea of what it's worth. It's just in the back lot."

Dupree eyed Nora. "Why would you want me to do that? I didn't exactly think we were friends."

"Let's just say, you're doing it for the daughter of a fallen policeman. I know how much you donate your money and time to them."

"Yeah, right."

"And, uh, I just wanted to apologize for what I said earlier. I'm not going to ask the police to investigate you. I was just feeling … I … was experiencing low blood sugar. So, could you please just look at my car? If I end up getting arrested for Adam Brockwell's murder, I'll need that money to pay a lawyer."

Dupree threw the toothpick into the trash can. "I suppose, but I can't take long. It's time I got back to some decent food in Louisiana."

"Oh, thank you. I really appreciate this."

Del Dupree stepped onto the pavement from the back door of the Tunie Hotel. Nora leaned up against the Dumpster. Max should be behind it. Hopefully Dupree wouldn't notice the hand holding a cell phone.

"So, where is this bucket of bolts?"

"I know," Nora said in almost a whisper.

Del snorted. "You know what?"

"I know you were blackmailing Adam Brockwell. You knew about his affairs and illegitimate children and that he was up for Piney Woods Pioneer."

"You're crazy. What proof do you have? Why would I do that?"

The smell of rancid fish drifted from the top of the trash heap to Nora as she lifted her chin in defiance. "So why did Adam Brockwell pay you so much money? You want to know what I think? I think you knew about my true parentage for years and were just waiting for the chance to cash in on that information. You were keeping up with Adam Brockwell, and when the Piney Woods Pioneer nominations came out, you went for the cash you knew he'd give you to keep quiet."

Del put his fingers in the rims of his pockets and shifted back and forth on his heels for a moment. "Once again, I have no idea what you're talking about."

Nora pulled her phone out of her pocket. "Let's just see what Tuck Watson thinks of this. He's a pretty good judge of character, but I don't think he's even begun to check you out. What will he find if he starts pulling up your record in Louisiana?"

"Sure. You have such a good track record with the local police around here yourself. Why should they believe you? They think you killed Adam Brockwell."

"Maybe so, but I'll call him anyway."

Del Dupree grabbed her hand, sending the cellphone flying. "Give me that damn phone. I'll say it again: you're just like your father. Your real father. I was on patrol with Ben Alexander and he told me all about your mother and her little bastard. Your father never did know when he was making a mistake. Even on the day he died he wasn't aware that I hung back. I could tell that whichever one of us went into that store would never come out again. Like I'm not going to use what information God gives me? After that, I just waited for the right opportunity. I didn't think it would take this long, but that was fine. Thank goodness for modern technology and a little thing they call a Google alert. Old Adam's name came up on my computer when the nominees were announced, and of course, I made my move. Adam Brockwell, future citizen of the year. You're thinking too hard, girl. What would the fine citizens of Piney Woods say if they found out that their citizen of the year had two bastards running around? Not quite the family man they thought he was."

Nora needed to make him say it twice just to make sure. "So you're saying you killed Adam?"

The corners of Del Dupree's mouth curled up in a smile, revealing a neat row of false teeth. "No. Didn't kill him either, just blackmail, darlin'. And for the record, I may be a lowdown swamp rat, but I don't kill people. No profit in it." Del advanced on Nora, pushing her up against the Dumpster. His hands went to her throat. "Now, I warned you once to stay out of my business. Do I need to reinforce what I'm sayin'?" Just as he pulled back one hand to wallop Nora, Max came around the other side of the Dumpster, tossing one of the old chairs that had been thrown away on Del's head and sending the man tumbling to the ground. Nora scrambled for her phone to finally make that call to Tuck. A tiny stream of blood began to drip from the back of Del's head onto the pavement. Max took one look and hit the parking lot with a thud.

# Chapter 37

TUCK WALKED ONTO the scene a few minutes later, as Nora leaned over Max, cradling his head in her lap, fanning him with a piece of discarded cardboard box.

"It's about time you got here."

"Don't worry, the ambulance is on its way. What happened to Max?"

"Max will be all right. He can't stand the sight of blood. He hit Del Dupree on the back of the head with a chair, and when Del started bleeding, Max went down."

The sirens grew stronger in the distance.

"And would you like to explain to me why Max attacked Mr. Dupree in the parking lot behind the hotel?"

"He had me pinned against the Dumpster and was about to hit me."

"Why would he want to do that? What is this thing you have with people wanting to hit you?" Tuck Watson reached down and put his fingers on Dupree's neck to feel his carotid artery. "He's still alive, anyway. I know Max will be relieved he doesn't have to defend himself on a murder charge."

"Especially seeing as how he might not have reached that volume of the online course yet."

The ambulance pulled up behind them, red lights flashing.

Max started to stir and looked into Nora's eyes. A gentle smile played on his round face. "Is this heaven?"

"It's not even Iowa. Do yourself a favor, Max, and keep your eyes on me. Let's see if we can get you up and away from here."

Nora helped Max to a standing position and walked him back inside, keeping his gaze away from the blood. Once she got him settled, she headed back to Tuck. Del Dupree was awake and rubbing the back of his head.

"That's her. She and her henchman ganged up on me."

Tuck looked at Nora. "I think I'll have you step over to the station and give me a statement about what happened here, Nora. Mr. Dupree is thinking of filing charges against you and Max."

Nora held up Max's phone in front of Tuck Watson's face. There was a video waiting. Nora reached over and pressed play. The silence was filled with Del Dupree talking to her about his scheme to blackmail Brockwell. Tuck's eyes darted from the video to Del.

"Mr. Dupree, I think I need to read you your rights." Tuck began rolling through Del Dupree's Miranda rights. After he finished, he shook his head. "Frankly, I think we've overlooked you in our investigation of Adam Brockwell's death."

The paramedics guided Mr. Dupree to the back of the ambulance. Tuck shut off the video.

"Tell Max I'll have to keep his phone until I get the video uploaded into the police computers for evidence."

"Okay. He will just have to play solitaire on the computers at work."

"I need to apologize. I should have looked more closely at Dupree."

She took a quick sharp breath as he drew closer to her. Taking a step back, she said, "Apology accepted."

Tuck's gaze roamed over her. "Well, I guess this could technically be called your collar."

"Pretty good for a hotel clerk." Nora returned his gaze. *Pretty good indeed.*

# Chapter 38

⎯⎯∼∼∼⎯⎯

MARTY ENTERED THE hotel lobby juggling two giant bags of toilet paper. Max was sitting on one of the red-velvet benches holding a bag of ice to his cheek.

"What happened to you, Max?"

"He faints at the side of blood," Nora said from behind the desk.

"What happened? Did one of the guests have an accident?"

"Sort of. Max hit him with a chair."

Marty dropped both bags of toilet paper and crossed her arms. "All right, you two. Spill."

Nora and Max told Marty about their successful attempt to trick Del Dupree into admitting to blackmail.

Marty sat next to Max on the bench and put her arm around him. "Max, you're a hero."

Max blushed. "Ah, shucks, it was nothing."

Nora came around the desk. "He came up with the idea. I was really surprised it worked."

"I was surprised it worked, too. And it's the first time I've ever attacked a man with a chair."

Marty scrunched her nose and grinned. "There is one little thing I'm not happy about."

"What? We kept the blood in the parking lot," Max said.

"And I appreciate that. Still, though, this is a business, and if any guests had seen that, it could have been a catastrophe. We're just getting our online reviews to improve. No one is going to stay at a hotel when they find out people are getting bashed over the head in the parking lot."

Max looked down. "You're right. I know the success of this place is very important to you. Heck, it's important to all of us. We shouldn't have done it."

"Or at least you could have let me know your plans. I would've loved to throw a few chairs."

Chastened, Nora said, "I know that since I've been here, I've caused trouble. It all comes back to Adam Brockwell. If you think about it, the office was broken into because of the diamond. That's turning out to be a problem. It's ironic one person wants it and my mother wouldn't have dreamed of taking it."

Marty's eyes widened. "You should count your blessings. I'd break into my own office for the infusion of cash that necklace could give me."

Max shifted the bag of ice for a moment, revealing a bruise that was forming. "Have you had it appraised yet?"

"Not yet. I'm still carrying it around with me. I'm afraid to leave it anywhere."

"Then you're officially off work for the day. Go to the bank. Get that thing under guard and then get our loan for the reunion."

"You sure?"

"Scoot." Marty turned her attention back to Max. She shifted the ice in the bag and gently placed it back on his forehead.

Max blushed again.

"Okay then. I guess I'm headed to the bank. Besides, I need

to visit my new sister. She's going to love hearing about what we just did to Del Dupree."

# Chapter 39

—✳—

A FEW MINUTES later, Nora opened the heavy glass door of Piney Woods Savings and Loan. It was a typical small-town bank with four teller windows. Along a side wall were several desks that seemed almost too large for the cubicles that housed them. The décor seemed to date back to the seventies when brown paneling was all the rage, but it didn't look bad, just worn. One of the tellers acknowledged Nora, but Nora pointed over to Lucy, who was back at work and talking on the phone. She wore a pumpkin-colored suit, with orange jewelry and matching shoes. Waving Nora over, Lucy looked happy to see her.

Nora grabbed a sticky note from a pad and scribbled on it.

> Del Dupree was just taken in for questioning. He was blackmailing Mr. Brockwell. Max and I got him to confess on video.

Lucy read the note while still listening to her caller. She shook her head in response to Nora's note and attempted to close out her call. "Well, I'm just so glad you made such a good return on it. All a part of my job. You have a great day. Goodbye." Lucy hung up the phone.

She held up the note. "He confessed?"

"Yes. I was filling in for Marty this morning at the hotel, and he came down. Max had this crazy plan to set him up. I knew he was here for more than a fallen police officer fund."

Lucy rocked back in her chair. "He seemed so nice at the police station yesterday."

"Yes, well, nobody crossed him. We all bought his cock-and-bull story about some sort of half-ass fund he set up for bereaved families. Guess what? I called over to Dealin' Del's and the person I talked to had never heard of it. Said he keeps every penny he can. When I confronted him, he looked like he was either going to strangle me or knock me across the parking lot. I can tell you, he was pretty surprised when Max brought the chair down on his head."

"I'll bet. No matter what anybody else says, Nora, you've got guts."

Nora turned as several feet shuffled behind her.

"There she is. Arrest her. Arrest both of them!" Corey Brockwell yelled from across the bank.

Tuck Watson and a couple of uniformed officers walked over to Lucy and Nora. "Mr. Brockwell was waiting for us when we brought Dupree in. You sure are keeping me busy today, Nora."

Corey stomped behind him, reminding Nora of a bull preparing to charge a red flag. He pointed a finger at her and Lucy. "You broke into my house. Both of you."

"What? We certainly did not," Lucy insisted, trying to sound indignant.

"Surveillance tape doesn't lie, sweetie. We have it all. I put them in right after my father's death," Corey yelled, even though he was now face-to-face with them.

Personal activity in the bank had come to a halt, and every person there was now watching the spectacle unfolding around Lucy's desk.

Nora and Lucy exchanged glances. Neither one of them had thought to check for cameras, especially after Mr. Brockwell bragged of not needing an alarm system.

Tuck shook his head in bewilderment. "Are you now *trying* to get me to arrest you?"

"As long as you're writing up charges, maybe you should check into how I ended up with bruises on me and why I had to steal my own necklace back from your victim, Corey," Nora answered. "Also, if you think about it, Mr. Brockwell is now only part owner of the house."

Lucy snapped her manicured fingers. "Right! His father left it to all three of us. Did you forget that little fact, brother dear?" Lucy's sarcastic tone made Corey's face turn a deep crimson.

"Arrest them!" he shouted at Tuck, sounding like a tired child about to go into full meltdown.

"What's the matter, bubba? Things not going the way you planned?" Lucy taunted, knowing he couldn't admit they'd taken back what he stole from Nora.

Tuck's phone rang, and he held up a finger and walked away. Nora clutched her bag as Corey Brockwell grabbed her by the neck. The on-looking policeman didn't seem to notice how hard he was pressing into her flesh.

"Once I get you in jail," he whispered, "I will personally make sure you never get out. You will never see a cent of my father's estate. You and Lucy over there. Trust me, baby. Money fixes everything, and it's about to fix you."

Lucy pushed Corey Brockwell away from Nora. "Cut it out, jerk."

A chill went through Nora. She couldn't let that happen. She'd also been around long enough to know what Corey Brockwell was saying was true. She'd be stuck in jail, and he could keep her there for as long as he wanted. It looked like he wanted her gone from his life for a very long time.

Nora spotted a fire alarm mounted on the wall behind Lucy's desk. Escaping Corey's grasp, she reached over and yanked the handle. As the alarm sounded, the bank managers appeared out of their private offices to evacuate the bank before panic ensued. In the chaos, Nora slipped out of the door, unnoticed.

# Chapter 40

Nora's feet pounded on the pavement as she dashed down the main street of Piney Woods, Texas. Yes, she'd always had a rebellious streak, but pulling a fire alarm and making a run for it was crazy, even for her.

She'd made a choice to run rather than submit to Corey Brockwell's plan to lock her up. Her mother had fallen prey to a Brockwell, and she had no intention of letting that happen again. The only problem with running was eventually you had to stop.

Nora needed a place to hide, a place where she could sort out her thoughts and plan what to do next. Maybe the police would think she'd left the building like everyone else but didn't get that she was expected to come back. Returning to the bed and breakfast was out of the question. The police would go there first, then the hotel. Where was the one place no one would expect her to go voluntarily? She knew where her mother would never expect to find her. It was if she guided her now.

When the idea hit her, Nora couldn't get there fast enough. She remembered a side door to the building, so she could enter unseen from the street. The side entrance connected the parsonage to the sanctuary. She hoped—no, prayed—it would be unlocked.

Nora tried the knob, and finding it open, darted inside. In the distance, the wail of sirens grew. She knew they were responding to the fire alarm she'd set off, but once they finished dealing with it, the police would be coming after her.

Once the door was shut, Nora was struck by the silence. The stagnant smell of wilting carnations on the altar of the First Congregational Fellowship was almost sickening. Nora hugged herself and crumpled into a pew.

How had her life become this nightmare? She wished her mother had never written that stupid letter. Why hadn't she just thrown it in the trash or mailed it, like any normal person? Nora could have gone on with her life and never set foot in Adam Brockwell's study. A sob bubbled up as hopelessness engulfed her.

The side door opened. Nora scrunched down in the long wooden bench, hoping she wouldn't be seen. Footsteps grew louder. Her heart was beating so rapidly she feared the sound would fill the quiet space of the sanctuary.

Nora heard a slight trickle of water and the whispering of the Trinity. It was Pastor Chilton. She hoped he hadn't seen her and hoped even more that if he did, he might help her.

"I know you're here. I heard all the sirens and looked out the window of the living room parsonage. It faces the door to the church. You might as well sit up."

Nora rose from her hiding place. Pastor Chilton walked over and sat next to her in the dimly lit sanctuary. His clerical collar was accented by a light-blue shirt tucked into black slacks and a black jacket.

His gaze went to the altar while he spoke. "Didn't expect you back so soon, Nora, especially given how you feel about the church."

"I'm more surprised than you are, I ..." Nora stammered.

Should she tell the pastor she was running from the police? If she did, would he give her refuge or report her? Pastors were law-abiding citizens. He would do the right thing and call the police on her.

"You what?" he asked with surprising gentleness.

Nora realized Pastor Chilton expected her to confess to killing his old friend. Maybe he'd been thinking she was the murderer all along. Nora couldn't face the idea of this good man thinking she'd done something so abhorrent. She blurted out, "I didn't do it."

Pastor Chilton turned to face her. "Of course you didn't. I know you didn't kill Adam. I've always known."

"You have?" An immense relief spread through her.

"From the very minute I met you, child. You might not be a churchgoer and 'of the world' as they say, but you are no killer. You're not quite the bad-ass you think you are, Nora Alexander." A smile played at the corners of his mouth.

Nora gasped at his use of profanity and then a giggle escaped her lips. Pastor Chilton chuckled. A sense of calm spread through Nora. With Pastor Chilton on her side, maybe she could fight this thing after all. He could protect her from Corey and his threat to lock her up indefinitely.

"The police are looking for me. Corey Brockwell is trying to get me arrested for breaking into his house. He told me he can make sure I stay in jail for a crime I didn't commit."

Nora put her head in her hands. "Tell me what to do, Pastor. I just don't know anymore."

She'd come to the right place for help. He would tell her what to do to get out of this mess.

Pastor Chilton fingered the cross he wore around his neck in an absentminded way and shifted his gaze back to the altar.

"You know, you were right. I didn't realize it until you said it the other day. I mean with regard to my brother, Arnie. He was a hero. He gave it all for his country. He knew what was right. I think it's why he left to join the service. He knew what

Adam did to your mother was wrong. He used her. Adam always intended to marry Corey's mother. Your mother wasn't the type of woman a Brockwell commits to. She'd been so innocent, and Adam had to have her. My brother loved her. Seeing her with Adam must have killed him. It must have been then he chose another path, one that took him away from here. A better path. Just as your mother did."

Chilton's eyes were like hardened glass. Staring straight ahead. Unblinking.

"I didn't believe it. I should have realized it. Adam gave so much of himself, so much of his money to the less fortunate. We gained so much from his generosity. You know ... I never saw my brother again. I lost him. Adam Brockwell was the false idol. When Arnie left for the army, he told me, 'Alton, you be careful. You're going to find out there are people who aren't who they portray themselves to be.' I just thought he was talking about hypocrites in the church. I was so in awe of Adam and his generosity. Not like my brother. Arnie will never be back. No matter what amends I make with my maker, Arnie's gone. No prodigal brother. No fatted calf."

Chilton rose. "Your mother's letter. It was the final proof. I knew then. I knew what Arnie was trying to tell me. Adam Brockwell was not a good man. He wasn't the town's benefactor. He wasn't anything like I thought he was. Nothing. Nothing at all. He fathered children out of wedlock. He used women and then just discarded them. Your mother, in her shame as a fallen woman, left the city, but in her final days she brought him to judgment. That took gumption. You have that same gumption, Nora. Adam Brockwell was a wolf in sheep's clothing. A demon wrapped in finery and good deeds to look like an angel. He used your mother and she lost her innocence. The shame she felt forced her to leave her home and family, and I now blame him for the loss of my brother as well."

In a jerky motion, Chilton's head riveted back to Nora, his eyes now maniacal. "You see, we've both suffered a great loss. I understand you, Nora. But this … this is my job. My calling. I had to do it. You, of all people, should understand why. It's my job to keep evil at bay."

"Y-you?" she stuttered. Her sense of peace evaporated. She'd escaped a madman and run right into the arms of a murderer.

"Yes, my child. I did it for you. I did it for me. I guess I even did it for Arnette Cooper and little Lucy. I did it for everyone who was ever hurt by that monster. Like the mighty archangel Michael, I fought the battle for good and won." Chilton slashed through the air with an imaginary sword.

Nora started to back out of the pew, hoping he was too caught up in the moment to notice her movement.

He reached out and clamped his hand down on her wrist. "But I do need to ask your forgiveness." He wasn't going to let her go.

"About what?" Nora tried to keep her voice calm.

"My works. My mission here on Earth. I have so much more work to do. I need to keep helping people. It's my calling." He spoke as if the church was full of people. His eyes became vacant and wide, his pupils dilated.

"Sure. Uh, I forgive you. Really. We're cool. Now, let go." Nora tried to pull away from Chilton, but he yanked her forward, getting an even better grip on her.

"Thank you so much. It means a lot to me. Now I know you'll understand why I have to do this." Chilton pulled a knife from out of his inside pocket. The glimmering steel caught the light coming through the stained-glass windows. He was going to kill her.

"I'll tell them you pulled this knife on me. I had to kill you in self-defense. You were crazed from the death of your mother. You were lashing out at the friend of the man who wouldn't accept you as his child—the man you killed. Don't worry, Nora. It will be over soon. This is a sacrifice we must both make."

He dragged her to the center aisle, and grabbing her around the neck, reached over to the large basin in the middle of the aisle. "A little holy water to set it right and I'm on my way."

Nora remembered the water splashed over her mother's letter as Brockwell held it in his dead hand. Now it made sense. That had been Chilton "setting it right."

Nora struggled in Chilton's grasp. "If you're ridding the world of evil, Pastor, why are you still here? Doesn't 'thou shalt not kill' mean anything to you? Or did you get the abridged version of the Ten Commandments?"

"Of course, taking a life means something to me. It's my sacrifice for the good of the people."

"Then what you did was no better than what Adam did. Even an unchurched sinner like me can figure out which is the worse sin."

"You don't understand. I'm a soldier. Like my brother, Arnie. He fought for his country. I'm fighting to eliminate evil in our world."

"It sounds pretty crazy to me. I trusted you and now you're going to kill me? Am I evil too? Can't you see how that is insane?"

"No. No. You must sacrifice your life and take the blame for Adam's murder. I have a mission to complete. *You* can do this for *me*." Chilton's voice rose, and he shook his head, making the craziness in his eyes even more evident.

Jabbing her elbow into his side, she then stomped as hard as she could on his foot. He loosened his grip before she could do any more damage. When he did, Nora pulled herself free and ran down the aisle. Where could she go? If she ran outside, Corey Brockwell would be waiting with the police. If she stayed inside, Chilton would kill her.

As she entered the church narthex, a beam of light from the afternoon sun played off a doorway. Nora flung open the door and took the stairs two at a time. Once she burst through into what she now knew was the steeple room, she noticed there was no lock to keep him out. Her escape might be short-lived. A single rope dangled in front of her. Above her, in the belfry, hung the town's first low-tech early warning system. Nora yanked at the rope with all her might, ringing the bell over and over. If what she'd been told was correct, the community would descend on them soon.

"Young lady!" Pastor Chilton was at the door, brandishing his knife. "Unauthorized personnel are not allowed to ring the church bell." He lunged at her with the knife, causing Nora to jump backward, breaking out a pane of glass with her elbow. A piece of broken glass punctured her arm. Sirens drew nearer as Chilton attacked again, this time making cuts on her upraised hands. She grabbed at the rope again and pulled as hard as she could.

"Stop!" he yelled, but Nora kept dodging the knife over and over, losing track of the times the blade bit into her flesh.

"This is my calling. This is your calling. This is why you were led here. Don't try to stop God's plan."

"Drop the knife, Pastor!" A red-faced Tuck Watson stood at the top of the stairs, his gun trained on Chilton.

Chilton turned. Still holding the knife, he put his hands on his knees and began gasping for breath. "Thank goodness you're here, Officer. She was trying to attack me."

Tuck's brow furrowed as he surveyed the scene. "But you're the one holding the knife." Watson held his gun steady.

"She just dropped it. I grabbed it. She was trying to …"

"… cut herself to make it look good? I don't think so, Pastor. Give me the knife."

Chilton dropped the knife, put his hand on the side of his face, and began speaking to the empty space above him. "This isn't right. I've failed. I'm so sorry. I've failed you …."

The pastor collapsed.

Nora had been right. Someone did believe in her innocence. Tuck Watson's gaze never left her as he put cuffs on the pastor. She could rest easy. He believed in her. Nora slid to the floor, and then felt Tuck's arms around her. It was like her dream. She could shut out the world around her. Taking a deep breath, she put her head on his shoulder. Nora felt very tired.

She heard the words, "Call an ambulance … she's going into shock …."

Nora felt a bustle of movement, and another set of arms went around her. The final thing she heard that day in the belfry was Bubby Tidwell shouting, "I've saved her. Number fifteen, everybody. Number fifteen …."

# Chapter 41

———— ≈ ————

"**W**E'RE GOING TO run out of ice!" Wiley yelled from the kitchen of the Hotel Tunie Restaurant.

"There's more in the back. Stay calm, Uncle Wiley. We haven't greeted a single guest yet."

Nora pulled at the neckline of the deep-green, tea-length gown Lucy had helped her pick out. The cut of the dress, with its full skirt and tight waist, reminded her of something Audrey Hepburn might have worn. It was also similar to the one her mother wore in the photograph in Mr. Tunie's collection. Nora was paying tribute to her mother and the history of the hotel. "It brings out the hues in your hair," Lucy had told her as Nora twirled around in front of the mirror. Tonight her hair was done up in a messy bun, wispy auburn strands framing her face.

The banquet room looked wonderful. Tatty took over the decorating, getting her ladies club to do the flower arrangements. They made copies of the old sign-in ledger and placed them on each table. To Nora's delight, the line of guests snaked around the block.

"Are you ready?" Marty stood at the door of the lobby.

"As I'll ever be."

"No turning back now …."

Marty opened the lobby door. "Welcome to the Tunie Hotel."

People filed past her, making their way into the banquet room. They were dressed in suits, dresses, and hats. It was just like the old days. No casual Friday this evening.

Even if they did run out of ice a time or two, the Tunie was filled like it hadn't been for decades. The Fredericks sisters entered in tandem, red lipstick applied to their creased lips and matching daisies clipped to their hair. Lucy came in behind them, her arm linked in Arnette's.

Lucy gave Nora a hug. "It's beautiful. Just beautiful."

"Do you think so?"

"I know so." Arnette reached out to hold her hand. "The town needed this old place back. A new Walmart will never make you feel like this."

A handsome gentleman in his forties walked over and stood next to Arnette.

"Nora," Lucy turned to the man who now stood so close to her mother, "I'd like you to meet Mr. Ellis. He knew my mother years ago when he taught in Piney Woods."

Was this the man who left town when Arnette became pregnant with Adam Brockwell's baby?

Nora pulled Lucy to the side. "Is he …?"

"Yes he is. The wonder of the internet. You can find anyone. He was living only two counties away. He told me our dear daddy ran him out of town, so when it became known Mama was pregnant, everyone would blame him. Like your mother, he didn't want to remain in the same town as Brockwell. He was afraid for us."

"What a legacy of damaged lives Adam Brockwell left."

"Yes, well, at least one good thing happened."

"What?"

"The paternity tests proved it. I now have a big sister. A big redheaded sister I can get into trouble with."

"Excuse me? I think *you* were the one who got *me* into trouble."

"Don't get me started," Lucy said with a playful wag of her forefinger. "Let's grab a table, Mama."

Lucy gave Nora a quick hug and followed Mr. Ellis as he walked with her mother into the Stephen F. Austin Banquet Room. As Nora watched them, she concluded it was worthy of its long name. The light fixtures had all been cleaned by Jolene and the newest staff member, her cousin Tammy. Now the light danced off of the shining silver and glassware.

A man cleared his voice behind her. "Nora, I brought … our … grandmother." Vernon, dressed in a suit a little too tight around the middle, stood holding Rosalyn's fragile hand.

"We had to make a visit first to the big reunion. Vernon took me by your mother's picture so I could see it again. She was so beautiful." Rosalyn's voice cracked. "I just wish she was here with us now."

Nora put her arm around Rosalyn's slight shoulders. A sadness came over her, as if her mother had died all over again. Nora wished for just one more chance to tell her she loved her. Instead, she focused on her grandmother. "But I found you. I'd like to think maybe she's here with us anyway."

Thanks to Marty's interview in the local paper and Mr. Tunie's photographic record, Nora and Marty had been able to spread the word about the Tunie reunion. People had come from miles around. Wiley's menu included his signature gumbo along with fried shrimp, crawfish, and biscuits so fluffy, they were compared to angel wings. Nora thought to place a "Save the Tunie" basket, along with some handpicked photos, on a table right next to the buffet. If all went as planned, not only would they be able to recoup the cost of their party, but Marty could also pay some of the bills she'd fallen behind on.

Even with the notable absence of Pastor Chilton, the entire First Congregational Fellowship had showed up. Maisie, who sat ensconced in the Class of 1979, glanced over and raised a glass to Nora. They were already in the process of calling another minister. Maybe, as Tuck had suggested when Marty hired her, the church would run a background check on their next shepherd.

One banquet room was set up with chairs for the presentation. Once everyone had made their way through the buffet line and taken their seats, Marty stood in front of a slide show of the treasured photos Nora had created. The mood was light and welcome now that the shock of finding out about the real Adam Brockwell and the real Pastor Chilton had begun to subside.

Wiley came over, drying his hands on a towel.

"How much is left?" Nora asked.

"We're good, even though Bubby Tidwell has come around the buffet three times. If he keeps eating like that, someone is going to have to rescue him. Looks like you're going to be seeing a lot of me. Marty wants me to run the restaurant full-time. Wiley McArdle, Restaurateur. It's a little scary, you know, all this responsibility."

He looked at the towel between his fingers. Nora put her hand over his.

She whispered in his ear, "You can do this, Uncle Wiley. I know you can."

"Maybe I can, maybe I can't, but we're sure going to find out." He locked eyes with Nora for a moment. "You know, before I met you, I was dying."

Nora's eyes widened.

"Not really. It's a figure of speech. We use those even in Texas, you know. Every day I'd get up and the only thing I felt like doing was having a drink. And then another. You see, I knew I let a bad thing happen. I let your mother down. I wasn't a good man."

Nora thought of Pastor Chilton aligning himself with who he thought was a "good man."

"Maybe we needed each other."

"You saved my life."

"Yeah, well. Keep going to meetings. Recovery is a long process. If you're going to run a restaurant, you're going to need some stress relief. Healthy, sober stress relief."

The door of the banquet room opened. Tuck Watson stood, hat in hand. His gaze took in Nora and her form-fitting deep-green dress.

"You look … wonderful," he offered with a smile. "I thought I'd find you here. I need to talk to you about Brockwell's charges. Got a minute?" His fingers played with the rim of his hat.

"Tonight?" Nora felt Wiley's scrawny yet protective arm go around her.

"Corey Brockwell has decided to drop the charges, especially after Harvey Mortensen reminded him you and Ms. Cooper can't be charged for breaking into a residence the two of you now have part ownership in—all proved by the positive results of the paternity tests. Although that just strengthened the case. Even with negative results, you were both in his will. Also, you could charge Corey for assault and theft after what he did to you. Yes, I know he's the one who hit you. I told him if he ever touched you again, he would have more than the law to deal with. Corey Brockwell is, well, shall we say, liquidating his assets."

Uncle Wiley stepped away from Nora, now flexing one thin arm into a small muscle. "You betcha. Just let him come around. We'll show 'em."

"Thank you, Uncle Wiley. I knew what we did was wrong but—"

"Hey," Tuck said, "I might have done the same thing if someone like Brockwell had pushed me around and hurt me." He looked around the room full of people. "Is there some place we can go and talk … in private?"

Pulling him away from the crowd, Nora led him to Marty's office. Once the door was closed, Tuck reached up and touched Nora's lip, his hand lingering. As he drew closer to her, his nearness made her head spin. He pulled her toward him, claiming her lips just as he'd done on their first night together.

Tuck dropped his hand. "When I saw you in that green dress …. It's against the official police rulebook to kiss a suspect. I'm so happy you're off that list."

As he tucked a strand of hair behind her ear, Nora reached up and kissed him back. This was so different for her. She was discovering an intimacy she never knew existed.

The door to the office opened abruptly, and Marty's expression changed from surprise to a grin. "I see you're working on those hospitality skills there, Nora." She began to close the door, but not before adding, "Carry on."

Tuck laughed and Nora reveled in the sound of it.

"Oh, and one more thing …" Tuck sighed and attempted to return to business. "Dupree lawyered up, and to no one's surprise there is no slain officers' fund after all. We just have to hope his admission on Max's phone will hold up in court."

"One less car salesman on the street—"

"And, to be honest with you, I'm awfully glad you're not a killer. I was going to have a hard time figuring out how to ask you out if I sent you to prison."

Nora's face heated. She was starting to like this town more and more.

"Of course, I had my doubts all along," he said with a smile. "I had trouble picturing you as a killer, and the blood on your shirt was not Adam's. It's just that there were no other viable suspects I could see."

When they re-entered the banquet room, the Fredericks sisters, standing at the buffet, were watching them with great interest. Nora gave a pleasant nod, and the sisters made a show of scooping up mashed potatoes from the metal serving dish.

Tuck nodded to the sisters. "Good evening, Miss Violet, Miss Azalea. Is there any food left? I'm starving."

"Good evening, Tuck. Yes, there's plenty of food." Miss Violet leaned in closer as if to let them in on some choice gossip. "It's all so delicious. You simply must try some."

"We used up all the plates," Wiley said as he finished refilling a heating dish. He raised a hand to reassure Tuck, "but I've got more in the kitchen. I'll run and get you one … that is, if you promise not to arrest my niece."

The Fredericks sisters tittered at his suggestion.

Tuck held up his hand. "I promise."

Wiley bowed and ran to the kitchen.

Tuck turned back toward Nora, taking her hand in his. "I should tell you, it wasn't until I saw Chilton going after you that I …"

"… finally decided I might be innocent after all?"

Tuck rolled his eyes and smiled with a lopsided grin. "Caught me. What gets me is my instincts are usually pretty good. It was like something was blocking my—"

"Spidey sense?"

Tuck laughed. "Must've been it."

Wiley returned with a stack of plates and set them next to the assortment of food on the table.

"So, have you eaten?" Tuck asked. "I hate to eat alone."

Nora's stomach grumbled. "Sounds like a wonderful idea."

Wiley nodded. "And it's about time, Nora girl. You're thin enough." He pulled silverware out of his apron pocket and handed it to Nora.

Max burst into the room, carrying a dusty picture frame. "Found it—Mr. Tunie! I found his picture. Once the place started looking better, Marty asked me to search for it. She had felt guilty hanging it up with everything so rundown."

Marty came over from the podium. Holding up the picture frame, she gazed at its subject. "I'll be darned. Sure brings back memories. Old man Tunie. He was quite dapper in his day."

Nora was taking a spoonful of Wiley's mashed potatoes when she looked at the picture and choked. Tuck tapped her on the back, his gentle touch complicating her attempts to get her breath.

"That's not Mr. Tunie," she gasped.

"Come on, Nora, everyone in this town knows this is Mr. Tunie," Max said.

"No. That's Mr. Birdsong. He comes here once a week and tells me about elegant evenings of dance. You've seen him, right?"

A blank look came across Max's face. "Who?"

"Mr. Birdsong. You know. The old guy with the bow tie. That's him."

Max shook his head and pointed to Nora's plate. "You've gone too long without eating. I knew I should've been watching you. I don't know who you think you saw, but that is the one and only Mr. Tunie."

As Nora looked at the faded photo of her regular visitor, she realized Marty was standing before the photo of her mother and Adam Brockwell. Nora took it off the wall and looked at the picture for what felt like the first time. There was someone dancing past her mother and the two men. It was Mr. Birdsong, tripping the light fantastic on his elegant evening of dance. Why had she never noticed him before?

"Oh, he was a great man. Kind of on the smallish side, and he always wore those bow ties." Max gestured at his neck as if straightening an invisible tie.

"He called me 'dear,' " Nora said, recalling his weekly visits. "I thought he didn't know my name, but now I think he knew exactly who I was. He was a gentleman. Part of the past."

The temperature around her grew chilly and there was a sudden breeze in the room, as if someone had walked by her. Or could it be ... danced by? She hugged herself.

"You okay, Nora?" Tuck asked.

"Yes. Yes, for the first time in years. I feel like I've come home. Home to a place I never knew existed."

Tuck gave her a smile as big as Texas. "Well, let me be the first to say, 'Welcome to Piney Woods, Nora Alexander.'"

**TERESA TRENT** LIVES in Houston, Texas, where she writes lighthearted cozy mysteries filled with small-town wisdom and plenty of quirky characters. She has won awards for her short stories with several Texas writers groups and is always in search of that next unusual character or plot. When she is not writing, she enjoys spending time with her family, singing, doing crafts, shopping with her daughter, and watching old mystery movies on television.

For more information, go to
www.teresatrent.com.

# From Camel Press
## and Teresa Trent

THANK YOU FOR reading *Murder of a Good Man*. We are so grateful for you, our readers. If you enjoyed this book, here are some steps you can take that could help contribute to its success and let you stay in touch with the Piney Woods Mystery series:

- Please think about posting a short review on Amazon, BN.com, and GoodReads.
- Check out Teresa's website (www.TeresaTrent.com) and blog (TeresaTrent.wordpress.com) and join her mailing list.
- Spread the word on social media, especially Facebook, Twitter, and Pinterest (teresa_trent/the-happy-hinter).
- "Like" Teresa's author Facebook page: www.facebook.com/teresatrentmysterywriter and the Camel Press page: www.facebook.com/CamelPressBooks.
- Follow Teresa (@ttrent_cozymys) and Camel Press (@camelpressbooks) on Twitter.
- Ask for your local library to carry this book and others in the series or request them on their online portal.

Good books and authors from small presses are often overlooked. Your comments and reviews can make an enormous difference.

MY TRENT, TERESA 02/18
Murder of a good man :
a Piney Woods mystery /

CPSIA information can be obtained
at www.ICGtesting.com
Printed in the USA
LVHW02s1720300118
564591LV00004B/884/P